1   2   3   4   5
85%   75%   60%   50%   30%

60% × 30% = $\frac{30}{60} = \frac{1}{2}$

Mental Health

Other Books in the Current Controversies Series:

Mental Health

Jennifer A. Hurley, *Book Editor*

David Bender, *Publisher*
Bruno Leone, *Executive Editor*

Brenda Stalcup, *Managing Editor*
Scott Barbour, *Senior Editor*

CURRENT CONTROVERSIES

6113468CBC)

Cover Photo: David Gifford/Science Photo Library

Library of Congress Cataloging-in-Publication Data

Mental health / Jennifer A. Hurley, book editor.
     p. cm. — (Current controversies)
    Includes bibliographical references and index.
    ISBN 1-56510-953-8 (lib. : alk. paper). — ISBN 1-56510-952-X
(pbk. : alk. paper)
    1. Mental health—Miscellanea. I. Hurley, Jennifer A., 1973–   .
II. Series.
RC344.M46   1999
616.89—dc21
                                             98-33944
                                              CIP

Contents

fairly attacked by those who feel that the drug is an "unnecessary self-indulgence." In truth, Prozac and other new antidepressants have miraculously cured most sufferers of depression. With the aid of Prozac, many people who were previously debilitated by depression are able to live normal and happy lives.

Children who suffer from attention deficit hyperactivity disorder (ADHD) have brains that are anatomically different from those of other children. The problems caused by this difference—hyperactivity, impulsivity, and inattention—can be safely and successfully treated with the drug Ritalin. This medication is a highly effective way of helping children who are diagnosed with ADHD.

No: Drugs Are Not the Most Effective Treatment for Mental Illness

Because most depression is caused by social and cultural factors, not biological problems, therapy is the most effective way to treat depression. While antidepressants can help alleviate depressive symptoms, therapy teaches people the life skills that they need to prevent further occurrences of depression.

Psychopharmacological drugs, particularly Prozac, are seen as the "magic pills" that promise to swiftly alleviate emotional disturbances. However, psychoactive medications treat only the symptoms of mental disorders, not the underlying psychological problems that cause these disorders. Because antidepressant drugs interfere with the mind's natural emotional processes, they should be used only as a last resort for treating depression.

Increasing numbers of doctors are prescribing the drug Ritalin to children whom they describe as having attention deficit hyperactivity disorder (ADHD). ADHD, however, is not an actual mental disorder; rather, it is a label for highly energetic children who "make trouble" for adults. Behavior-modifying drugs such as Ritalin are used to subdue these children so parents can more easily control them.

Chapter 3: What Non-Drug Therapies Effectively Treat Mental Illness?

Electroconvulsive Therapy (ECT)—a procedure in which an electrical stimulus is used to induce a seizure in the patient's brain—can benefit severely depressed patients who have failed to respond to other treatments. In fact, ECT has been found to allay major depression in at least 80 percent of patients. Furthermore, the procedure is quick, painless, and has no lasting side effects.

exposure to artificial or natural light alleviates the symptoms of SAD.

Chapter 4: How Should the Legal System Respond to the Mentally Ill?

cal treatment for their disorders—and as a result, often present a danger to society and to themselves. Involuntary commitment would allow the mentally ill to get the treatment they need in order to live happy, productive lives.

Involuntary commitment laws give the legal system the authority to confine the mentally ill—without their consent—in hospitals or institutions. Because involuntary commitment deprives law-abiding citizens of their right to freedom, it is unconstitutional. If society is to uphold the Declaration of Independence's promise of "liberty and justice for all," involuntary commitment laws must be abolished.

Chapter 5: How Should Society Deal with the Mentally Ill?

Society's treatment of the mentally ill has undergone dramatic changes during the twentieth century. Following the expansion of federal entitlement programs in the 1960s and 1970s, long-term psychiatric patients were released from mental hospitals back into society. This process—referred to as "deinstitutionalization"—was based on the premise that with the appropriate social support systems, the mentally ill could make a successful transition to community homes or independent living. While deinstitutionalization freed thousands of patients from obsolete mental institutions that provided little or no psychiatric care, it also led to a severe increase in the homeless mentally ill population. This outcome has instigated debate over whether policies should be reformed to allow long-term hospitalization of the mentally ill.

Treatment costs for mental illness—which afflicts as much as 20 percent of the adult population—have become a heavy burden to taxpayers and to the employers who fund health insurance for their employees. However, untreated mental illness has high costs to society in terms of lost wages, homelessness, and crime. Without sacrificing accessibility and quality of care, managed care companies, by stressing early intervention, are able to provide services for the mentally ill at a reasonable cost.

Managed care can make it difficult—in some cases impossible—for the mentally ill to obtain the treatment they need. Because insurers have the final word in treatment decisions, many mentally ill patients are denied care, especially if the requested treatment is not considered to be cost-effective. Furthermore, because psychiatrists must negotiate with insurers for treatment authorization, they often end up divulging confidential information about their patients' conditions.

Because the treatment of mental illness can be expensive, those who fund health care often restrict mental health care benefits. However, many mental illnesses are caused by chemical imbalances in the brain that can be inexpensively corrected with medication. Furthermore, untreated mental health problems lead to greater health care costs in the long run. Providers of health care coverage should be required to offer mental health care benefits equal to those offered for physical care.

Foreword

By definition, controversies are "discussions of questions in which opposing opinions clash" (Webster's Twentieth Century Dictionary Unabridged). Few would deny that controversies are a pervasive part of the human condition and exist on virtually every level of human enterprise. Controversies transpire between individuals and among groups, within nations and between nations. Controversies supply the grist necessary for progress by providing challenges and challengers to the status quo. They also create atmospheres where strife and warfare can flourish. A world without controversies would be a peaceful world; but it also would be, by and large, static and prosaic.

The Series' Purpose

The purpose of the Current Controversies series is to explore many of the social, political, and economic controversies dominating the national and international scenes today. Titles selected for inclusion in the series are highly focused and specific. For example, from the larger category of criminal justice, Current Controversies deals with specific topics such as police brutality, gun control, white collar crime, and others. The debates in Current Controversies also are presented in a useful, timeless fashion. Articles and book excerpts included in each title are selected if they contribute valuable, long-range ideas to the overall debate. And wherever possible, current information is enhanced with historical documents and other relevant materials. Thus, while individual titles are current in focus, every effort is made to ensure that they will not become quickly outdated. Books in the Current Controversies series will remain important resources for librarians, teachers, and students for many years.

In addition to keeping the titles focused and specific, great care is taken in the editorial format of each book in the series. Book introductions and chapter prefaces are offered to provide background material for readers. Chapters are organized around several key questions that are answered with diverse opinions representing all points on the political spectrum. Materials in each chapter include opinions in which authors clearly disagree as well as alternative opinions in which authors may agree on a broader issue but disagree on the possible solutions. In this way, the content of each volume in Current Controversies mirrors the mosaic of opinions encountered in society. Readers will quickly realize that there are many viable answers to these complex issues. By questioning each author's conclusions, students and casual readers can begin to develop the critical thinking skills so important to evaluating opinionated material.

Current Controversies is also ideal for controlled research. Each anthology in the series is composed of primary sources taken from a wide gamut of informational categories including periodicals, newspapers, books, United States and foreign government documents, and the publications of private and public organizations. Readers will find factual support for reports, debates, and research papers covering all areas of important issues. In addition, an annotated table of contents, an index, a book and periodical bibliography, and a list of organizations to contact are included in each book to expedite further research.

Perhaps more than ever before in history, people are confronted with diverse and contradictory information. During the Persian Gulf War, for example, the public was not only treated to minute-to-minute coverage of the war, it was also inundated with critiques of the coverage and countless analyses of the factors motivating U.S. involvement. Being able to sort through the plethora of opinions accompanying today's major issues, and to draw one's own conclusions, can be a complicated and frustrating struggle. It is the editors' hope that Current Controversies will help readers with this struggle.

Greenhaven Press anthologies primarily consist of previously published material taken from a variety of sources, including periodicals, books, scholarly journals, newspapers, government documents, and position papers from private and public organizations. These original sources are often edited for length and to ensure their accessibility for a young adult audience. The anthology editors also change the original titles of these works in order to clearly present the main thesis of each viewpoint and to explicitly indicate the opinion presented in the viewpoint. These alterations are made in consideration of both the reading and comprehension levels of a young adult audience. Every effort is made to ensure that Greenhaven Press accurately reflects the original intent of the authors included in this anthology.

Introduction

In September of 1989, Joe Wesbecker, a long-time employee at the Standard Gravure printing plant in Louisville, Kentucky, walked into work carrying an AK-47 and three spare clips. He opened fire on his coworkers, killing eight, maiming two, and wounding ten more. The assault ended when Wesbecker shot himself with an automatic pistol.

The incident mimicked other workplace shootings except for one key factor: Wesbecker, who had been diagnosed with depression, had just recently started taking the antidepressant drug Prozac. Claiming that the drug was responsible for Wesbecker's violent behavior, the widows of Wesbecker's victims brought suit against Eli Lilly, the company that makes Prozac. Eli Lilly won the suit after a settlement had been made in which the company paid the plaintiffs to exclude certain evidence from the trial.

The Wesbecker suit marked the first of several allegations that Prozac incites violent behavior—none of which has succeeded in court. In fact, Prozac's success seems virtually immune to such charges. Despite the Wesbecker case, Prozac sales skyrocketed in the early 1990s. In 1995, Prozac was the most commonly prescribed medicine internationally, with sales totaling over $2 billion. The drug, which has been authorized to treat depression, obsessive-compulsive disorder, and bulimia, is awaiting approval for the treatment of such diverse conditions as chronic fatigue syndrome and premenstrual syndrome. Prozac impacts a wide range of personality disorders, researchers claim, because it increases brain activity. Along with other selective serotonin reuptake inhibitors (SSRIs), Prozac works by raising the brain's level of serotonin—a chemical that regulates behavior. Psychiatrist Michael J. Norden describes serotonin as "a surrogate parent" because it "discourages behavior that might get us in trouble and comforts us when trouble nevertheless arrives—soothing worry, pain and most forms of stress."

In addition, proponents contend that SSRIs, unlike other antidepressants, have no serious side effects. Previously, the best drugs available for depressed patients were tricyclic antidepressants, which bring on frightening symptoms such as heart problems and memory loss—and can be extremely dangerous when mixed with alcohol. With the introduction of Prozac and other SSRIs, researchers maintain, people suffering from depression and similar disorders can obtain relief without the risks of harsh side effects, addiction, or overdose.

Since SSRIs have been lauded as an antidote for everything from timidity to compulsive eating, it is hardly surprising that Prozac has acquired an almost cultlike following. In 1995 alone, nearly 19 million prescriptions for Prozac were dispensed in the United States—a number that continues to rise. Furthermore, some veterinarians are even prescribing it to antisocial dogs and cats. Enthusiasts have an easy explanation for Prozac's popularity: It works. According to psychiatrist Peter Kramer, one of Prozac's most avid proponents, Prozac can "do in a matter of days what psychiatrists hope, and often fail, to accomplish by other means over a course of years." Some psychiatrists see no end to the potential uses of Prozac. For example, Dr. Joel Yager of the University of California at Los Angeles says that "he has no qualms with the use of SSRIs to smooth over troublesome personality characteristics, even when a clinical disorder is not apparent." According to Yager and other psychiatrists, if Prozac will improve a person's quality of life, there is nothing wrong with prescribing it.

Critics, on the other hand, balk at the notion that antidepressants should be freely dispensed. Some fear that the popularity of Prozac brings society closer to the one depicted in Aldous Huxley's novel *Brave New World*, in which the fictional drug Soma was used to subdue all unpleasant emotions. Critics contend that the prescription of antidepressants should be limited to clinically depressed individuals who demonstrate a genuine need for drug intervention.

Others maintain that Prozac is not an effective way of treating depression. According to Peter Breggin, a vocal opponent of Prozac, "Many people . . . on Prozac . . . react with a narrowing of their emotional spectrum. They lose touch with themselves and others, and may perceive this as a kind of relief. . . . [Prozac] disconnects a person from the rest of the world and from his or her own real-life issues." Breggin and others argue that while Prozac alleviates depressive symptoms, it fails to address the underlying issues behind these symptoms; therefore, it is a temporary fix, not a long-term solution.

Other protests against Prozac center around a different issue: the use of Prozac on children. As of this writing, Eli Lilly is awaiting Food and Drug Administration (FDA) approval for a peppermint-flavored children's Prozac. However, doctors can legally write children prescriptions of adult Prozac—and many have not hesitated to do so. In fact, Arianna Huffington reports that "children's prescriptions of adult antidepressants have soared from 342,900 in 1994 to 579,700 in 1996." Criticisms of this practice range from fears that Prozac may affect children's brain development to moral questions about whether it is right to treat children's emotional problems with medication. Some warn that Prozac teaches children that pills, rather than personal responsibility, are the way to solve problems. According to columnist Cal Thomas, "If drugs are used to alter the mood of a child, what moral authority do adults have to persuade a teenager not to alter his or her mood with marijuana, heroin or cocaine?"

The debate over Prozac reflects the larger question of whether drugs are the best way to treat mental illness. Those in favor of Prozac believe that drug treatments have revolutionized mental health care. They contend that mental illness is caused by chemical imbalances in the brain that can be easily corrected with drug therapies. On the other hand, critics of Prozac argue that the popularity of SSRIs is emblematic of a dangerous cultural trend toward the desire to solve problems instantaneously and easily. They allege that Prozac and other mind-altering medications eliminate normal human responses to life problems. This debate is among the topics addressed in *Mental Health: Current Controversies.* Throughout this anthology, authors offer contrasting perspectives on the medical, social, and legal issues surrounding mental illness.

Chapter 1

How Serious Is the Problem of Mental Illness?

Chapter Preface

The *Diagnostic and Statistical Manual of Mental Disorders* (DSM), often referred to as the "psychiatrist's bible," is used by doctors, therapists, and health insurers as a complete reference of mental illnesses. The fourth edition of the manual, published in 1994, lists more than 350 mental disorders. The increase in the number of documented mental disorders, up from 60 disorders listed in the first version of the DSM, has generated debate over whether mental illness is being too broadly defined.

Critics of the DSM-IV contend that the American Psychiatric Association, which publishes the manual, has stretched the definition of mental disorders to include behaviors demonstrated by nearly everyone. According to Stuart A. Kirk and Herb Kutchins, "Insomnia, worrying, restlessness, getting drunk, seeking approval, reacting to criticism, feeling sad and bearing grudges are all considered possible signs of mental illness." Skeptics claim that some of the new classifications verge on the ridiculous: The "Disorder of Written Expression," for example, is marked by a poor use of grammar and punctuation, not to mention sloppy handwriting. Those who believe mental illness is too broadly defined also criticize such entries as "Antisocial Personality Disorder," which is demonstrated by "a pervasive pattern of disregard for . . . the rights of others" and "an inflated and arrogant self-appraisal." Critics of the DSM-IV warn that defining personality flaws such as these as mental disorders encourages people to deny responsibility for negative behavior.

On the other hand, those who defend the DSM-IV's definitions of mental illness maintain that the manual provides an accurate documentation of existing mental disorders. In response to charges that the new classifications are too encompassing, defenders of the DSM-IV contend that while many people may demonstrate individual symptoms of a mental disorder, it is the combination and severity of symptoms that determine whether a person is mentally ill. Furthermore, proponents argue, the manual's new classifications, by showing how common mental disorders are, help to break down the stigma surrounding mental illness.

The controversy over how to define mental illness reflects ideological differences about the pervasiveness of mental illness. Some believe that mental disorders occur as frequently as physical health problems, while others allege that mental conditions requiring medical attention are relatively rare. In the following chapter, psychiatrists, psychologists, and others debate the prevalence of mental illness.

Mental Illness Is Widespread

by Michael J. Norden

About the author: *Michael J. Norden is a psychiatrist and clinical associate professor at the University of Washington in Seattle. He is the author of the book* Beyond Prozac, *from which the following viewpoint is excerpted.*

Mental illness now strikes nearly all of us, although with vast differences in form and degree. And the numbers are mounting steadily. In particular, serious depression has risen astonishingly in recent years, as emphasized by the late Dr. Gerald Klerman, a leading figure in American psychiatry. He termed the hunt for the mysterious cause of this epidemic "the search for Agent Blue."

To claim that nearly everyone will suffer mental illness may seem absurd, for many of us still think of it only in its most extreme forms. But let's recast the issue. Let's ask: How many people suffer emotionally or physically from stress? Indeed, the harried, floating anxiety that accompanies stress *is* a type of mental illness, and most of us, even if we do not care to admit it, have experienced it to some degree. However, stress is much more than that harried feeling, which originates in the brain. Biologically, it includes almost anything that puts an extra burden on an organism. For example, extreme heat falls under the heading. Mental illness is certainly stress related, but most people find *stress-related illness* a far more acceptable term, for then their condition joins the respectable company of high blood pressure, ulcers, and the many other stress-caused illnesses.

Ironically, many of the people we most admire are included in this stigmatized group. A study of three hundred biographies of history's most accomplished scientists, politicians, philosophers, and artists found evidence that some three out of four had suffered serious mental illness. For example, two of Western culture's most revered leaders, Abraham Lincoln and Winston Churchill, wrote in detail of their struggle with incapacitating depression. At one point Lincoln concluded: "I am now quite certainly the most miserable man alive."

As the above study shows, the mentally ill are, overall, quite disproportionately gifted and achieving. We fear such illness probably because at some level it reminds us of our own vulnerability. That we don't understand how these conditions develop has made them seem even more frightening. Fortunately, the more we learn about the causes of mental illness and how to treat it, the less stigma is attached to it.

> *"Serious depression has risen astonishingly in recent years."*

We now know that many mental disorders are actually biological in origin, which puts them on the same plane as angina or arthritis, for example. Apart from biological factors, many psychiatric conditions are simply the result of poor learned responses to life. Fortunately, these can readily be unlearned through cognitive or behavioral therapy. There's nothing terribly mysterious or threatening about such cases. . . .

How Widespread Is Mental Illness?

When I first began looking at the puzzle of rising mental illness rates, best estimates were that about one in five people were afflicted at some time during their life. Just as the first large-scale, rigorous study of sexuality in America produced big surprises, the first such study on mental illness produced rather shocking results.

Published in 1994 in *Archives of General Psychiatry*, but curiously receiving little publicity, the study found that among people between the ages of eighteen and fifty-four, nearly half had already met the formal diagnostic criteria for at least one of fourteen serious psychiatric illnesses. These people did not merely feel bad for the occasional few days; nearly one-third of them had had a disorder lasting over a year. The elderly, who were not included in the study, are at particularly high risk for psychiatric conditions. Thus, over a lifetime, clearly a majority of us will undergo serious mental illness.

Mental illness is certainly stress-related but genetics plays a role, as it does with stress-related physical illness. However, a recent study found that stress played the greater role in causing depression.

The Role of Stress

I cannot emphasize strongly enough that all stress-related conditions are similar, whether manifested as psychiatric or as general medical problems. Indeed, a majority of primary care physician visits concern stress-related illness. This mental-physical overlap is further demonstrated in that roughly two-thirds of those who suffer depression also suffer at least one of the following: hypertension, arthritis, advanced coronary artery disease, diabetes, gastrointestinal disorders, chronic back pain, chronic lung problems, and angina. Insomnia falls somewhere in the netherland between psychiatry and general medicine. The National Commission on Sleep Disorders Research estimates that occasional "tossing and turning" troubles more than 90 percent of the U.S. population, with more shall 30 percent reporting the problem as serious and chronic.

Certainly, stress-induced mental illness is no more deserving of shame, fear, or prejudice than are similarly induced medical conditions.

Charting the Epidemic

"Generation X," the group of people born between about 1960 and 1970, has a particularly high depression rate—but so do generations "X – 1" and "X + 1." Since World War II, depression has been increasing steadily across international, cultural, and ethnic boundaries. A national collaborative group recently evaluated these trends in various countries, including Germany, Italy, France, Lebanon, and Taiwan. Some of the studies found that depression in men born after World War II continues to rise, while women's rates have flattened, although twice as many women suffer from depression as men. Disturbingly, suicide rates among adolescents and young adults are also climbing.

According to Paul Greenberg and others, the economic burden that depression inflicts on the United States reaches over $44 billion annually. While other psychiatric conditions have not been studied to the extent

"Over a lifetime, . . . a majority of us will undergo serious mental illness."

that depression has, we see that most other forms of mental illness are certainly increasing. Some, such as anorexia and bulimia, were virtually unknown until recently.

The Prevalence of Minor Depression

A recent study headed by Dr. Louis Judd, former director of the National Institute of Mental Health, found that many people who do not meet the current diagnostic criteria for depression nonetheless suffer real impairment due to one or more symptoms of the illness. This milder depression, which Judd has labeled "subsyndromal symptomatic depression," befalls four times the number who meet the full definition of depression.

Just how bad is this lesser depression? A recent study found that surprisingly the impairment associated with minor depression often exceeded that caused by medical conditions such as heart disease, diabetes, and arthritis. Further, people with minor depression may use even more psychiatric and other medical services than do those who suffer the full condition. The mildly depressed also take a greater economic toll on society in lost workdays than do their formally diagnosed counterparts.

Curiously, people with minor depression sometimes *lack* the symptom of depressed mood. (The three most common symptoms reported are sleep disturbances, fatigue, and thoughts of death.) Perhaps even more curious, those who do not experience lowered mood account for twice the number of disability days than those who *do* have the symptom.

To understand this, we must first realize that depression often arrives without noticeably lowering one's mood. In order to qualify for the diagnosis of major depression, one need have only five symptoms, and depressed mood need *not* be among them.

I developed the following mnemonic as a diagnostic aid and use it when I lecture on depression.

Symptoms of Depression

Physical Symptoms

A: Appetite and/or weight (e.g., 5 percent in a month) reduction or increase

P: Psychomotor retardation or agitation

E: Energy reduction (fatigue)

S: Sleep reduction or increase

Psychological Symptoms

S: Suicidal ideas or thoughts of death

W: Worthlessness or feelings of excessive/inappropriate guilt

I: Interest or pleasure-marked diminution in most activities

M: Mental ability diminution (difficulty thinking, concentrating, or deciding)

The *Diagnostic Statistical Manual IV* diagnosis of a major depressive episode in adults requires either loss of interest or depressed mood plus four other of the above symptoms to be present nearly every day during the same two-week period, and that these symptoms represent a change from previous functioning (suicidal ideation need not meet the nearly-every-day requirement).

Why Depression Is Not Diagnosed

Ask the right questions, and diagnosing depression is usually easy enough. So, *why isn't it happening?* I have come to suspect that primary care doctors, perhaps from fear of offending their patients, actually avoid inquiring into their state of mind.

The survey finding that nearly half the U.S. population had undergone a serious, diagnosable psychiatric condition also determined that only 40 percent of them had ever sought pro-

> *"Suicide rates among adolescents and young adults are . . . climbing."*

fessional help. So perhaps the most common psychiatric "condition" of modern times is massive denial. While some do engage in effective self-help programs, many resort to self-medication, which rarely cures anything and often leads to greater problems. Those who drink heavily often know quite well that they do

22

so to quell the stresses of work and personal life. A study of smokers found that those who could not quit generally suffered a high incidence of mood disorders, suggesting that smoking is too valuable a coping device for them to abandon.

It is now clear that mental or physical stress-related illness, and even serious, formal psychiatric disorders (usually involving anxiety depression or drug/ alcohol abuse), afflict the vast majority of us. And these problems are rapidly growing worse, making the task of identifying Agent Blue even more critical.

Depression Is Often Undiagnosed

by Nancy Wartik

About the author: *Nancy Wartik is a Brooklyn, New York, writer who specializes in psychology and health issues.*

It often strikes when people are young and vital. It may linger for years and become as debilitating as diabetes or arthritis. It affects one in 10 Americans annually, more than half of them women. What's the disorder? Depression. Fortunately, thanks not only to the Prozac revolution, but also to effective psychological treatments, 80% to 90% of sufferers can now find relief.

So why are most of them still not getting it? In January 1997 an expert panel convened by the National Depressive and Manic-Depressive Association in Washington sounded an alarm. "The vast majority of patients with chronic major depression are misdiagnosed, receive inappropriate or inadequate treatment or are given no treatment at all," the panel reported in *The Journal of the American Medical Association.* "It's shocking to realize that so many depressed people actually seek a doctor's help and are improperly treated," says NDMDA acting director Donna DePaul Kelly. "The system is failing them."

The situation has reached crisis dimensions, according to Ron Kessler, Ph.D., a professor of health care policy at Harvard Medical School. "In a given year, only about a third of depressed Americans get good care," he says. "The costs are enormous. Depression steals the most productive years of people's lives." Meanwhile, the specter of the ailment looms larger than ever. A 1996 World Health Organization study predicted that by 2020, depression will be the second-greatest cause of disability worldwide, preceded only by heart disease.

An Urgent Problem for Women

The question of why such a devastating ailment remains so neglected holds special urgency for women. Myrna Weissman, Ph.D., an epidemiologist at Columbia University in New York City, ranks depression among the top five health concerns confronting women today. "Despite the fact that women use

Reprinted from Nancy Wartik, "Missed Diagnosis: Why Depression Goes Untreated in Women," *American Health*, June 1997, by permission of *American Health*.

the health care system more than men do, many of their depressive symptoms aren't being diagnosed," she says. "I believe that's because they're not taken seriously."

That rings true for Laura Tracey [not her real name] of Fort Wayne, IN. Tracey, a 49-year-old chef and single parent of three, saw her mother die in a car crash when she was a child. The trauma, she believes, triggered her decades-long struggle with depression. "I tried drowning my sorrows in

> *"The vast majority of patients with chronic major depression are misdiagnosed."*

alcohol," she says. "Just dragging myself out of bed was an effort. But my doctors just kept telling me that I had PMS, that I was hysterical and that I was stressed because I'm a single mother." It wasn't until Tracey tried to commit suicide at age 43 that she finally got antidepressant treatment and therapy. "When the doctor told me I had clinical depression, I asked, 'What's that?'" she recalls. "Until then, I'd bought the idea that it's normal for a woman to have these kinds of problems."

A Sign of Weakness

Still, the chief factor in depression's undertreatment, many experts believe, is the stigma associated with mental illness. "There's a widespread belief that a general medical problem is beyond our control but that a psychiatric illness is our own fault," says Robert Hirschfeld, M.D., chairman of the department of psychiatry at the University of Texas in Galveston, who headed the NDMDA panel. "That's ludicrous. We know now that people are born with proclivities to mental illness. Yet patients are reluctant to accept a psychiatric diagnosis, doctors undervalue psychiatric problems and insurers discriminate in coverage for mental illness."

A case in point: More than half of the people who responded to a 1996 National Mental Health Association (NMHA) survey viewed depression as "a sign of weakness." This pervasive scorn makes it hard for even the well-informed to acknowledge the disease. Anne Suess [not her real name], 31, of Dallas, is a psychiatric nurse, so she knows the symptoms of depression well. But Suess suffered from bouts of extreme fatigue, irritability and suicidal feelings for 10 years before she realized that she was clinically depressed herself. "Even when you work with psychiatric illness every day, it's hard to see it in yourself," she says. "It was the type of thing I didn't want to tell anyone about."

Since a psychiatrist diagnosed her and prescribed the antidepressant Zoloft, Suess's perspective on the disease has changed. "I'd get treatment again in a second," she says. "There's no shame in a diabetic's needing insulin or nutritional counseling and no shame in my needing antidepressants or mental counseling."

Ignorance about depression's symptoms also stops people from seeking help or prevents family members from recognizing the disease in a loved one. It's not widely known, for instance, that physical ailments such as fatigue, sleep disturbances and body aches frequently characterize mood disorders. And spouses or friends who don't understand that anger and irritability can be a sign of depression often feel alienated instead of sympathetic. Another stumbling block: Because depression impairs thinking, it's difficult for sufferers to recognize it in themselves, says Ellen Leibenluft, M.D., a psychiatrist at the National Institute of Mental Health in Bethesda, MD. "Depressed people tend to be self-critical and pessimistic, which means they blame themselves for what they feel."

Explaining Away Depression

People also tend to explain away depression as an expected response to an upsetting event. "They say, 'Of course I'm depressed; my business is failing,'" says Jean Endicott, Ph.D., a professor of clinical psychology at Columbia University Medical Center and an NDMDA panel member. "But not everyone goes on to develop major depression when they suffer a setback. Some people are more biologically vulnerable than others." Similarly, depression that accompanies common life stressors such as bereavement or illness is often dismissed as normal.

Increasingly, experts stress that leaving such depressions untreated not only is a mistake, but also may speed the course of certain diseases. For example, 18% to 20% of heart disease patients also suffer from depression, and their mortality rates are higher than their nondepressed peers. And in a 1993 Montreal Heart Institute study, depressed heart attack patients were three to four times as likely to die within six months as patients who weren't depressed.

Depression Goes Undetected

Unfortunately, many doctors overlook depression, either because they aren't familiar with the symptoms or because they don't explore what's happening in a patient's life. "Talking to patients is undervalued in our medical training and culture, especially today," says Dr. Leibenluft. "It takes time, and you have to create a comfortable atmosphere to do it. You can't just stick in a needle, take blood and make the diagnosis."

Indeed, primary-care doctors spend only about 16 minutes with each patient, which may partly explain why they fail to detect serious depression in 40% to 60% of cases, according to a 1989 Rand study. Even patients diagnosed with depression don't necessarily get the right treatment: Only 5% to 10% of depressed patients in the Rand study were referred to mental health specialists.

"By 2020, depression will be the second-greatest cause of disability worldwide, preceded only by heart disease."

Another barrier to appropriate diagnosis and treatment is money—or the lack of it. In a study of 101 depressed New York City area residents, conducted by Dr. Endicott, 36% said one reason they didn't get treatment was that they couldn't afford it. The fact that insurance coverage for mental health is often woefully inadequate exacerbates the problem, according to the NDMDA report. While the panel didn't single out managed care, they pointed to such worrisome industry trends as a tendency to push doctors toward prescribing older, cheaper antidepressants instead of pricier but more effective medications, or putting un-realistic limits on the number of treatments or therapy sessions allowed.

Positive Strides in Mental Health Care

The overall picture isn't completely gloomy, however. In 1996, Congress passed an amendment mandating that companies with 50 or more workers offer equal benefit limits for mental and medical health care (both annual and life-time) starting in 1998. This amendment is a "good first step," says NMHA spokesperson Patrick Cody. "Now we need equal access to an appropriate num-ber of treatments, whether the illness is psychological or physical."

Perhaps more important, the gap between scientific knowledge and practical treatment of depression is narrowing. Due to vastly improved medication and increased public awareness, a third of those with depression today get adequate treatment, compared with just 10% in 1980. "We've made a lot of progress, though not nearly enough," says Dr. Hirschfeld. "We can't always treat cancer and we can't always treat heart disease, but we can nearly always treat depres-sion. It makes no sense that people are suffering needlessly."

Dissociative Identity Disorder Is a Common Response to Childhood Trauma

by the Sidran Foundation

About the author: *The Sidran Foundation is a nonprofit organization whose mission is advocacy, education, and research on behalf of people with psychiatric disabilities.*

The growing recognition of psychiatric conditions resulting from traumatic influences is a significant mental health issue of the 1990s. Until recently considered rare and mysterious psychiatric curiosities, Dissociative Identity Disorder (DID) (until very recently known as Multiple Personality Disorder—MPD) and other Dissociative Disorders (DD) are now understood to be fairly common effects of severe trauma in early childhood, most typically extreme, repeated physical, sexual, and/or emotional abuse.

In 1994, with the publication of the American Psychiatric Association's *Diagnostic and Statistical Manual of Mental Disorders-IV*, Multiple Personality Disorder (MPD) was changed to Dissociative Identity Disorder (DID), reflecting changes in professional understanding of the disorder, which resulted largely from increased empirical research of trauma-based dissociative disorders.

Post-Traumatic Stress Disorder (PTSD), widely accepted as a major mental illness affecting 9–10% of the general population, is closely related to Dissociative Identity Disorder and other Dissociative Disorders. In fact, as many as 80–100% of people diagnosed with DID also have a secondary diagnosis of PTSD. The personal and societal cost of trauma disorders [including DID, DD, and PTSD] is extremely high. For example, recent research suggests the risk of suicide attempts among people with trauma disorders may be even higher than among people who have major depression. In addition, there is evidence that

Reprinted from *Dissociative Identity Disorder (Multiple Personality Disorder)*, a brochure published by the Sidran Foundation, ©1994. Reprinted with permission.

people with trauma disorders have higher rates of alcoholism, chronic medical illnesses, and abusiveness in succeeding generations.

What Is Dissociation?

Dissociation is a mental process which produces a lack of connection in a person's thoughts, memories, feelings, actions, or sense of identity. During the period of time when a person is dissociating, certain information is not associated with other information as it normally would be. For example, during a traumatic experience, a person may dissociate the memory of the place and circumstances of the trauma from his ongoing memory, resulting in a temporary mental escape from the fear and pain of the trauma and, in some cases, a memory gap surrounding the experience. Because this process can produce changes in memory, people who frequently dissociate often find their senses of personal history and identity are affected.

Most clinicians believe that dissociation exists on a continuum of severity. This continuum reflects a wide range of experiences and/or symptoms. At one end are mild dissociative experiences common to most people, such as daydreaming, highway hypnosis, or "getting lost" in a book or movie, all of which involve "losing touch" with conscious awareness of one's immediate surroundings. At the other extreme is complex, chronic dissociation, such as in cases of Dissociative Identity Disorder and other Dissociative Disorders, which may result in serious impairment or inability to function. Some people with DID can hold highly responsible jobs, contributing to society in a variety of professions, the arts, and public service. To co-workers, neighbors, and others with whom they interact daily, they apparently function normally.

> *"Dissociative Disorders . . . are now understood to be fairly common effects of severe trauma in early childhood."*

There is a great deal of overlap of symptoms and experiences among the various Dissociative Disorders, including DID. For the sake of clarity, this viewpoint will refer to DID as a collective term. Individuals should seek help from qualified mental health providers to answer questions about their own particular circumstances and diagnoses.

How Does DID Develop?

When faced with overwhelmingly traumatic situations from which there is no physical escape, a child may resort to "going away" in his or her head. This ability is typically used by children as an extremely effective defense against acute physical and emotional pain, or anxious anticipation of that pain. By this dissociative process, thoughts, feelings, memories, and perceptions of the traumatic experiences can be separated off psychologically, allowing the child to function as if the trauma had not occurred.

DID is often referred to as a highly creative survival technique, because it allows individuals enduring "hopeless" circumstances to preserve some areas of healthy functioning. Over time, however, for a child who has been repeatedly physically and sexually assaulted, defensive dissociation becomes reinforced and conditioned. Because the dissociative escape is so effective, children who are very practiced at it may automatically use it whenever they feel threatened or anxious— even if the anxiety-producing situation is not abusive.

"Current research shows that DID may affect 1% of the general population and perhaps as many as 5–20% of people in psychiatric hospitals."

Often, even after the traumatic circumstances are long past, the left-over pattern of defensive dissociation remains. Chronic defensive dissociation may lead to serious dysfunction in work, social, and daily activities. Repeated dissociation may result in a series of separate entities, or mental states, which may eventually take on identities of their own. These entities may become the internal "personality states," of a DID system. Changing between these states of consciousness is described as "switching."

People with DID may experience any of the following: depression, mood swings, suicidal tendencies, sleep disorders (insomnia, night terrors, and sleep walking), panic attacks and phobias (flashbacks, reactions to stimuli or "triggers"), alcohol and drug abuse, compulsions and rituals, psychotic-like symptoms (including auditory and visual hallucinations), and eating disorders. In addition, individuals with DID can experience headaches, amnesias, time loss, trances, and "out of body experiences." Some people with DID have a tendency toward self-persecution, self-sabotage, and even violence (both self-inflicted and outwardly directed).

Who Gets DID?

The vast majority (as many as 98 to 99%) of individuals who develop DID have documented histories of repetitive, overwhelming, and often life-threatening trauma at a sensitive developmental stage of childhood (usually before the age of nine), and they may possess an inherited biological predisposition for dissociation. In our culture the most frequent precursor to DID is extreme physical, emotional, and sexual abuse in childhood, but survivors of other kinds of trauma in childhood (such as natural disasters, invasive medical procedures, war, and torture) have also reacted by developing DID.

Current research shows that DID may affect 1% of the general population and perhaps as many as 5–20% of people in psychiatric hospitals, many of whom have received other diagnoses. The incidence rates are even higher among sexual abuse survivors and individuals with chemical dependencies. These statistics put DID in the same category as schizophrenia, depression, and anxiety, as one of the four major mental health problems today.

Most current literature shows that DID is recognized primarily among fe-
males. The latest research, however, indicates that the disorders may be equally
prevalent (but less frequently diagnosed) among the male population. Men with
DID are most likely to be in treatment for other mental illnesses, for drug and
alcohol abuse, or incarcerated.

DID survivors often spend years living with misdiagnoses, consequently
floundering within the mental health system. They change from therapist to
therapist and from medication to medication, getting treatment for symptoms
but making little or no actual progress. Research has documented that on average, people with DID have spent seven years in the mental health system prior
to accurate diagnosis.

This is common, because the list of symptoms that cause a person with DID
to seek treatment is very similar to those of many other psychiatric diagnoses.
In fact, many people who are diagnosed with DID also have secondary diagnoses of depression, anxiety, or panic disorders.

Do People Actually Have Multiple Personalities?

Yes, and no. One of the reasons for the decision by the psychiatric community to change the disorder's name from Multiple Personality Disorder to Dissociative Identity Disorder is that "multiple personalities" is somewhat of a
misleading term. A person diagnosed with DID has within her two or more entities, or personality states, each with its own independent way of relating, per-
ceiving, thinking and remembering about herself and her life. If two or more of
these entities take control of the person's behavior at a given time, a diagnosis
of MPD can be made. These entities previously were often called "personalities," even though the term did not accurately reflect the common definition of
the word as the total aspect of our psychological makeup. Other terms often
used by therapists and survivors to describe these entities are: "alternate personalities," "alters," "parts," "states of consciousness," "ego states," and "identities." It is important to keep in mind that although these alternate personality
states may appear to be very different, they are all manifestations of a single
person.

Dissociative Disorders are highly responsive to individual psychotherapy, or
"talk therapy," as well as to a range of other treatment modalities, including
medications, hypnotherapy, and adjunctive therapies such as art or movement
therapy. In fact, among comparably severe psychiatric disorders, DID may be
the condition that carries the best prognosis, if proper treatment is undertaken
and completed. The course of treatment is long-term, intensive, and invariably
painful, as it generally involves remembering and reclaiming the dissociated
traumatic experiences. Nevertheless, individuals with DID have been successfully treated by therapists of all professional backgrounds working in a variety
of settings.

Mental Illness Is Too Broadly Defined

by Sheila M. Rothman

About the author: *Sheila M. Rothman is a senior research scholar at the College of Physicians and Surgeons of Columbia University.*

In recent years, the types of behavior that are labeled as diseases have increased dramatically. Modern psychiatry is ready to treat not only acute depression and schizophrenia, but also moodiness, anxiety and poor self-esteem, feelings most of us have experienced at one time or another.

Nowhere is this development clearer than in editions of the psychiatrists' desk manual, *Diagnostic and Statistical Manual of Mental Disorders*, or DSM. Published by the American Psychiatric Association, the first edition, which came out in 1952, listed 60 categories, including schizophrenia, paranoia and other aberrant forms of behavior. By contrast, the fourth edition or DSM-IV, which came out in 1994, has more than 350 listings (by my count). Many of the disorders it describes have overlapping criteria and subtle manifestations and each may have six or more symptoms. Patients who exhibit three or more are given the diagnosis.

Is Everyone Mentally Ill?

Since many of us have suffered from at least some of the symptoms that characterize the new illnesses, their status as disorders raises the prospect of defining us all as mentally ill. The proliferation of disease categories is beginning to blur the distinction between health and illness, between person and patient. And by offering to relieve us of the moods and anxieties that are part of everyday life, doctors are providing something other than cures for given ailments: They are ready to help make us better than normal.

Take one of the newly classified diseases, body dysmorphic disorder. BDD, as it is known, is characterized by spending excessive time examining oneself before a mirror and by great concern with the size or shape of a body part. But how do you distinguish the disease from vanity? In her book, *The Broken Mir-*

Abridged from Sheila M. Rothman, "There's a Name for What Ails You," *The Washington Post National Weekly Edition*, April 21, 1997, p. 25. Reprinted with permission.

ror, Katharine Phillips, a psychiatrist at Brown University School of Medicine who helped to establish BDD's criteria, says that more than 5 million Americans (men as well as women) suffer from it. She concedes that the "difference between BDD and normal appearance concerns may be largely a matter of degree." But that does not dissuade her, or the American Psychiatric Association, from labeling it a disorder—and including it in DSM-IV.

Another new disease, premenstrual dysphoric disorder (PMDD) is marked by irritability, tension, sadness, lethargy, headaches and weight gain. What transforms these commonplace symptoms into a disease is their timing; they generally appear one week before menstruation and disappear a few days afterward. But are symptoms that are unremarkable and transitory truly indicative of a disease? Is an (imperfect) correlation with a normal bodily rhythm and hormonal shift sufficient grounds to find pathology? With PMDD the line between the normal and abnormal becomes murky.

Expanding the Definition of Mental Illness

The editors of DSM-IV are comfortable in expanding further the already broad categories of mental disorders. Under the heading "Other Conditions That May Be a Focus of Clinical Attention," they include the "partner relational problem, sibling relational problem, age-related cognitive decline, bereavement, academic problem, occupational problem, and phase of life problem." Put all these categories together and the division between patient and person virtually disappears.

This is also evident in the expanding group of diseases associated with known eating disorders. The first to be widely recognized, in the 1970s, was anorexia nervosa, the symptoms of which include an intense fear of gaining weight, amenorrhea (the absence of menstruation) and a distorted body image, so that sufferers think they are fat even when they're underweight or emaciated. Anorexia was joined in the psychiatric literature of the 1980s by bulimia nervosa, which is characterized by binge eating or chronic dieting and a persistent concern with body shape and size. Both these disorders represent very real problems for sufferers, but since the symptoms may sporadically appear in healthy individuals, psychiatrists were obliged to evaluate "the context in which the eating occurs," according to the manual. What is "excessive consumption at a typical meal might be considered normal during a celebration or holiday meal." To look at it any other way, we would all be candidates for psychiatric treatment at Thanksgiving.

"Modern psychiatry is ready to treat not only acute depression and schizophrenia, but also moodiness, anxiety and poor self-esteem."

In a *New England Journal of Medicine* article entitled "Running: An Analog of Anorexia?" Alayne Yates writes that regular exercise can be symptomatic of disease. Exercise that is too regular—or, in psychiatric terms, compulsive—indicates an "activity disorder," writes Yates. At issue is not the timing of the behavior (as in PMDD) or its context (as in bulimia nervosa), but its purpose. In Yates's view, excessive running to lose weight or to control weight becomes pathological. The behavior may well be included in the next edition of DSM: Psychiatry is clearly troubled by tracks, fitness centers and gyms.

The fading distinction between normal and abnormal that these newly defined diseases suggest is still more evident in so-called "shadow syndromes." Proposed by John Ratey, a psychiatrist at Harvard Medical School whose book takes the term for its title, the syndromes represent "hidden psychological disorders." People who are "a little bit" depressed or anxious or display bad tempers suffer from them. Although Ratey concedes that the manifestations are too mild to fit what he calls "the DSM's concrete blocks," he nevertheless argues that feelings of this sort pose genuine risks: "People's lives can and do crash . . . because of small problems."

This extraordinary expansion of psychiatric illnesses coincides with our increasing interest in biological determinism. Indeed, the two trends reinforce one another. The new field suggests that characteristics once believed to be individual and fluid are, to the contrary, hard-wired into us. Biologists and geneticists are encroaching on the field of psychiatry, hypothesizing that biochemical deficiencies, often caused by a genetic defect, are trig-

> *"Are symptoms that are unremarkable and transitory truly indicative of a disease?"*

gering depression, aggression and anxiety. Although they concede that family dynamics may be relevant, they put nature firmly over nurture. In their view—and in contrast to the accepted psychiatric thinking of most of the 20th century—biology matters most. Not surprisingly, this orientation is generating in the public a kind of genomic anxiety, which recent reports on cloning only exacerbate. Perhaps we really are puppets at the end of a DNA string—our temperaments, like the possibility that we'll develop cancer, defined by our genes.

"Disturbed Brain Chemistry"

The most frequently invoked biological explanation for many forms of irregular behavior involves deficiencies in serotonin, one of the brain's natural chemicals that transmit signals between nerve cells. In *The Broken Mirror,* Phillips relates body dysmorphic disorder to an "abnormality in the serotonin neurotransmitter system." Other psychiatrists have attributed eating and exercise disorders, shadow syndromes and even PMDD to low serotonin levels. What is their evidence? That patients feel better once their serotonin levels are raised through the administration of medications called selective serotonin reuptake inhibitors (SSRIs), of which Prozac is the most often prescribed. Because patients with BDD seem to respond to these drugs, Phillips insists that "disturbed brain chemistry plays an important role" in the disease.

Phillips's reasoning fits neatly with the arguments Peter Kramer put forward in his bestseller, *Listening to Prozac*. Both psychiatrists use the same circular reasoning: The existence of a disease is confirmed because treatment sparks a positive pharmacological response. Once upon a time doctors diagnosed the disease and then discovered a cure. Now doctors have interventions that inspire them to create new diseases.

Accept for the moment that a heightened concern with appearance or a little bit of depression does constitute a disease. What type of physician does one go to and for what kind of treatment? Psychiatrists insist that despite the biological cause of these illnesses, they are behavior-related and are therefore best treated by psychiatric methods. Although some psychiatrists still rely on long-term psychotherapy, essential to almost everyone's practice today is Prozac or one of its pharmacological equivalents. And patients with a wide variety of complaints appear to improve on Prozac. Their "self-esteem and self-confidence get a boost," Phillips reports. They "feel more normal."

Although clinical trials confirming claims like Phillips's are in short supply, enthusiasm is rampant. Prozac and similar SSRIs have been successfully used in treating classic obsessive-compulsive disorders (sufferers may not be able to leave the house because hand washing or floor washing consumes the day). Since many of the newly discovered diseases are also characterized by repetitive behavior or concerns, many psychiatrists are convinced that SSRIs will work for them as well. Meanwhile, anecdotes substitute for data. "Prozac," Kramer maintained, "seemed to give social confidence to the habitually timid, to make the sensitive brash, to lend the introvert the social skills of the salesman." Phillips concurs: "The scientist in me wants to be cautious." However, "my treatment of many patients, many of whom have suffered for decades and who have responded well—sometimes miraculously—to these approaches leads me to advocate them.". . .

Is Normalcy Enough?

The new disease categories are also prompting physicians to minimize the differences between cure and enhancement, between returning patients to normal and making them better than normal. Kramer coined the term "cosmetic psychopharmacology" to describe the treatment of patients whose behavior was optimized through Prozac. And Ratey uses SSRIs to treat shadow syndromes on the grounds that: "For many of us, normalcy is not enough.

> *"Doctors have interventions that inspire them to create new diseases."*

The fact that a dark temper or a pessimistic character may be normal does not mean it is easy to live with." Yet, to the extent that physicians make enhancement their goal, all of us become perpetual patients. With this reasoning, the criterion for visiting a doctor's office will become an existential vision of the person one might be. What a heady task for physicians, and what an anguished position for the rest of us.

No one wants to forgo the therapeutic benefits that 21st century medicine will bring; some of us may even wish to gain a competitive edge through enhancement. But how we can achieve these ends without losing our personal identities or becoming perennial patients is one of the most critical challenges posed by the new psychiatry, biology and genetics. After all, none of us wants to spend the better part of life in physicians' waiting rooms.

> *"To the extent that physicians make [personality] enhancement their goal, all of us become perpetual patients."*

Physical Ailments Are Commonly Mistaken for Mental Illnesses

by Allen P. Wilkinson

About the author: *Allen P. Wilkinson is a legal writer and consultant in Whittier, California.*

Millions of Americans suffer from real or apparent mental disorders and seek psychiatric treatment for them. However, a significant number of psychiatric symptoms are caused by an underlying physical condition. Many psychiatric patients are actually suffering from a physical illness.

Studies of 4,500 psychiatric patients showed that 58 percent referred for psychiatric care suffered from an undiagnosed, significant physical abnormality. In about 22 percent of those cases, the physical condition was directly related to the psychiatric symptoms. However, only in half of those cases did the psychiatrist correctly diagnose the underlying physical problem.

Another study of 3,500 psychiatric patients found that more than half had a physical disease. Of these, 23 percent were discharged from psychiatric care after they received appropriate medical treatment for their physical condition.

Mistaking Physical Illness for Mental Illness

Psychiatrists generally focus primarily or even solely on the psychiatric aspects and mental symptoms of a patient's condition, an approach reinforced by the *Diagnostic and Statistical Manual of Mental Disorders* (fourth edition), published by the American Psychiatric Press. Because of this mindset, physical illnesses are sometimes overlooked or discounted as somatic manifestations of the mental illness.

A patient whose apparent mental disorder is caused by a physical condition may wind up spending thousands of dollars and years in therapy without receiving appropriate treatment for the real problem.

Excerpted from Allen P. Wilkinson, "Psychiatric Malpractice: Failure to Diagnose Physical Illness," *Trial*, May 1997; ©1997 by Allen P. Wilkinson. Reprinted with permission.

Patients may undergo unnecessary, lengthy psychiatric hospital stays, be involuntarily committed, or even commit suicide as a result of the mental manifestations of the untreated physical illness. They may be put on powerful psychotropic (mind-altering) drugs that will do nothing to treat the underlying physical condition. These drugs can cause serious, even lethal, side effects and may exacerbate the actual physical illness.

"A significant number of psychiatric symptoms are caused by an underlying physical condition."

The failure to diagnose the physical condition may allow it to deteriorate to the point that surgery or other drastic medical intervention is necessary. In some cases, if a physical problem is left untreated long enough, any treatment may be too late.

A Psychiatrist's Duty

A psychiatrist has a duty to exercise the requisite standard of due care in diagnosing a patient's illness and will not be liable for an erroneous diagnosis so long as that standard of care is met. As a medical specialist, a psychiatrist owes a higher duty of skill and care toward patients than a nonpsychiatrist.

In most states, the duty of care awed by a psychiatrist is measured by a national standard. That duty is generally described as the degree of care expected of other psychiatrists with similar skills acting under the same or similar circumstances. In determining a psychiatrist's standard of care, advances in the profession and the resources available to the psychiatrist must be taken into account.

Courts usually take pains to point out that the diagnosis of mental illness is not an exact science. One court noted that "diagnosis with absolute precision and certainty is impossible."

Courts also realize that, in addition to considering the psychiatric aspects of mental illness, psychiatrists must think about possible physical causes of apparent mental disorders. For example, a federal district court in Maryland acknowledged this duty of care when it stated, "The psychiatrist's primary responsibility is to evaluate and treat the patient's mental condition. *Since many psychological problems have an organic basis, this responsibility includes determining whether there might be an organic etiology for the psychological problems."*

Ignoring Possible Physical Causes

Psychiatrists are medical doctors, but they generally use little, if any, of their nonpsychiatric medical training in their practices. Some have let their medical knowledge of the body and physical disorders atrophy. Their offices usually lack the facilities and medical equipment needed to perform a competent, thorough physical examination. In the typical psychiatrist's office, not even a stethoscope rests on the desk, let alone on the doctor's shoulders. For these reasons, many psychiatrists are no longer qualified to perform even the most basic physical examination.

One study found that only 8 percent of psychiatrists did any physical examination of their patients at all, and then only on selected outpatients. Another study of 100 psychiatrists revealed that none performed routine physicals. Accordingly, most psychiatrists, in the exercise of due care, should refer patients to other physicians competent to perform thorough exams to rule out possible physical causes of psychiatric symptoms.

In referring a patient for a physical examination, the psychiatrist should specify particular physical illnesses that the general practitioner or internist should look for or tests that should be performed. For example, a psychiatrist referring a depressed patient for a physical examination should ask the examining physician to perform, among other things, a full panel of thyroid function tests on the patient to see whether hypothyroidism (an underactive thyroid) is the culprit.

Thyroid disorders can cause a wide variety of physical and mental ailments. Hypothyroidism can result in fatigue, lethargy, excess sleeping, weight gain, dry and puffy skin, thinning hair, disorganized thought processes, speech changes (such as a deeper or hoarse voice), and even incoherence. Many of these symptoms are also associated with clinical depression.

The Importance of Differential Diagnosis

The process of considering all possible causes—both physical and mental—for a patient's symptoms is known in medical terms as making a "differential diagnosis." *Stedman's Medical Dictionary* defines this as "the determination of which of two or more diseases with similar symptoms is the one from which the patient is suffering, by a systematic comparison and contrasting of clinical findings." Only by conducting a differential diagnosis, in which all possible physical as well as mental causes are considered, can the psychiatrist or examining physician make an accurate diagnosis and provide effective treatment. Otherwise, patients are denied the help they need.

For example, one woman who suffered from despondency, cognitive problems, and fatigue went through a year of psychotherapy that did nothing to alleviate her symptoms. After her second suicide attempt, she was hospitalized. Hospital doctors examined her carefully and ordered appropriate diagnostic blood and thyroid tests, which revealed that she was suffering from

> *"[A] study of 3,500 psychiatric patients found that more than half had a physical disease."*

hypothyroidism. With synthetic thyroid supplements, the woman recovered fully and became free of psychiatric symptoms.

Patients who have been negligently misdiagnosed have the right to take their grievances to court. In one case, the federal government was held liable for the failure of psychiatrists at a Veterans Administration hospital to diagnose a patient's benign brain tumor. The patient had been treated for paranoia and depression before the tumor was detected.

One woman who brought suit was treated for three years for a "hysterical personality," when in fact she was suffering from a spinal cord tumor. However, judgment for the defendants was affirmed on appeal. The court held that the plaintiff's claim—that the woman would have survived if the doctors had diagnosed and begun treating her tumor earlier—was too speculative.

An Example of Differential Diagnosis

A case encountered by psychiatrist Sydney Walker III, director of the Southern California Neuropsychiatric Institute in La Jolla, illustrates the type of thinking and diagnostic steps that lead to a correct diagnosis. He examined a 40-year-old man who believed everyone was out to get him, heard voices in his head when women tried to speak to him, and thought people talked about him frequently, among other symptoms. A previous psychiatrist had diagnosed psychotic disorder not otherwise specified; possible schizophrenia; and possible bipolar mood disorder, mixed state (manic depression with simultaneous symptoms of both mania and depression).

Walker recognized the man's complaints as potentially symptomatic of Wilson's disease, a genetic disorder that causes an excess of copper to accumulate in bodily tissues, especially the liver, brain, kidneys, and cornea.

> *"One study found that only 8 percent of psychiatrists did any physical examination of their patients at all."*

It can cause severe liver disease, tremor, rigid muscles, dementia, and behavioral symptoms ranging from sexual exhibitionism to psychosis. These symptoms often appear before any signs of liver disease show up.

As part of his differential diagnosis, Walker looked closely into the man's eyes and found the telltale sign of Wilson's disease: golden brown or green rings on the periphery of his corneas. Diagnostic tests were performed that confirmed Walker's suspicions. The patient was properly treated for his physical condition, and the mental manifestations resolved themselves. . . .

A Call for Higher Standards

Requiring psychiatrists to put more emphasis on possible physical causes of apparent mental disorders places no greater duty on them in diagnosing patients' true illnesses. Too many psychiatrists are not performing or ordering the necessary diagnostic physical workups to discover the actual causes of patients' ailments. But custom does not equate with standard of care.

In the words of the U.S. Supreme Court, "What usually is done may be evidence of what ought to be done, but what ought to be done is fixed by a standard of reasonable prudence, whether it usually is complied with or not."

Therapists Diagnose Mental Illness Without Basis

by Scott D. Miller, Mark A. Hubble, and Barry L. Duncan

About the authors: *Scott D. Miller, Mark A. Hubble, and Barry L. Duncan are associates at the Institute for the Study of Therapeutic Change in Chicago, Illinois.*

Some time ago, the authors of this article conducted a little experiment. We showed to a group of therapists who had come to our center for training, a videotape of a family we had interviewed. Following the videotape, we asked the therapists to use their skills to describe what they had observed. They quickly began describing the family and its various members.

The mother, the therapists agreed, was obviously an "angry and controlling woman" who was frustrated with her marriage and overwhelmed by her child-rearing responsibilities. Several group members pointed out, however, that the woman's outward expression of anger was merely the superficial manifestation of an underlying depression. On the other hand, her husband, the father of their three children, was described as "cutoff and distant" from the family. A few therapists with backgrounds in drug and alcohol counseling even identified the signs of a "hidden" drinking problem in the father. In particular, they pointed out how the wife consistently "enabled" the man to remain aloof with her and the children during the interview.

When asked for recommendations, nearly all of the therapists agreed that the family should continue with some sort of family therapy. In addition. they recommended that the mother be referred to a psychiatrist, the father to an addictions specialist, and the daughter to her own individual therapist.

Once the therapists were finished with their descriptions and recommendations, we informed them that watching the videotape had actually been part of an experiment designed to teach therapists about how their beliefs affect their

Excerpted from Scott D. Miller, Mark A. Hubble, and Barry L. Duncan, "Counseling for Change," *Professional Counselor*, February 1997. Reprinted by permission.

clinical observations. In reality, the videotape they had all seen was not an actual therapy session and the subjects were not real clients. Moreover. far from being sick, the individuals on the tape were actually part of a healthy, well-functioning family—neighbors and long-time friends of ours—who were discussing and planning an upcoming family picnic.

Each time we conducted the experiment, the results were largely the same. At no time did any therapist who viewed the tape discover our ruse. More troubling, however, is that so few therapists noticed any signs of mental health in this obviously healthy, well-functioning family. How could this be?

Dwelling on Sickness

Precious little professional training time is spent on the contribution that mental health makes to change in psychotherapy. Rather, the majority of clinical education—in the form of course work, professional publications, and continuing education seminars—is spent on "sickness." The result, as our study so clearly demonstrates, is that the field is often more adept at identifying problems as opposed to solutions; deficits as opposed to capabilities; weaknesses as opposed to strengths.

Of course, there is a kind of commonsense appeal to the domination of mental health problems in the professional discourse. After all, the reasoning usually goes, people don't seek out a therapist when they are doing well. In the last analysis, however, the nearly exclusive focus on problems in modern mental health treatment results in a professional who seems more capable of diagnosing a client's problems than solving them.

Overstating Mental Illness

As an example of how problems dominate the professional discourse, consider the staggering rise in the number of diagnostic categories of mental illness that has taken place over the last 40 years. Since the *Diagnostic and Statistical Manual of Mental Disorders* was first published in 1952, the number of diagnostic categories included in the volume has increased a whopping 300 percent,

even though there is no evidence that the huge increase in diagnostic categories in any way reflects a similar increase in the incidence of mental illness in the general population.

Furthermore, in the clinical literature, clients are most often portrayed as the "unactualized" message-bearers of family dysfunction, manufac-

> *"The field [of therapy] is often more adept at identifying problems as opposed to solutions; deficits as opposed to capabilities; weaknesses as opposed to strengths."*

turers of resistance, and in most therapeutic traditions, targets for the presumably all-important technical intervention. For example, experts insist that 96 percent of the American public grew up in a dysfunctional family and that upwards of 230 million Americans are suffering the negative effects of an alcoholic home.

Portraying Clients as Damaged

Consider how clients have been portrayed in the lead articles of recent issues of *Professional Counselor.* In the February 1996 issue, for example, a variety of mental "health" experts basically described their clients as "unfulfilled and disconnected personality disorders living in an antisocial society"; "young, wounded spirits with hardened hearts"; and "borderline addicts." Later in the year, clients were referred to as "shaken victims"; "self-destructive adolescents full of self-hatred"; and "numb, shattered, dependent, passive and psychologically impaired victims of intergenerational abuse."

> *"Experts insist that 96 percent of the American public grew up in a dysfunctional family."*

It is curious that the very profession that makes helping a virtue has made a virtual cult out of client incompetence. As Bernie Zilbergeld observed in *The Shrinking of America,* "In the [modern] therapeutic view, people [may not be] regarded as vile or as having done anything they should feel guilty about, but *there is certainly something wrong with them."*

Multiple Personality Disorder Is Induced by Therapists

by Paul R. McHugh

About the author: *Paul R. McHugh is director of psychiatry at Johns Hopkins University School of Medicine in Baltimore, Maryland.*

Where's hysteria now that we need it? With the fourth edition of the *Diagnostic and Statistical Manual of Mental Disorders* (DSM-IV), psychiatrists have developed a common language and a common approach to diagnosis. But in the process of operationalizing diagnoses, we may have lost some concepts about patient behavior. The term "hysteria" disappeared when the third edition of the *Diagnostic and Statistical Manual of Mental Disorders* (DSM-III) was published in 1950; without it, psychiatrists have been deprived of a scientific concept essential to the development of new ideas: the null hypothesis. This loss hits home with the epidemic of multiple personality disorder (MPD).

The work of Talcott Parsons, David Mechanic, and Isidore Pilowsky taught psychiatrists to appreciate that phenomena such as hysterical paralyses, blindness, and pseudoseizures were actually behaviors with a goal: achieving the "sick role." Inspired by Parsons, Mechanic and Pilowsky used the term "abnormal illness behavior" in lieu of hysteria. Their approach eliminated the stigma of malingering that had been implied in hysteria and indicated that patients could take on such behavior without fraudulent intent. They were describing an old reality of medical experience.

Some people—experiencing emotional distress in the face of a variety of life circumstances and conflicts—complain to doctors about physical or psychological symptoms that they claim are signs of illness. Sometimes they display gross impairments of movement or consciousness; sometimes the features are subtle and changing. These complaints prompt doctors to launch investigations in laboratories, to conduct elaborate and sometimes dangerous studies of the

Excerpted from Paul R. McHugh, "Resolved: Multiple Personality Disorder Is an Individually and Socially Created Artifact," *Journal of the American Academy of Child and Adolescent Psychiatry*, July 1995, vol. 34, no. 7, p. 957. Reprinted with permission.

brain or body, and to consult with experts, who examine the patient for esoteric disease. As the investigation proceeds, the patient may become still more persuaded that an illness is at work and begin to model the signs of disorder on the subtle suggestions of the physician's inquiry. For example, a patient with complaints of occasional lapses in alertness might—in the course of investigations that include visits to the epilepsy clinic and to the electroencephalogram (EEG) laboratory for sleep studies, photic stimulation, and nasopharyngeal leads— gradually develop the frenzied thrashing movements of the limbs that require the protective attention of several nurses and hospital aides.

Eventually, with the patient no better and the investigations proving fruitless, a psychiatric consultant alert to the concept of hysteria and its contemporary link to the "sick role" might recognize that the patient's disorder is not an epileptic but a behavioral one. The patient is displaying movements that attract medical attention and provide the privileges of patienthood.

Defining the "Sick Role"

Talcott Parsons, the Harvard sociologist, pointed out in the 1950s that medicine was an organized component of our society intended to aid, through professional knowledge, the sick and the impaired. To accomplish this, certain individuals—physicians—are licensed by society to decide not only how to manage the sick, but to choose and distinguish the sick from other impaired people. Such an identification can provide these "sick" individuals with certain social privileges, i.e., rest, freedom from employment, and support from others during the reign of the condition. The person given the appellation "sick" by the social spokesman—the physician—was assumed by the society to respond to these privileges with other actions, i.e., cooperating with the intrusions of investigators of the illness and making every effort at rehabilitation so as to return to health. The hidden assumption is that the burdens and pains of illness act to drive the patient toward these cooperative actions with the physicians and thus to be happy to relinquish the few small pleasures that can be found in being treated as a victim of sickness.

However, because there are advantages to the sick role, there are some situations in which a person might seek this role without a "ticket of admission," a disease. This is hardly a remarkable idea as almost anyone has noticed the temptation to "call in sick" when troubles are afoot. But in some patients—those with emotional

> *"The distressing symptoms [of MPD] continue as long as therapeutic attention is focused on finding more alters."*

conflicts, weakened self-criticism, and high suggestibility—this temptation can be transformed, usually with some prompting, into the conviction that they are infirm. This kind of patient may, in fact, use more and more information from the medical profession's vities to amplify the expression of the infirmity.

The Case of Hysteroepilepsy

Psychiatrists have known about these matters of social and psychological dynamics for more than 100 years. They were brought vividly to attention by the distinguished pupil of Jean-Martin Charcot, Joseph Babinski (he of the planter response). Like Sigmund Freud and Pierre Janet, Babinski had observed Charcot manage patients with, what Charcot called, "hysteroepilepsy." But Babinski was convinced that hysteroepilepsy was not a new disorder.

> *"MPD is [a] behavioral disorder . . . in distressed people who are looking for help."*

He believed that the women at Charcot's clinic were being persuaded—and not so subtly—to take on the features of epilepsy by the interest Charcot and his assistants expressed. Babinski also believed that these women were vulnerable to this persuasion because of distressing states of mind provoked in their life circumstances and their roles as intriguing patients and the subject of attention from many distinguished physicians who offered them a haven of care. . . .

Babinski wrote that just as hysteroepilepsy rested on persuasion, so a form of counterpersuasion could correct it. He demonstrated that these women improved when they were taken from the wards and clinics where other afflicted women—epileptic and pseudoepileptic—were housed and when the attention of the staff was turned away from their seizures and onto their lives. These measures—isolation and countersuggestion—had the advantage of limiting the rewards for the behavior and of prompting a search for and treatment of the troubles in the personal life.

How Therapists Induce MPD

All this became embedded in the concept of hysteria and needs to be reapplied in the understanding of MPD. The patients I have seen have been referred to the Johns Hopkins Health System because elsewhere they have become stuck in the process of therapy. The histories are similar. They were mostly women who in the course of some distress sought psychiatric assistance. In the course of this assistance—and often early in the process—a therapist offered them a fairly crude suggestion that they might harbor some "alter" personalities. As an example of the crudity of the suggestions to the patient, I offer this published direction by S.E. Buie of how to both make the diagnosis and elicit "alters":

> The *sine qua non* of MPD is a second personality who at some time comes out and takes executive control of the patient's behavior. It may happen that an alter personality will reveal itself to you during this [assessment] process, but more likely it will not. So you may have to elicit an alter personality. . . . To begin the process of eliciting an alter, you can begin by indirect questioning such as, "Have you ever felt like another part of you does things that you can't control?" If she gives positive or ambiguous responses, ask for specific examples. You are trying to develop a picture of what the alter personality is like.

. . . At this point, you might ask the host personality, "Does this set of feelings have a name?" Occasionally you will get a name. Often the host personality will not know. You can then focus on a particular event or set of behaviors and follow up on those. For instance, you can ask, "Can I talk to the part of you who is taking those long drives to the country?"

Once the patient permits the therapist to "talk to the part . . . who is taking those long drives," the patient is committed to having MPD and is forced to act in ways consistent with this role. The patient is then placed into care on units or in services—often titled "the dissociative service"—at the institution. She meets other patients with the same compliant responses to therapists' suggestions. She and the staff begin a continuous search for other "alters." With the discovery of the first "alter," the barrier of self-criticism and self-observation is breached. No obstacles to invention remain.

Countless numbers of personalities emerge over time. What began as two or three may develop to 99 or 100. The distressing symptoms continue as long as therapeutic attention is focused on finding more alters and sustaining the view that the problems relate to an "intriguing capacity" to dissociate or fractionate the self.

Challenging MPD Diagnoses

At Johns Hopkins, we see patients in whom MPD has been diagnosed because symptoms of depression have continued despite therapy elsewhere. Our referrals have been few and our experience, therefore, is only now building, probably because our views—that MPD may be a therapist-induced artifact—have only recently become generally known in our community.

We seem to challenge the widely accepted view and to "turn back the clock." The referrals that come to us often arrive with obstacles to our therapeutic plans. Patients and their referring therapists often wish to stay in regular contact (two to three times weekly) and to continue their work on MPD. At the same time, we at Hopkins are expected to treat the depression or some other supposed "side issue." We, however, following the isolation and countersuggestion approach, try to bring about, at least temporarily, a separation of the patient from the staff and the support groups that sustain the focus on "alters." We refuse to talk to "alters" but rather encourage our patients to review their present difficulties, thus applying the concept of "abnormal illness behavior" to their condition. . . .

> *"[The diagnosis of MPD] will obscure the real problems in [the patients'] lives and render psychotherapy long, costly, and pointless."*

Charcot had quite reliable ways of diagnosing hysteroepilepsy. It just did not exist as he thought it did, but rather it was a behavior seeking the sick role. It is my opinion that MPD is another behavioral disorder—a socially created artifact—in distressed people who are looking for help. The diagnosis and subsequent procedures for exploring MPD give them a coherent posture toward themselves and others as a particular kind of patient: "sick" certainly, "victim" possibly. This posture, if sustained, will obscure the real problems in their lives and render psychotherapy long, costly, and pointless. If the customary treatments of hysteria are provided, then we can expect that the multiple personality behaviors will be abandoned and proper rehabilitative attention can be given to the patient.

Chapter 2

Are Drugs the Most Effective Way to Treat Mental Illness?

The New Antidepressants: An Overview

by Julie Marquis

About the author: *Julie Marquis is a staff writer for the* Los Angeles Times.

It's just a little green and white pill, but it's got the name recognition—and some would say the devoted following—of a rock star.

Twice, the antidepressant Prozac has been featured on the cover of *Newsweek*. It has been the subject of several books, including one bestseller.

But not everyone is an avid fan. Critics say that it is grossly overprescribed and that its long-term effects are unknown. Others say it is no replacement for a stint on the psychotherapist's couch.

Rising Popularity

Meanwhile, more than 20 million people in 100 countries have partaken of this flagship drug, the first in a new generation of antidepressants called selective serotonin reuptake inhibitors (SSRIs). In 1995, sales climbed 24% to $2 billion.

And the competitors are coming up fast: The makers of another serotonin-enhancer, Zoloft, sold $1.4 billion worth of the drug in 1995, a 45% rise over 1994. Third-ranked Paxil's manufacturer sold $782 million worth, up 51%.

What accounts for these medication-sensations?

Oddly enough, it isn't so much that they are more effective than their predecessors. About two-thirds of patients respond to any given antidepressant. Eli Lilly, Prozac's manufacturer, puts its effectiveness at 70%.

These drugs are simply more tolerable. They can be prescribed more widely, for a longer period, with less risk of serious side effects. Patients are more likely to stick with the program. The drugs are nonaddictive, they don't produce an amphetamine-like "high" and they are nearly impossible to use, by themselves, as a means of committing suicide.

"It is *not* a happy pill," Dr. Steven Paul, vice president of Lilly Research Laboratories, said of Prozac.

SSRIs, however, are more than just antidepressants. Prozac and Paxil are approved by the Food and Drug Administration to treat obsessive-compulsive disorder, and Zoloft is awaiting the FDA nod. Paxil is also approved for panic disorders.

The drugs are also prescribed legally by physicians for such "off-label" uses as treating bulimia, weight problems, premenstrual syndrome, alcohol and nicotine addictions—even gambling and compulsive shopping.

How SSRIs Work

Although the precise reasons for their widespread powers are not known, University of California at San Diego (UCSD) researcher Stephen M. Stahl points to activity in four serotonin pathways in the brain—each of which mediates different effects. The drugs prolong the effects by enhancing the neurotransmitter's concentration in the synaptic cleft (the space between brain cells, or neurons).

There is a downside. The SSRIs have their own set of side effects: occasional nausea and vomiting, anxiety, insomnia, headaches and sexual dysfunction.

"The reality is they are pretty damn good," said Stahl, an adjunct professor of psychiatry at UCSD. "But they aren't as good as some people say."

Voices of Dissent

Critics' concerns range from the physical to the philosophical.

Shortly after Prozac rose to prominence in the early 1990s, allegations surfaced, in lawsuits and anecdotes, that it prompted violence and suicide.

But the drug companies, along with other clinicians and researchers, have fairly successfully dismissed these as unproven. "There is no credible, objective evidence," Paul said.

Dr. Peter Breggin, a Maryland psychiatrist who has made a side career out of lambasting what he considers "toxic" psychiatric drug treatments, laments that Prozac may have become "our national prescription drug."

"In less than a generation, we have rejected the motto, 'Just say no to drugs,' and adopted the motto, 'Take this drug to improve your life,'" Breggin writes in his 1994 book, *Talking Back to Prozac*. "It is time for opposing voices. It is time to talk back to Prozac."

Breggin also was talking back to

> *"The [new antidepressants] are nonaddictive, they don't produce [a] 'high' and they are nearly impossible to use, by themselves, as a means of committing suicide."*

Peter Kramer, a psychiatrist who in 1993 published a provocative, sometimes whimsical bestseller, *Listening to Prozac*. The book is an exploration of the author's experience treating patients who may not meet the definition of clinical depression, yet find themselves positively transformed by the drug.

After the Kramer book, even Eli Lilly felt the need to stress Prozac's primary mission as an antidepressant. In 1994 advertisements, the company warned that it ought to be prescribed only "where a clear medical need exists."

Widely Prescribed

In reality, however, Prozac and other SSRIs are prescribed for a variety of purposes, often by general practitioners not necessarily well-schooled in the intricacies of mental illness.

Some mental health experts believe the drugs are overprescribed without a good understanding of whether side effects will emerge, say, 20 years from now.

"Unfortunately, we've got an experiment going on right now with . . . millions of people," said David Antonuccio, a psychology professor at the University of Nevada School of Medicine.

SSRI proponents point out that diabetics take insulin for life and patients with high blood pressure take anti-hypertensives without drawing the same outcry. And Prozac's maker says the drug, approved by the FDA in 1988, shows no signs of trouble. "It's not 20 years, but things look good," Paul said.

It is always useful to consider non-drug treatments, says Dr. Steven Hyman, Director of the National Institute of Mental Health. But "if somebody is suffering a depression-like distress, and they take a medication and they get a lot better, who could rightly tell them to stop it?"

> *"The SSRIs have their own set of side effects: occasional nausea and vomiting, anxiety, insomnia, headaches and sexual dysfunction."*

Some clinicians warn that a drugs-only approach to treatment assigns minimal importance to such intangibles as human will and courage.

"We know that Winston Churchill had manic-depressive illness—but he had a country to run; he had a war to fight. There are people who would be totally incapacitated by that," said University of California at Los Angeles psychiatrist Jeffrey Schwartz. "Am I saying they are weak? No. Am I saying that Churchill was heroic? Yes, I am."

"The [strictly] biological people are making an egregious error by removing the heroic struggle of some people against their illness. It's not all about chemicals . . . not all left to doctors."

A Decline in Psychotherapy

Psychotherapy, as traditionally practiced, is under enormous pressure. Many patients don't bother with therapy anymore, relying on their general practitioner to dash off a prescription instead.

For patients, drug treatment often is less expensive. A visit to a medical doctor is often reimbursed more fully than one to a counselor.

The very nature of psychotherapy is changing, largely because of the pressures of managed care. But Prozac and drugs like it often are seen by employers and insurers as better investments than long-term therapy.

Psychotherapists are under pressure to prove that their techniques work as well—and as fast. Hence the push toward "time-limited" sessions and by-the-book approaches that are easier to monitor.

"Prozac and other SSRIs are prescribed for a variety of purposes, often by general practitioners not necessarily well-schooled in the intricacies of mental illness."

The issue isn't simply effectiveness, but cost-effectiveness. For psychotherapists, this is a sore point because they see what they offer as more than time-limited relief.

Economics aside, researchers sometimes disagree on what works best—psychotherapy, drugs or a combination. Concerning depression, studies comparing older antidepressants to therapy have reached conflicting conclusions.

The point, say mental health advocates, is to expand treatment options, not to lop them off in the name of short-run savings. Therapy and drugs should not be either-or propositions, they say.

"For our population, a pill is often necessary," said Laura Lee Hall, a neuroscientist and deputy director at the National Alliance for the Mentally Ill. "But a pill alone is usually not enough."

Psychoactive Drugs Successfully Treat Most Mental Illnesses

by Judith Hooper

About the author: *Judith Hooper is a writer for* Time *magazine.*

The disease is known to doctors as "irrational rationality" because it forces its victims to defy reason while seeming to embrace it. Characters as disparate as Howard Hughes, Lady Macbeth and Freud's sexually conflicted "Rat Man" are among its victims. Today, in every elementary school of 200 pupils or so, three or four youngsters are likely to suffer from it. Howard Hughes' symptoms included an insistence on having a germ-free environment and all his windows permanently sealed. The schoolchildren are more inclined to count cracks in the blacktop (for them, "Step on a crack, break your mother's back" is frighteningly literal) or meticulously arrange their crayons in neat rows, again and again, to avert some imagined catastrophe.

All of them are suffering or have suffered from a mental disease known as obsessive-compulsive disorder (OCD), which torments its victims with clouds of horrific anxieties and forces them, like primitive priests propitiating unknown gods, to indulge in senseless and repetitive rituals. Not long ago, this disease—along with most other so-called mental illnesses—was considered to be a chronic, untreatable condition, a psychological crippler whose roots lay hidden deep within the brain's mysterious recesses.

But the brain is finally giving up its secrets, and the biggest secret of all is that this 3-lb. maze of nerves and tissue is also a veritable laboratory of chemicals whose workings and interactions largely determine the state of our mental health, down to the latest mood swing. Many mental illnesses once thought to be purely psychological conditions—among them schizophrenia, panic disorder, post-traumatic stress disorder and OCD—turn out to be caused by specific chemical imbalances. Those who suffer from them are racked not by toilet-training traumas or the "unceasing terror and tension of the fetal night" (as an early psychoanalyst put it) but by something as simple—and complex—as an imperfectly mixed chemical cocktail. The Oedipus complex has been reduced to a matter of molecules.

The good news is that many if not most of these brain afflictions can now be remedied by increasingly precise psychoactive drugs. In the past few years, scientists have joined disciplines and come up with a whole new pharmacopoeia of compounds to deal with mental disorders. "Today the psychiatrists who treat patients are working hand in hand with the 'wet-brain guys'—the pharmacologists, chemists and molecular biologists," says Dr. Steven Hyman, director of the National Institute of Mental Health (NIMH) in Bethesda, Maryland. While the effects of earlier psychiatric drugs were discovered largely by trial and error, the latest compounds are aimed at exact targets in the brain. "When you wanted to develop a new drug, you used to copy an old one that worked, add a little twist to the molecule and test it out on patients," explains Dr. Kenneth Davis, chairman of psychiatry at Mount Sinai School of Medicine in New York City. "If you were lucky, you got a drug that worked as well as the old one but had fewer side effects. Now we can be very specific and say, 'Let's go after the D3 receptor or the D4 receptor.'"

Scientists consider receptors—which are specially tailored protein molecules—and the substances that bind to them to be the critical junction in the ongoing chemical processes that underlie thinking, feeling, dreaming and remembering. For an electrical signal to travel from neuron to neuron in the brain, it must cross a minuscule gap, the synapse, between them. A number of different chemical messengers known as neurotransmitters ferry the signal across the synapse and then lock on to receptors that lie on the membrane of the next nerve cell in line.

Some neurotransmitters induce other neurons to fire; others dampen neuron activity. In either case, once the chemical locks on to the receptor, it sets in motion a cascade of chemical events in the receiving cell. This ongoing dance of neurotransmitters and receptors is the intricate code that brain cells use to communicate with one another.

Many psychoactive drugs—including opiates, the Valium-type compounds and angel dust—mimic the action of neurotransmitters by binding to particular receptors and influencing the neuron's firing. Pharmacologists have acquired the tools to screen new drugs quickly, testing their affinity for particular receptors by cloning, or duplicating, the receptors and then designing molecules that bind to them. So refined are the new techniques that scientists now know of 14 different receptors for serotonin, the ubiquitous chemical messenger that plays a critical role

"Many mental illnesses once thought to be purely psychological conditions . . . turn out to be caused by specific chemical imbalances."

in sleep, mood, depression and anxiety. They have also discerned five different receptor subtypes for dopamine, a neurotransmitter thought to be involved in schizophrenia. By formulating compounds that selectively bind to particular dopamine receptors, for example, drug designers can craft schizophrenia drugs that curb hallucinations without triggering disabling Parkinsonian symptoms.

The development of drugs for schizophrenia, one of the most perplexing and devastating of all mental illnesses, was an early success story. After several decades as a hopeless research backwater, the schizophrenia field was reborn in 1989, when the U.S. Food and Drug Administration approved a remarkable drug, clozapine (brand name: Clozaril). Made by the Swiss pharmaceutical firm Sandoz, Clozaril was aimed at patients who did not benefit from other drugs. While traditional antipsychotic drugs such as chlorpromazine (Thorazine) and haloperidol (Haldol) work by blocking dopamine receptors, Clozaril appears to bind to serotonin receptors as well. "It is what we call a dirty drug," says Mount Sinai's Davis. "It probably binds to a whole bunch of receptors. We used to think that was a bad thing. Now we think that's maybe a good thing." Perhaps because of its affinity for serotonin receptors, Clozaril is largely free of the Parkinsonian side effects (the "Thorazine shuffle" and so on) that plague the classic antipsychotic drugs. It was also the first drug to ameliorate symptoms of schizophrenia that are resistant to other drugs. But Clozaril has a major drawback: a life-threatening side effect called agranulocytosis, a drastic drop in white blood cells that requires patients to undergo expensive weekly blood monitoring.

> *"Many . . . brain afflictions can now be remedied by increasingly precise psychoactive drugs."*

Now scientists are exploring an entire spectrum of what Dr. Steven Paul, vice president for central-nervous-system research at Eli Lilly, calls "Clozaril wannabes" that they hope will work as well without triggering agranulocytosis. One of the wannabes, risperidone (Risperdal), made by Belgium-based Janssen Pharmaceutica, entered the market in 1993, and four others are nearing approval by the FDA, including Lilly's Zyprexa and Abbott Labs' Serlect. Meanwhile, further down the drug-development pipeline are a number of third-generation Clozaril cousins, some of which are specifically targeted at the little-known D3 and D4 receptors.

"We're not curing schizophrenia with these new antipsychotics," says Paul. "But we can treat it better. What would happen if we designed a drug that was 10 times better than Clozaril?" Mount Sinai's Davis, on the other hand, thinks future schizophrenia drugs might well be based on altogether different chemical-messenger systems. "There is evidence that schizophrenics have abnormalities in two very common neurotransmitters, GABA [gamma-aminobutyric acid] and glutamate," he says. "None of the current drugs do anything for the most incapacitating symptom of schizophrenia, the cognitive deficits. Maybe it's time to get off the dopamine merry-go-round we've been on for 40 years."

New drugs have also drastically altered the outlook for panic disorder, a chronic illness characterized by recurrent panic attacks and a lifetime of fear in between. The symptoms of an attack—among them palpitations, breathlessness, sweating, dizziness, tingling sensations, hot flashes or chills, as well as a sense of impending doom—seem so dire and life-threatening that patients frequently turn up in emergency rooms convinced they are having a heart attack or going insane. Thirty percent of the 2.4 million Americans with panic disorder go on to develop agoraphobia, the fear of leaving home lest they succumb to panic on the freeway, in a store or at a concert. Some 20% of patients attempt suicide.

> *"New drugs have also drastically altered the outlook for panic disorder, a chronic illness characterized by recurrent panic attacks and a lifetime of fear in between."*

Panic disorder probably results from a "combination of a genetic predisposition and some number of traumatic separations in childhood," according to Dr. Jack Gorman, a Columbia University psychiatrist. But whatever the cause, the brain of a person who suffers from it is different from that of someone who does not. Stimulation studies using the drug yohimbine have revealed an abnormal firing rate in an area of the brain stem called the locus ceruleus, which is rich in cells that release the neurotransmitter norepinephrine, the trigger for human fight-or-flight response. This primal alarm system has obvious survival value—useful for fleeing man-eating tigers and such. But in patients with panic disorder, it appears to kick in at too low a threshold.

A decade ago, many a panic-disorder patient ended up as a tragic, misunderstood recluse. But today panic disorder is one of the most treatable mental illnesses. Studies have shown that 70% of patients benefit from cognitive behavioral therapy, which includes breathing training, "cognitive restructuring" and "exposure therapy." Most patients can be helped by short-acting antianxiety drugs such as Xanax and long-acting antidepressants such as desipramine and imipramine.

The superstar of the hour, however, is the family of antidepressant drugs known as SSRIs (selective serotonin re-uptake inhibitors). There is evidence linking panic disorder to a serotonin deficiency, and these compounds appear to work by boosting serotonin levels. The best known of all this family is Prozac, Eli Lilly's $2.1 billion-a-year baby, which has become a societal catchword for relief from anxiety. But another family member, Paxil (manufactured by SmithKline Beecham), is the first to be approved by the FDA specifically for the treatment of panic disorder. While drug therapy by itself is successful in 70% of cases—the same rate as cognitive behavioral therapy alone—preliminary, unpublished research suggests that the success rate might climb as high as 90% when the treatments are combined. But Gorman cautions that this needs to be studied in more detail. . . .

The multifaceted SSRIs have also dramatically altered the treatment of depression, which remains the most common form of mental illness. Although no more efficacious than traditional antidepressants, they do not produce many of the unpleasant side effects, such as sedation and weight gain, that have caused thousands of potential patients to shun treatment. "SSRIs have revolutionized, and continue to revolutionize, the comfort levels with which psychiatrists and family practitioners treat depression," says Dr. David Kupfer, chairman of psychiatry at the University of Pittsburgh School of Medicine. "Suddenly, physicians are more willing to prescribe these medications for people who truly need them, and people suffering from a depression are more willing to take them and stay on them."

Even patients who have been chronically depressed for five years or more respond well in 65% to 70% of cases, Kupfer points out, and recent research underlines the importance of remaining on the medications long enough to prevent a relapse. "New studies show that the dosage that got you better will keep you better," he says. "Depression is a chronic, lifelong illness, and we're beginning to think of these drugs as being similar to insulin for diabetes."

Still, a new generation of medications—perhaps tailored to particular serotonin receptors—is urgently needed for the 20% of depressed patients who do not benefit from existing drugs. Researchers hope to come up with compounds that begin acting immediately rather than in a period of weeks. "The Holy Grail of new antidepressant treatment is rapid onset," asserts Dr. John Ascher, a research physician at Glaxo Wellcome in Research Triangle Park, North Carolina. "We're talking about medicine that takes effect in just a day or two."

Ultimately, scientists would like to figure out how genetic defects cause depression, and then to design drugs to correct whatever has gone awry. Gene mapping would be particularly helpful to people at risk for manic-depressive illness: although lithium and related drugs usually relieve the manic episodes, current antidepressants are often ineffective against the acute depressive ones. Says Ascher: "That's the real frontier."

Obsessive-compulsive disorder, which affects 1% to 3% of Americans, was until recently considered a chronic, untreatable condition. Victims more ordinary than Lady Macbeth and Howard Hughes are haunted by persistent, intrusive thoughts or worries (obsessions), and may spend countless hours performing repetitive rituals (compulsions) such as hand washing, counting, hoarding old clothes, arranging napkins in a meaningless symmetry or checking a hundred times to make sure the electric coffeemaker is turned off. Themes of dirt, contamination or germs rule their thoughts, and other

> *"Some 75% to 80% of [obsessive-compulsive disorder] patients today get substantial relief—sometimes complete remission—from [medication].*

common obsessions center on horrific or violent images, a need for symmetry or exactness, or an exaggerated sense of sin or morality.

A key breakthrough in OCD treatment came about in the late 1980s, when researchers discovered that a particular antidepressant, clomipramine hydrochloride (brand name: Anafranil), relieved obsessions and compulsions as no others did. The presumed secret of its success was its ability to inhibit the reabsorption of serotonin in the brain. A few years later, the advent of the SSRI family made it even more obvious that obsessive-compulsive disorder was at least in part a serotonin problem. Some 75% to 80% of OCD patients today get substantial relief— sometimes complete remission—from one or another member of the SSRIs. . . .

More secrets of the brain are emerging every day. There is evidence, for instance, that long-term use of antidepressants changes the intracellular environment permanently, even turning certain genes on or off. And new molecular techniques have revealed that individual receptors come in various genetic forms, or polymorphisms. This kind of knowledge opens the gateway to a whole panoply of fresh possibilities. The brain is a vast continent, and scientists have barely landed on its shores.

Drugs Can Remedy the Symptoms of Depression

by Minette Marrin

About the author: *Minette Marrin is a writer for the* Sunday Telegraph, *a British newspaper.*

Prozac is a name that is too often taken in vain. This wonderful drug, which has eased the despair of millions of the mentally ill, is now usually spoken of as an unnecessary self-indulgence. For years now it has been thought of as little more than a mood-lifter for the fashionable, the butt of bitchy little jokes; Diana, Princess of Wales took it, Sarah Ferguson took it. Even American cats and dogs took it. Now Camille Paglia, the excitable American media feminist, has decided it is time for her to let the world know how much she, too, despises Prozac.

Prozac, she says, is "the drug of choice for glum politically correct sentimentalists unable to face the spiritual deficiencies at the heart of their own decaying liberalism . . . what a bore". In her view the only way to relax and to stay clear-headed is with fine wine and food "in the Mediterranean manner". This is just a pretentious, unsympathetic, polysyllabic way of saying that people should pull themselves together; perhaps Camille Paglia was more interested in attacking the glum politically correct sentimentalists than the drug, but either way it is outrageous that someone of her fame and influence should add her voice to the ignorant and irresponsible attacks on Prozac.

Remarks such as hers only add to the shame and confusion that surround mental illness. For too long people suffering from depression have been tormented by advice to pull themselves together, as though depression were some sort of moral weakness. For too long most people have failed to distinguish between degrees of normal sadness and pessimism, and the pathological kind. For too long people have been bullied into thinking that taking drugs for depression is either, on the one hand, quite unnecessary, or, on the other, something only raving nutters do. The widespread abuse of Prozac in America has only made

Reprinted from Minette Marrin, "Ignore the Bullies and Take the Drugs," editorial, *Sunday Telegraph* (London), November 30, 1997, by permission of the author.

these problems worse; however, just because a great many silly Americans pop pills they don't need, it doesn't mean that nobody needs them, or that they don't work.

Clinical depression affects millions of people. According to the Royal College of Psychiatrists, it is the most common, most overlooked and most treatable mental illness. Those like Camille Paglia, who seriously think it can be treated with good food and wine "in the Mediterranean manner", clearly have not the slightest imaginative understanding of the terrible anguish involved even in fairly mild cases of depression—the self-loathing, the rage, the anxiety, the tearfulness, the inability to concentrate, the destruction of relationships and the waste of talent, to name a few of the usual symptoms. I suppose it is not entirely surprising that Camille Paglia appears to have little insight into those who are unduly low; she herself appears to be unduly excitable whenever I see her on television, talking a blue and mean streak and gesticulating wildly. If I had to guess which mental illness she might be prone to, I would immediately suggest hypomania, and prescribe sedatives, which might prevent her from talking about things she doesn't, apparently, understand.

> *"For too long people have been bullied into thinking that taking drugs for depression is . . . unnecessary."*

Drugs achieve miracles with real depression. How often does it need to be said? Friends, counsellors and talking cures work well with sadness and confusion, but for deep, settled depression there is nothing to touch brain chemicals. Why should not depression have a physical basis? Every other aspect of personality and consciousness does.

The Effects of Prozac

It is a matter of fact that when the first antidepressants were discovered in the 1950s and 1960s, the mental hospitals were emptied, and the inmates emerged to lead more or less normal lives. These drugs had unpleasant side effects, but Prozac and its successors have very few. These days it is inspiring to see the effects of these new antidepressants on people who have led lives of terrible despair. Suddenly they stop longing to be dead. Suddenly they are able to rejoin the rest of humanity. Suddenly they stop being angry, churlish, negative, reclusive and dull. Suddenly they feel they have become their "real" selves again.

To sneer at Prozac is like sneering at antibiotics or painkillers. These inventions are triumphs of the 20th century, which, though it has inflicted so much pain, has assuaged so much as well. Camille Paglia's "glum politically correct sentimentalists and their decaying liberalism" are no doubt a terrible bore. But their bad faith may well have driven them into deep and settled depression, and some of them may genuinely need antidepressants. Prozac would help a great deal more than any amount of Valpolicella or tiramisu.

Medication Helps Children with Attention-Deficit Hyperactivity Disorder

by Jerry Wiener

About the author: *Jerry Wiener, a physician, is on the faculty of George Washington University Medical School in Washington, D.C.*

In defending the current use of Ritalin for treating attention deficit hyperactivity disorder (ADHD), it's important first to emphasize that the disorder really exists.

Telling whether a child has ADHD is more complicated than a diagnosis of the mumps or chickenpox, but the diagnosis of ADHD can still be as valid as any in medicine. An analogous health problem would be multiple sclerosis: As with ADHD it's a distinct disease, yet we don't know what causes the problem and have no laboratory test for diagnosing it.

Is ADHD a Biological Problem?

Since the 1950's, what we now call ADHD has been a well-recognized syndrome involving, as all syndromes do, a group of signs and symptoms that occur together. Years of research have documented that some children differ from their peers in being inattentive and hyperactive as well as impulsive. Extensive field trials and numerous studies have established that hyperactivity and impulsivity are at the core of the diagnosis, with inattention a consequence of the other two, especially in school-age boys.

Adding to the evidence that ADHD is a legitimate clinical problem are recent results of magnetic resonance imaging (MRI) studies showing that children diagnosed with ADHD have subtle but significant anatomical differences in their brains compared with other children. Furthermore, studies of families suggest there is a genetic component for many cases of ADHD. More specifically, recent research has found a possible link between ADHD and three genes that code for receptors (proteins that jut from the surface of cells) that are activated by dopamine, a neurotransmitter (a chemical that conveys messages from one nerve cell to another). Defects in these genes could mean a reduced response to dopamine signals, perhaps accounting for the uninhibited behavior observed in ADHD.

How Is ADHD Diagnosed?

A child suspected of having ADHD should be evaluated by a trained and experienced clinician who takes the time to assess the child's development, family history and behavior at school and at home. The clinician should require that the criteria set forth in the current *Diagnostic and Statistical Manual of Mental Disorders* (DSM-IV) are met before concluding that a child has ADHD.

To receive the diagnosis of ADHD, a child should display a significant number of symptoms and behaviors reflecting hyperactivity, impulsivity and inattention—and the symptoms and behaviors must be more persistent and severe than normally occur in children of that age. In addition and importantly, there must be impaired functioning in school, at home and/or social relationships.

Are mistakes made in diagnosing ADHD? Of course. They usually occur when the clinician is rushed, inexperienced, untrained, pressured or predisposed either to "find" ADHD or to overlook it. As a result, there is both over- and underdiagnosis of ADHD. The reported fivefold increase in Ritalin prescriptions from 1991 to 1996 is reason to reflect about possible overusage. However, repeated findings of a three percent prevalence rate of ADHD among school-age children gives as much cause for concern about underdiagnosis as for overusage: At these prevalence rates, up to 30 percent of children with ADHD may not be receiving sufficient treatment.

> *"Children diagnosed with ADHD have subtle but significant anatomical differences in their brains compared with other children."*

Treating ADHD

While there is no cure for ADHD, there is a very effective treatment to minimize its symptoms—through the use of stimulant medications such as Ritalin. Such drugs are by far the most effective treatment for moderating and controlling the disorder's major symptoms—hyperactivity, inattention and impulsivity—in 75 percent to 80 percent of children with this disorder.

The safety and effectiveness of Ritalin and other stimulant drugs, including Dexedrine (dextroamphetamine) and Cylert (pemoline), have been established more firmly than any other treatment in the field of child and adolescent psychiatry. Literally scores of carefully conducted blind and double-blind controlled studies have repeatedly documented the improvement—often dramatic—in symptoms of ADHD following the use of stimulant medication, with

Ritalin the most common choice. By contrast, no other treatment, including behavior modification, compares with stimulant medication in efficacy; and in fact, no treatment besides these medications has had much success at all in treating ADHD.

Medication for ADHD Is Not Prescribed Enough

Stimulant medication is so effective that a parent with a child diagnosed with ADHD should receive an explanation if the clinician's judgment is *not* to prescribe medication. Appropriate considerations for not opting for Ritalin and similar drugs include a history of tic or Tourette's disorder, the presence of a thought disorder, significant resistance to such medications in the patient or family or insufficient severity of the symptoms or dysfunction. Other classes of drugs, such as antidepressants, can be effective and can be used when there is concern about the use of a stimulant medication or when side effects occur.

> *"The safety and effectiveness of Ritalin . . . [has] been established more firmly than any other treatments in the field of child and adolescent psychiatry."*

The issue should not be whether stimulants are overprescribed but the risk that they may be misprescribed. The most common example: children who are described as overactive or impulsive but who do not meet the criteria for the diagnosis of ADHD. Another example is use of stimulants as a diagnostic "test" by a rushed or inexperienced clinician who may not realize that a favorable response was due to the placebo effect and therefore mistakenly assumes that the diagnosis of ADHD has been confirmed.

The Role of Therapy

As effective as Ritalin can be for treating the symptoms of ADHD, it should rarely if ever, be the only treatment for someone with the problem. The child or adolescent may also benefit from remedial work for any identified learning disability and from family therapy or psychotherapy for problems of self-image, self-esteem, anger and/or depression.

Is Ritalin overprescribed? Not when it's used for children who meet the criteria for the diagnosis of ADHD, including the requirement that the child's ability to function must be "significantly impaired." All too often, the mistakes in prescribing Ritalin are errors of omission, where children who could benefit from the drug never receive it. Instead, they go through school labeled as troublemakers, or as unmotivated or hostile. They'll have missed out on the opportunity for at least a trial on a medication that could have significantly improved their symptoms and allowed for improved academic performance, self-esteem and social interaction.

Therapy, Not Medication, Is the Best Treatment for Depression

by Michael Yapko

About the author: *Michael Yapko is a clinical psychologist and marriage and family therapist in private practice in Solana Beach, California. He is also the author of the book* Breaking the Patterns of Depression.

Currently, the most common mental health disorder in America—and one of the most costly—depression racks up a staggering $54 billion a year in costs from work absenteeism, reduced productivity, lost earnings and treatment expenses, according to a 1995 study by the National Institute of Mental Health. Depression is also among the most medicalized of psychiatric diagnoses; indeed, family doctors, not psychiatrists, write up to 70 percent of antidepressant prescriptions, with a wide array of meds to choose from. With the lion's share of mental health research dollars going into psychopharmacology, as of 1997 there are five major classes of antidepressants on the market. Seven new medications have been introduced since 1987, and about 15 more are now being tested by the pharmaceutical companies.

But does the wide prevalence of depression, the staggering popularity of drugs to treat it and the obvious zeal for medicalizing the whole problem constitute prima facie proof that it is a disease? Can we now reduce the complex phenomena of depression, with all its emotional, cognitive, relational, social and biological elements, to a simple neurochemical mistake? Or is it possible that most depressed people are *not* "sick," and that biology only represents one component in the reasons for their depression and the way they experience it? . . .

Are Behaviors Based on Biology?

The rising fascination with evolutionary psychology and biological determination has led some experts to proclaim, without much evidence, that all emotional

From Michael Yapko, "Stronger Medicine." This article first appeared in the *Family Therapy Networker* (January/February 1997) and is excerpted here with permission.

states (including depression) are ultimately based on biology. One study published in *Psychological Science* in 1990 by Robert Plomin, Robin Corley, John DeFries and David Fulker, for example, suggests that one's amount of television viewing may be genetically determined. A 1992 study in the same journal by Matt McGue and David Lykken indicates that the tendency to divorce is also biologically determined. Do we really have genes for TV and divorce? Where and how in human history would we have acquired such genes (that only seem to have been activated in the last 30 or so years)? Indeed, as psychologist Stanton Peele writes in *Diseasing of America,* it is currently fashionable to view all kinds of self-defeating personal behaviors, including eating disorders, excessive shopping and too much sex, as evidence of disease.

The push to redefine depression as a disease is aided and abetted by the managed care industry, which encourages the use of antidepressant medication as a treatment approach. According to psychiatrist Matthew Dumont, "It seems that if we so much as inquire whether a depression might be related to the stresses or losses of life before blasting it with a chemical, we are virtually guilty of malpractice."

Depression and Culture

But this devaluation of therapy that inevitably accompanies the new emphasis on biological approaches is wrongheaded on two fronts. In the first place, epidemiological, social and cultural data indicate that, for most people, depression is not a disease of biological origin. Increasing in prevalence among all age groups, it is growing most rapidly among late adolescents and young adults. The average age of onset for a first major depressive episode has been steadily decreasing and is now the mid-twenties. Since gene pools and biochemistry do not tend to change so markedly in so short a time, the evidence supports an argument for social and cultural causes for depression in most cases. Since 1945, when the first of the baby boomers, who suffer disproportionately from depression, were born, our cultural mores have changed profoundly. The breakup of the family, explosive technological growth, dwindling resources, violence, terrorism and the threat of nuclear disaster have undermined our sense of social stability and cast deep shadows over future expectations. Writing in the *Archives of General Psychiatry* in July 1985, psychiatrist Gerald Klerman and his colleagues identified some of the social stresses they believe account for the higher rates of depression. These include urbanization, changes in family structure, new gender roles and occupational shifts. All of these trends unsettle people, uproot them from traditional mores and meanings, confuse them about who they are and what is expected of them and create many new opportunities for experiencing inadequacy and failure. Psychology

> *"For most people, depression is not a disease of biological origin."*

researcher Martin Seligman suggests that, as a people, we tend to be more self-absorbed than our forebears, and thus more hypersensitive to each transient mood. Seligman thinks that we may also have unrealistically high expectations of ourselves and others, even as we increasingly feel both more helpless and hopeless about controlling our lives. This dichotomy is even more confounding for our own emotional well-being.

> *"Therapy is as effective or more effective than drugs are for treating depression, with lower rates of relapse."*

Rates of depression and symptomatology vary widely from culture to culture and between genders, also lending support to the theory that the interplay of social, cultural and psychological factors is generally more important than biology. The Amish, for example, have considerably lower rates of depression than do other Americans. Their lower incidence of depression presumably relates to cultural factors, including vital religious beliefs, close-knit community ties and a reliance on their own labor rather than technology. Women in this country are two or three times more likely to be diagnosed as depressed than men, in part for biological reasons (reproductive events like postpartum depression and possibly premenstrual syndrome), but more likely because of systemic social inequities and cultural conditions.

There is no question that genetics and biochemistry play a part in depression, but the best data from identical- and fraternal-twin studies indicate that genetics can be identified as a cause of unipolar depression less than 20 percent of the time. But, if, as the evidence now shows, cultural and social forces contribute more to the onset of depression than does biology, medication is only a partial solution.

The Best Medicine for Depression

More important, there is now abundant evidence that therapy is as effective or more effective than drugs are for treating depression, with lower rates of relapse. In the January 1994 issue of *American Psychologist,* Ricardo Muñoz, Steven Hollon et al. reviewed guidelines for treatment of depression developed by the Agency for Health Care Policy and Research (AHCPR) that compared thousands of treatment outcome studies using drugs alone, psychotherapy alone or a combination. Evaluating the guidelines, the authors concluded that psychotherapy was at least as efficient as drugs for relieving depression. And, on many measures, including treatment-dropout rate, social adjustment, symptom improvement and relapse rate, psychotherapy performed better than meds. Several metanalyses of many controlled studies involving thousands of patients have reached the same conclusion. One is a recent review by David Antonuccio et al. of numerous studies comparing drugs to therapy and the value of both approaches combined, published in the December 1995 issue of *Professional Psy-*

chology: Research and Practice, which reports substantial evidence for the superior effectiveness of therapy. There is "no stronger medicine" for depression than psychotherapy, writes Antonuccio in a recent issue of the *American Psychologist.* So, while medications can help relieve symptoms, and possibly help clients take better advantage of therapy, the reputation of Prozac or Zoloft as miracle cures for depression, rendering therapy obsolete, is simply not supported by research.

How Effective Is Therapy?

In late 1995, the position of therapy was buttressed even more by the largest survey ever conducted of people who had undergone outpatient psychotherapy treatment, published in the November 1995 issue of *Consumer Reports* and based on extensive reader-response questionnaires submitted by 4,000 subscribers. Unlike standard efficacy studies, with their random assignments of clients meeting rigid eligibility requirements to standardized treatments, the *Consumer Reports* survey caught the experience of therapy as it really is for most people—with therapists who typically offer an eclectic mix of approaches and adjust their work to individual clients.

Of respondents to the survey, 87 percent said they felt better after treatment. There was no significant difference between psychotherapy alone and in combination with medication for any disorder, including depression. And social workers, psychologists and psychiatrists all had roughly the same rates of success. Most surprising, perhaps, to a field giving increased emphasis to brief therapy, respondents reported better results for longer treatment. Among those with similar levels of emotional difficulty, those who stayed in therapy more than six months said they made greater progress than those who left earlier. Not surprisingly, people whose choice of therapist or whose length of treatment was dictated by insurance coverage improved less than those who freely chose the clinician and modality.

Although the *Consumer Reports* study is not without problems—low response rate to the questionnaire, lack of specificity to the depression diagnosis and other possibly distorting factors—it broke new ground. By going directly to the mental health consumer, it produced the most naturalistic view of the actual experience of therapy of any study of the field

> *"The reputation of Prozac or Zoloft as miracle cures for depression, rendering therapy obsolete, is simply not supported by research."*

ever conducted. According to psychology researcher Martin Seligman, principal consultant on the survey, writing in the December 1995 *American Psychologist,* "[The survey] is large-scale; it samples treatment as it is actually delivered in the field; it samples without obvious bias those who seek out treatment; it measures multiple outcomes . . . ; it is statistically stringent and finds clinically meaningful results. . . . Its major advantage over the efficacy method for study-ing the effectiveness of psychotherapy and medications is that it captures how and to whom treatment is actually delivered and toward what end. . . . It pro-vides a powerful addition to what we know about the effectiveness of psy-chotherapy and a pioneering way of finding out more."

A Vital Aspect of Treatment

While medications are often invaluable for symptom relief of depression, their effectiveness is not evidence for an underlying physical pathology. Medi-cations work because they have a relevant chemical effect, indicating a correla-tion between their impact on specific neurotransmitters and mood. But while there are some cases in which medications may help depression sufferers with-out additional treatment, the consensus among most depression experts is that only prescribing medications is generally a disservice to the client. Most people require much more substantial psychotherapeutic help to learn the skills neces-sary for solving problems and avoiding future difficulties, if their medication-improved mood is to endure.

"Just as there is no single cause for depression, . . . there can be no all-purpose panacea, like the simple act of taking a pill, that resolves life's difficulties."

What is it about psychotherapy that makes it so vital to treatment, that gives depressed clients some-thing they cannot obtain from medi-cations? People become and stay de-pressed partly because they tend to explain life's ordinary defeats and disappointments in terms of their personal inadequacies and failures, and then believe their own negative opinion of themselves. Others have deeply pessimistic worldviews that influence their mood states and tend to engender self-fulfilling prophecies. A healing relation-ship with a therapist can provide the kind of personal support and teaching that can clear up the misperceptions that contribute to the negativistic view of life typical of depressed people. Therapy can help clients see life events from dif-ferent perspectives and reattribute experience by assigning alternative explana-tions for life events that are less damaging to themselves than the typical de-pressive worldview. The ability to see and interpret events from new perspectives is critical to mental health. . . .

An Active Approach

Therapy works with depressed people because it draws on the clinical skills and adaptability required to understand a complex disorder—skills no pill can mimic. Therapists also need to emphasize active, solution-oriented treatments over pathology-based passive ones. Rather than search the dim past for causes of presumed deficits, therapists need to actively teach clients the specific skills they need to manage their feelings and develop what author Daniel Goleman calls their "emotional intelligence.". . .

Just as there is no single cause for depression, which is the personal and idiosyncratic response of individuals to a multitude of biological, psychological and social factors, so there can be no all-purpose panacea, like the simple act of taking a pill, that resolves life's difficulties. The idea that depression is a disease reflects, in part, the benign intention to destigmatize the suffering it causes and, less benevolently, the economic pressures to find a cheaper cure. Americans have a history of valuing quick-fix solutions to difficult problems. But this simplistic approach to depressive disorders underestimates the remarkable human capacity for self-transformation. We have the ability to use imagination and intelligence to change our life circumstances, our attitudes and emotions, even, to some extent, our personalities.

2105
  47

2058

Drugs Are Overprescribed for Mental Illness

by David Shanies

About the author: *David Shanies writes for* Miscellany News, *a newspaper published by Vassar College in New York.*

"One cubic centimeter of Soma cures ten gloomy," or so people were told in Aldous Huxley's *Brave New World.* In Huxley's world, a disturbing commentary on the dehumanization of society leading to widespread mind control, everyone was taught that the answer to their problems was simple: With chemical stabilization, no one ever needs to be unhappy again.

Unfortunately, this manner of thinking is one of the many ways in which Huxley's vision of our society's future rings alarmingly true. As psychopharmacological drugs continue to gain expansive use and increased acceptance in America, it is becoming clear that the "magic pill" mentality prevails in our culture. As this trend continues, however, many are growing wary of its implications. It is clear to me that the overprescription and overuse of psychoactive medications are responsible for a dangerous tendency to seek a quick fix to our personal and emotional problems.

Conditions like depression and attention deficit disorder (ADD) are particularly susceptible to misdiagnosis and mistreatment because the criteria for defining them are more subjective and ambiguous than those for other diseases. This calls into question whether many cases of "depression" are really just life's typical hard times, and whether an individual identified as having ADD might really just be particularly energetic or lack self-discipline.

The Fastest, Easiest Solution

This is not meant to suggest that genuine cases of depression, ADD or other psychological disorders do not exist; I believe that they do. But I also believe that in many cases, the decision to medicate patients to remedy these symptoms is made quickly and without exploring other options. It is no secret that in our fast-paced consumer culture, we seek the fastest, easiest solutions to our prob-

Reprinted from David Shanies, "Prozac Becoming America's Soma," *Miscellany News* via *University Wire*, February 20, 1998, by permission of the publisher.

lems. This used to apply mainly to our constant search for technological improvements which would make everyday tasks more simple, but the fact that it now extends to apply to making our psychological and emotional problems go away—via chemical intervention—sets a dangerous precedent.

Antidepressants like Prozac (Fluoxetine HCl) and drugs to treat ADD like Ritalin (Methylphenidate [MPH]) work by altering the levels of certain chemicals in the brain; Prozac alleviates depression by increasing serotonin levels, while MPH stimulates dopamine (a frontal lobe chemical which aids concentration) production. Although these can be helpful in certain cases, they often serve as a substitute for other treatment options.

Sedating Children

In the case of ADD treatment, which is far more prevalent among youth than adults, many parents of children diagnosed with the disorder have become alarmed by some doctors' willingness to diagnose patients with ADD and to quickly prescribe a drug like MPH. Others have expressed an opinion similar to that which Dr. Peter Breggin put forth in his May 20, 1996 letter to the editor in *The New York Times*, entitled "Whose Attention Disorder Does Ritalin Treat?" Breggin suggested that a lack of discipline, attention and affection at home can cause many of the behavior problems that doctors aim to treat with drugs like MPH. Still others believe that many "symptoms" of ADD can be attributed to a creative, energetic personality, one which children can be taught to channel into more productive behavior rather than simply be sedated with drugs like MPH.

I myself demonstrated many of these "symptoms" as a child and still often have trouble getting myself to concentrate. When my parents took me to a doctor as a child, however, he said that I did not in fact have an attention or behavioral disorder, but that I was just somewhat hyperactive and energetic. Though diagnosis of ADD was not as prevalent then as it currently is in America, I would not be surprised if a child just like me were diagnosed with ADD by a physician today. I say this not to suggest that physicians are incompetent and make poor judgments, but rather to demonstrate that as a society, we are increasingly inclined to look for a "textbook" explanation

> *"As psychopharmacological drugs . . . gain expansive use . . . in America, it is becoming clear that the 'magic pill' mentality prevails in our culture."*

with a designated set of medical treatment options. In my case, I simply needed to learn patience and self-control—something a pill, no matter how effective in the short term, could never teach me.

The U.S. Drug Enforcement Administration released a report in late 1995, stating that while the U.S. produces and consumes five times as much MPH as the rest of the world combined, "Every indicator . . . urges greater caution and more restrictive use of MPH."

Similarly, and to perhaps an even greater extent, the treatment of depression, manic depression and other similar disorders too often centers on pharmacological solutions rather than therapeutic and emotional processes. This does not mean that drugs cannot have positive effects; on the contrary, I know many people who have benefited from using psychoactive medications to get them through depression. I see two major problems with this approach, however: that medication, while it may help a patient's mood, may not be a necessary or logical form of treatment; and that in the cases where it does work, it does not allow patients to get to the root of their problems.

As far as the first issue is concerned, the overdiagnosis of depression and related disorders (and the excessive use of medication to treat them) is a well documented and often-discussed phenomenon. As an example, about a year ago in my town (a suburb on Long Island), I went to the local CVS pharmacy to pick up a prescription, only to find out that they didn't have the medication I needed in stock. As I was leaving, the pharmacist commented, "Too bad it's not like Prozac. We'll never run out of that!" Indeed, I know many people who experience life's ups and downs and are in therapy with psychiatrists who have no reservations about writing out a prescription for a drug like Prozac. As I heard one psychiatrist reason, "There are very, very few side effects, so the worst that can happen is it won't work for you." As a result, many Americans who have emotional problems will go into therapy and ask their doctor about Prozac, and soon enough, they'll be filling their prescriptions from the local pharmacy's never-ending supply.

> *"The decision to medicate patients [who experience psychological disorders] is made quickly and without exploring other options."*

"A Sacrament of Helplessness"

Even more serious, though, is the second problem I mentioned. When people are too hasty to throw up their hands and declare that they are helplessly plagued by depression, they rob themselves of the opportunity to take responsibility for their lives and work out their problems on their own. Breggin, in his book *Talking Back to Prozac*, contended that in many cases, taking medication like Prozac is "a sacrament of helplessness, a statement that the suffering is unendurable and beyond one's own means, that less suffering is preferable to an intact brain and drug-free mind." This is indeed a strong statement to make, so one should take caution before identifying medication as the solution to one's problems. Seeking such a simple and short-term solution can actually rob the individual of the opportunity to learn about himself, work out his problems (with help from others, if necessary) and learn from the experience.

There are genuine cases of depression where the temporary use of medication is a necessary intermediate step in the process of attacking the patient's true problems, but there are simply too many cases where it is either unnecessary or interferes with the patient's emotional processes. In fact, a recent piece in *Newsweek* mentioned a study that found that individuals can alter their own serotonin levels to some extent by making a conscious effort to change their attitudes and outlooks on life.

"Psychopharmacological solutions to our emotional problems should be used as a last resort."

We should not be so eager to give up control of our most precious resources: our minds. Psychopharmacological solutions to our emotional problems should be used as a last resort, with the true emphasis placed on self-betterment. Unless we want to live in a world like that which Huxley envisioned, in which we sacrifice our mental freedom and character in exchange for a worry-free life, Americans ought to realize what a dangerous trend overdiagnosis and overmedication of emotional and psychiatric disorders represent, and take steps to reverse it.

Behavior-Modifying Drugs Should Not Be Prescribed for Children

by Peter R. Breggin

About the author: *Peter R. Breggin is a psychiatrist practicing in Bethesda, Maryland, and the author of* Toxic Psychiatry, Talking Back to Prozac, *and* Talking Back to Ritalin.

In recent years, the basic principle of adult responsibility for children has been drastically eroded by a scientific medical approach to educating and rearing children. Health professionals began telling many adults—parents as well as teachers—that they have no responsibility for the misconduct or failures of the children under their care. Similarly, these adults are told that they cannot take responsibility for improving the lives of troubled or troublesome children. Instead, parents and teachers are taught to believe that millions of children suffer from exotic psychiatric maladies such as attention-deficit disorder, oppositional-defiant disorder and conduct disorder. These mental disorders supposedly make children unable to adjust to school or family life, regardless of the quality of teaching or parenting. Difficult children thus are labeled incorrigible through the subtle means of psychiatric diagnosis.

Overall, there probably are more than 2 million youngsters in the United States taking the stimulant drug Ritalin. Millions more have been given prescriptions for other psychiatric medication such as Prozac and lithium—that have not even been FDA-approved for children. More ominously, since the early 1990s, there has been an enormous escalation in the prescription for children of Ritalin and similar medications.

Does ADHD Really Exist?

The diagnosis most often used to justify this medicating of children is attention-deficit hyperactivity disorder, or ADHD. According to the American

Psychiatric Association's *Diagnostic and Statistical Manual of Mental Disorders*, fourth ed., ADHD takes two forms—hyperactivity-impulsivity and inattention. For hyperactivity-impulsivity, the chief diagnostic symptoms in descending order are the following: "Often fidgets with hands or feet or squirms in seat; often leaves seat in classroom; often runs about or climbs excessively in situations in which it is inappropriate; often has difficulty

> *"ADHD is really a catchall label for children who frustrate or anger adults."*

playing or engaging in leisure activities quietly." For diagnosing the inattention form of ADHD, the most common symptoms are defined as these: "Fails to give close attention or makes mistakes in schoolwork; often has difficulty sustaining attention; often does not seem to listen when spoken to directly; fails to follow instructions or to finish chores or schoolwork."

Daydreaming by a girl used to be considered a sign of boredom in a bright child; restlessness in class on the part of a spunky boy was considered a disciplinary problem. Now these behaviors are considered symptoms of mental disorder.

Many of us are concerned that ADHD is really a catchall label for children who frustrate or anger adults, especially when the adults are unable or unwilling to give them sufficient attention. Even the diagnostic manual recognizes that the symptoms commonly disappear when the child is "under very strict control, is in a novel setting, is engaged in especially interesting activities, is in a one-to-one situation." In my office, most ADHD children show remarkable capacities for concentration as they sit with their parents to discuss problems in the family or at school. Often the children do fine during vacations or in the care of other adults.

Whose Attention Deficit?

The "symptoms" of ADHD should not be used to red-flag children as suffering from mental disorders. The "attention deficit" is not in the child but in the adults who need to attend better to the child's needs. Children don't become bored, inattentive, undisciplined, resentful or violent in the home or school because of something innately wrong with them. To the contrary, these children usually are more energetic and more spirited than most. To fulfill their special promise, they need a more disciplined, interesting and loving child-oriented environment. When they get it, they often become our most creative, outstanding and responsible members of society.

Blaming the distress and misconduct of children on mental disorders recently reached a boiling point when the federal mental-health establishment claimed that inner-city children suffer from genetic and biochemical defects that predispose them to violence. In 1992 and 1993, proposals were made to focus federal research on finding supposed biological markers for violence with the aim of treating inner-city children with drugs. Ginger Ross Breggin and I sounded an alarm about these plans, creating a national controversy. We described this in our book, *The War Against Children*, resulting in the government withdrawing its overall plan.

A Class Difference

While working with parents from the inner city, we found that most of them rejected the medical diagnosis and drugging of their difficult or disturbed children. Unhappily, we discovered a far different attitude among mainstream Americans, including parents and teachers in the affluent suburbs of Washington. Conditioned intellectually to accept the modern psychiatric viewpoint, they often embraced the idea that a large proportion of their children are inherently incorrigible and hence in need of drug treatment.

In any suburban public elementary classroom, several children are likely to be taking prescribed medication to control their behavior. In more specialized public- and private-school classes, half or more may be on Ritalin or other medications. Often the parents and teachers of these students are taking Prozac and therefore assume that Ritalin might be good for the children.

"Bad" or "Mentally Ill"?

Health professionals frequently tell ADHD children that the reason they must take drugs is that they have "crossed wires" or a "biochemical imbalance" in their heads. Advocates of this approach say that medical explanations relieve children of guilt and shame about their problems or misconduct. Instead of being "bad" the child is encouraged to view himself or herself as "sick." But what's better for a child—to think of himself or herself as bad or as mentally ill? It is far more demoralizing for a child to believe that he or she has a defective mind or brain. That makes the child feel deformed, like a freak, cheated of a normal mind. The child is robbed of the concept of self-discipline or self-control, and the future can seem hopelessly limited.

I have treated adults who found their lives stifled by the demoralizing effects of these childhood diagnoses. One 25-year-old man came to me for a second opinion after his psychiatrist wanted him to resume Ritalin. Instead, we worked on learning to deal with the underlying emotional turmoil that disrupted his attention, as well as on how to impose self-discipline. He now has gone on to a successful medication-free college career.

> *"In any suburban public elementary classroom, several children are likely to be taking prescribed medication to control their behavior."*

It not only is demoralizing to attribute the child's problems to a brain disorder, it also is untrue. There is no compelling evidence that children diagnosed with ADHD have anything physically wrong with them. Since the diagnosis in reality reflects conflict between children and adults, it is unlikely that its "cause" will ever be found to reside in the child's brain.

I have described the medical hazards associated with controlling children through the use of psychotropic drugs in my books, *Toxic Psychiatry* and *The War Against Children*. In both works I argue that there's little scientific justification for the practice. In Great Britain, Sweden and Denmark, these diagnoses rarely are made and the drugs are almost never used.

The Medical Approach to Raising Children

While the use of Ritalin in the United States at present only affects a relatively small percentage of children, some advocates estimate that up to 10 percent of boys should be on medication. Meanwhile, the philosophy guiding the enthusiasm for medication has changed profoundly how we view children in general. Today, a "difficult child" typically is referred to professionals for medication. Not only are we drugging our most energetic and potentially most creative children, we are intimidating all of them.

In a vicious circle, the medical approach escalates the deterioration of school and family life by blaming inadequacies or failures on disorders in the children; this removes any incentive for the adults to improve the child's family and school life.

> *"There is no compelling evidence that children diagnosed with ADHD have anything physically wrong with them."*

Every national commission on education has found that our schools fail to respond to the moral, social and educational needs of youngsters. Meanwhile, it's also apparent that too many families are unable, ill-equipped or unwilling to raise children in a secure, disciplined and loving manner.

A Cruel and Unethical Approach

But, drugging children is not the remedy for dysfunctional families. This is a cruel and unethical approach to problems that lie with the adults in the child's life. The vulnerable child is not the cause of these problems: We are. The national debate about family values has the potential to promote the well-being of children but, thus far, the debate has overlooked this psychiatrically induced crisis in our values. Millions of parents and teachers are being taught by medical and psychological experts that they cannot and should not take responsibility for the lives of their children.

On the contrary, adults do play the determining role in the lives of children, since adults provide them with nutrition, medical care and shelter, as well as protection from physical, sexual or emotional abuse. All children need adults to offer them unconditional love—to treasure them for themselves. They also need adult guidance in developing self-esteem through the mastery of age-appropriate tasks. Children need grown-ups to discipline them in a rational manner and to teach them personal responsibility and respect for others. They need their teachers and parents to instruct them in academic and social skills in a manner that's consistent with their individual vulnerabilities and strengths.

Adults Are Responsible for Their Children

For reasons that often are beyond their control, teachers and parents commonly feel overwhelmed and in need of relief. The scientistic medical approach reassures them: "You are not to blame for the problems of your children." This may temporarily assuage adult guilt. But this approach cannot be taken without undermining the most fundamental family value of all—that adults are responsible for the lives of their children.

As a psychiatrist, I call upon my medical colleagues to stop blaming the problems of children on some chemical defect in the children themselves and to rededicate themselves to meeting children's authentic needs. As a parent, I remind all parents that we cannot take pride in how well our children do in life while disavowing responsibility for their problems.

Chapter 3

What Non-Drug Therapies Effectively Treat Mental Illness?

Chapter Preface

For people suffering from depression, medication, the most common treatment, is not always a suitable choice. Some depressed patients find the side effects of antidepressants—which include a "drugged" feeling, insomnia, and sexual dysfunction—to be intolerable. Other patients believe their mental disorders are not serious enough to warrant drug intervention. Still others categorically reject the idea of using medication to alleviate mental problems. Of the patients who refrain from taking antidepressants, many opt for non-drug therapies such as meditation, exercise, or dietary supplements. One such supplement that is gaining widespread attention is the herb St. John's wort.

St. John's wort, a yellow-flowered plant whose Latin name is *Hypericum perforatum*, has been used therapeutically for over 2,000 years. Today, the herb is Germany's leading treatment for depression—and its popularity in the United States is growing rapidly. Although St. John's wort's effectiveness has not been proven, existing studies suggest that the herb relieves depression. For example, a study conducted by the *Journal of Geriatric Psychiatry and Neurology* found that after four weeks of treatment with St. John's wort, "80 percent [of depressed patients] either felt better or became completely free of symptoms." Physicians and therapists attribute much of the herb's popularity to the fact that it is virtually free of side effects: Only 2.4 percent of patients studied reported experiencing restlessness, gastrointestinal irritations, and mild allergic reactions as a result of taking St. John's wort.

While research suggests that St. John's wort is safe, the herb is not without critics. Because the Food and Drug Administration (FDA) classifies St. John's wort as a dietary supplement, it is not subject to rigorous quality control. Skeptics, citing a case in which a tainted batch of an amino acid supplement killed forty people, claim that St. John's wort presents a similar danger. According to Esther Sternberg, a researcher at the National Institute of Mental Health, "Without an unbiased third party like the FDA policing these supplements, a disaster could happen again." Furthermore, some physicians fear that the herb's availability may lead people to self-medicate without consulting a health professional.

Despite these cautions, the number of people taking St. John's wort for depression is rising. St. John's wort is only one non-drug therapy available for the treatment of mental illness. Other non-drug options—including shock treatment, biofeedback therapy, and exercise—are discussed in the following chapter.

Electroconvulsive Therapy Is a Safe and Effective Treatment for Severe Mental Illness

by the American Psychiatric Association

About the author: *The American Psychiatric Association is an organization of psychiatrists dedicated to studying the nature, treatment, and prevention of mental illness.*

Electroconvulsive Therapy, more commonly known as "ECT," is a medical treatment performed only by highly skilled health professionals—including doctors and nurses—under the direct supervision of a psychiatrist, who is a medical doctor trained in diagnosing and treating mental illnesses. Its effectiveness in treating severe mental illnesses is recognized by the American Psychiatric Association, the American Medical Association, the National Institute of Mental Health and similar organizations in Canada, Great Britain and many other countries.

A course of treatment with ECT usually consists of six to twelve treatments given three times a week for a month or less. The patient is given general anesthesia and a muscle relaxant. When these have taken full effect, the patient's brain is stimulated, using electrodes placed at precise locations on the patient's head, with a brief controlled series of electrical pulses. This stimulus causes a seizure within the brain which lasts for approximately a minute. Because of the muscle relaxants and anesthesia, the patient's body does not convulse and the patient feels no pain. The patient awakens after five to ten minutes, much as he or she would from minor surgery.

How ECT Works

The brain is an organ that functions through complex electrochemical processes, which may be impaired by certain types of mental illnesses. Scientists

---

Reprinted from "Fact Sheet on Electroconvulsive Therapy" (1997), by permission of the author, the American Psychiatric Association.

believe ECT acts by temporarily altering some of these processes.

Electroconvulsive therapy is generally used with severely depressed patients when other forms of therapy—such as medications or psychotherapy—have not been effective, cannot be tolerated, or (in life-threatening cases) will not help the patient quickly enough. ECT also helps patients who suffer with most forms of mania (a mood disorder which is associated with grandiose, hyperactive, irrational and destructive behavior), some forms of schizophrenia, and a few other mental and neurological disorders. ECT is also useful in treating these mental illnesses in older patients for whom a particular medication may be unadvisable.

Psychiatrists are very selective in their use of Electroconvulsive Therapy. According to the National Institute of Mental Health, approximately 33,000 hospitalized Americans received ECT in 1980, the last year for which NIMH has figures. That comes out to only about two tenths of one percent of the 9.4 million who suffer with depression, the four million who suffer with schizophrenia and the more than one million who suffer with mania during any given year. Some patients—a minority—also undergo ECT as an outpatient procedure.

ECT's Effectiveness

Numerous studies since the 1940s have demonstrated ECT's effectiveness. Clinical evidence indicates that for uncomplicated cases of severe major depression, ECT will produce a substantial improvement in at least 80 percent of patients. ECT has also been shown to be effective in depressed patients who do not respond to other forms of treatment. Medication is usually the treatment of choice for mania, but here too certain patients don't respond. Many of these patients have been successfully treated with ECT.

Any medical procedure entails a certain amount of risk. However, ECT is no more dangerous than minor surgery under general anesthesia, and may at times be less dangerous than treatment with antidepressant medications. This is in spite of its frequent use with the elderly and those with coexisting medical illnesses. A small number of other medical disorders increase the risk associated with ECT, and patients are carefully screened for these conditions before a psychiatrist will recommend them for the treatment.

Immediate side effects from ECT are rare except for headaches, muscle ache or soreness, nausea and confusion, usually occurring during the first few hours following the procedure. Over the course of ECT, it may be more difficult for patients to remember newly learned information, though this difficulty disappears over the days and weeks following completion of the

> *"Psychiatrists are very selective in their use of Electroconvulsive Therapy."*

ECT course. Some patients also report a partial loss of memory for events that occurred during the days, weeks, and months preceding ECT. While most of these memories typically return over a period of days to months following ECT, some patients have reported longer-lasting problems with recall of these memories. However, other individuals actually report improved memory ability following ECT, because of its ability to remove the amnesia that is sometimes associated with severe depression. The amount and duration of memory problems with ECT vary with the type of ECT that is used and are less a concern with unilateral ECT (where one side of the head is stimulated electrically) than with bilateral ECT.

Myths About ECT

Researchers have found no evidence that ECT damages the brain. There are medical conditions, such as epilepsy, that cause spontaneous seizures which, unless prolonged or otherwise complicated, do not harm the brain. ECT artificially stimulates a seizure, but ECT-induced seizures occur under much more controlled conditions than those that are "naturally occurring" and are safe. A recent study by Coffey and colleagues found no changes in brain anatomy with ECT, as measured by very sensitive scans of the brain using magnetic resonance imaging (MRI) equipment. Other research has established that the amount of electricity which actually enters the brain (only a small fraction of what is applied to the scalp) is much lower in intensity and shorter in duration than that which would be necessary to damage brain tissue.

"For uncomplicated cases of severe major depression, ECT will produce a substantial improvement in at least 80 percent of patients."

The idea of ECT is frightening to many people, thanks in part to its depiction in the film *One Flew Over the Cuckoo's Nest*. Some may not know that muscle relaxants and anesthesia make it a safe, practically painless procedure.

Some people who advocate legislative bans against ECT are former psychiatric patients who have undergone the procedure and believe they have been harmed by it and that the treatment is used to punish patients' misbehavior and make them more docile. This is untrue.

It is true that many years ago, when psychiatric knowledge was less advanced, ECT was used for a wide range of psychiatric problems, sometimes even to control troublesome patients. The procedure was frightening for patients because it was then administered without anesthesia or muscle relaxants, and the uncontrolled seizures sometimes broke bones.

Today, the American Psychiatric Association has very strict guidelines for ECT administration. This organization supports use of ECT only to treat severe, disabling mental disorders, never to control behavior.

Patient Rights

No psychiatrist simply "decides" to treat a patient with ECT. Before he or she can administer ECT, he or she must first obtain written consent from the patient or (in most states), if the patient is too ill to make decisions for him or herself, from a court-appointed guardian (usually one of the patient's family members).

Under the APA's recommended "informed consent" protocol, permission to administer ECT comes after a careful review of the treatment. This review is not a simple recitation of dry, confusing facts; the psychiatrist explains in clear language what ECT involves, what other treatments might be available, and the benefits and risks these procedures may entail. The patient or family member is informed of when, where, and by whom the treatment will be administered and the number of treatments expected. Questions are encouraged. The person consenting to the procedure is kept informed of progress as the treatment continues, and may withdraw consent at any time.

> *"ECT is no more dangerous than minor surgery under general anesthesia."*

The costs for any psychiatric treatment vary widely, depending on the state and the facility administering it. Usually, however, ECT costs between $300 and $800 per treatment, an amount which covers the psychiatrist, anesthetist, and a variety of hospital charges. With eight as the average number of treatments, this means a course of ECT treatment will usually cost between $2,400 and $6,400. The cost of ECT is at least partially reimbursed by most insurance plans offering coverage for mental disorders. In cases where the use of ECT shortens the duration of a hospital stay, its net cost may be substantially less.

Electroconvulsive Therapy Causes Permanent Brain Damage

by Michael Chavin

About the author: *Michael Chavin, an anaesthesiologist who assisted in 2,000 electroconvulsive therapy (ECT) procedures, is now an outspoken critic of ECT. He is a commissioner with the Citizens Commission on Human Rights International, an organization that works to abolish human rights abuses in the field of psychiatry.*

To begin with, electro-convulsive therapy is never referred to as shock treatment by those who profit from it. The word "shock" carries too many true, but threatening, connotations. Psychiatrists are more likely to tell you it is called "electrotherapy" or "electro-convulsive therapy" to blur any negative response. They'll tell you openly that they don't know how it "works," nor that they have any scientific reasoning for why they think it is a good idea to destroy your brain cells.

The procedure is quick and straightforward. The patient is not allowed to eat or drink for four or more hours prior, to prevent vomiting during the procedure. A half hour before, a drug such as Atropine or Robinol, a medication that reduces secretions in the mouth and air passages, is given. This cuts down the risk of suffocation and other complications that could arise if the patient should swallow his own saliva.

Dentures, jewelry, and hair ornaments are removed to avoid injury during the convulsion. The person is placed on a bed. A cart nearby contains life-saving equipment, including a "defibrillator" for jump-starting a heart in cardiac arrest.

A jelly is applied to the temples to improve electrical conductivity and to prevent burns. An anesthetic is injected into the vein, rendering the patient unconscious. A muscle relaxant is then administered, causing a virtual shutdown of muscular activity. The person is then placed on an artificial respirator until he

Reprinted, with permission, from "Psychiatry Destroys Minds," by Michael Chavin, published by the Citizens Commission on Human Rights (1997), at www.cchr.org/ect/eng/page06.htm.

resumes breathing on his own after treatment.

A rubber gag is placed in the mouth to stop the patient from breaking his teeth or biting his tongue. The electrodes are placed on the temples.

A button is pushed and between 180 to 460 volts of electricity sends a current searing through the brain from temple to temple (bilateral ECT), or from the front to the back of one side of the head (unilateral ECT). This creates a severe convulsion or seizure of long duration, called a "grand mal" convulsion, which is identical to an epileptic fit. Because the muscle relaxant masks the body's normal response to the shock, the administering psychiatrist usually looks for a curling up or twitching of the toes to determine if the shock has "worked." Without this sign, multiple electric shocks can be given until the desired effect is achieved.

> *"The purpose of shock treatment is to create brain damage."*

The entire procedure takes between five and fifteen minutes. For this, the psychiatric industry in the U.S. alone makes an estimated $3 billion per year.

Most patients are given a total of six to twelve shocks: one a day, three times a week. On top of this, most patients are given more than one series of treatments because they never experience permanent relief from it. In the U.S., this can increase a psychiatrist's annual income by $27,300. (The average psychiatrist made $131,300 in 1993!)

The American Psychiatric Association (APA) has estimated that more than 88,600 people are given ECT each year in the U.S., with the total number of treatments estimated at 260,000. However, this figure is only an estimate based on the APA's collection of statistics for 1976. It would seem that psychiatrists have no desire to monitor their systematic social crippling of tens of thousands of people each year. Newspaper articles in 1993 state that the number of Americans undergoing ECT each year could be as high as 110,000.

ECT's Purpose

The purpose of shock treatment is to create brain damage. There is a shock wave through the brain, causing the brain to discharge energy in a very chaotic type of state. And this increases metabolism to a very high level which deprives the brain of oxygen and can actually destroy brain cells. This brain damage is what brings about the memory loss and learning disability, as well as the spatial and time disorientation which always follows shock treatments.

All physical damage done to the brain by ECT is permanent and irreversible. There is evidence that the damage, once begun by ECT, is progressive and feeds on itself, leading to further brain deterioration, including physical shrinkage of the brain and a shortening of the life of the victim. . . .

Why is shock treatment so devastating to those receiving it? This is a simple description of some of the basic ways in which electric shock treatment permanently and irreversibly damages the brain:

1. When the high-voltage electric shock hits the brain, it overwhelms the brain's normal protective mechanisms that keep nerve cells from overstimulating each other. A massive electrical storm instantly takes off through the organ. This is called a grand mal epileptic seizure. Sweeping back and forth randomly through the brain, it can last for several minutes.

2. Even though the brain is only about two percent of the body's weight, it normally uses about 20 percent of the body's oxygen. Because of the massive electrical activity during the seizure, there is a huge increase in the brain's demand for oxygen. Blood flow to the brain increases by as much as 400 percent, as does the brain's need for oxygen. This increase in oxygen demand lasts not only for the duration of the seizure, but remains elevated for some time following it.

To meet this oxygen demand, the blood pressure can increase by as much as 200 percent. This extremely high brain blood pressure overwhelms the brain's blood pressure regulation mechanisms and frequently ruptures small and large blood vessels. This is called hemorrhaging. Human autopsy studies have confirmed that many of the deaths that have occurred both during and after ECT are due to this phenomenon.

3. Electric shock causes damage to the blood-brain barrier, compromising the brain's ability to isolate itself from harmful toxins and foreign substances. [The "blood-brain barrier" is a set of defenses that the brain uses

> *"Each successive 'treatment' creates new injuries and escalates [brain] damage in the areas already affected."*

to keep itself healthy and protect itself from damage: the blood vessels in the brain bring needed substances to the organ; they also carry away those undesirable substances that would otherwise harm the brain—such as an over-concentration of proteins, toxic substances (like drugs), and other foreign matter. These blood vessels prevent an excess of undesirable substances from leaking out of the vessels and contacting the brain tissue.]

4. The combination of raised brain blood pressure, hemorrhaging and ruptures in the blood-brain barrier can force undesired substances and fluids to "leak" out of the blood vessels and into the brain tissue, causing swelling to occur.

This cycle, once started, becomes a vicious circle: as the pressure within the skull rises due to the swelling, brain capillaries (tiny blood vessels) close off. This denies oxygen which then damages the linings. The result is that they become more leaky. This leads to more swelling and more damage. Nerve cells and other tissues become starved for oxygen and can die. Later, after the swelling has subsided, the brain will be seen to have shrunk; fluids will have been absorbed. An analogy might be like squeezing dirty water out of a sponge.

[Note that providing oxygen to the patient during ECT may not prevent permanent brain damage since supplying oxygen only prolongs the seizure, much like throwing fuel onto a fire. The neurons (nerve cells) die when the available substances they use as fuel are exhausted. The subsequent coma that follows a seizure can occur from a lack of necessary nutrients—even though an adequate amount of oxygen was present. Any apparent benefits of supplying oxygen to the patient are thus negated by the subsequent brain damage that occurs.]

5. The increase in blood pressure causes the swelling to spread to wider areas of the brain. Leakage of undesirable substances across the blood-brain barrier occurs.

6. This cycle of blood pressure–induced damage is not prevented by the "modern" use of muscle relaxants and anesthetics simply because it is the brain's enormous demand for oxygen during the seizure that causes the high blood pressure. During the seizure, this demand exists whether the patient is anesthetized or not.

7. Each successive "treatment" creates new injuries and escalates the damage in the areas already affected. A usual course of ECT involves six to twelve shocks over a period of weeks.

8. The chemical composition of the brain is changed by electric shock. Cellular activity is altered for hours after the "treatment." Abnormal levels of neurotransmitters (chemical substances that assist in the transmission of electrical impulses between nerve cells) and enzymes (protein substances) appear. The switchboard-like function of the brain becomes scrambled and impaired. Memory loss, confusion, and loss of space and time orientation result.

9. Following ECT there is a marked rise of a substance called arachidonic acid (an unsaturated fatty acid obtained from lecithin) that can cause small strokes to occur throughout the brain. The damage is random, accumulates over many treatments, is not limited to the area directly assaulted with the electric shock, and can lead to death.

10. The physiology of the brain is changed from normal to abnormal by ECT. There are profound alterations in brain function which are measured as EEG changes (EEG: Electroencephalogram: a recording of the brain's electrical activity). These represent extremely long-lasting, probably permanent, abnormalities of brain function. Peter Sterling, Associate Professor of Neurobiology at the University of Pennsylvania School of Medicine, describes these alterations in brain function as "similar to . . . epilepsy . . . and other neuropathologies." According to Sterling, ". . . the biochemical basis for convulsive therapy is similar to that of cranial cerebral trauma."

> *"The physiology of the brain is changed from normal to abnormal by ECT."*

As early as 1942, studies showed ECT to cause brain damage. Dr. Bernard J. Alpers, who carried out the first post-ECT autopsies, found in two cases hemorrhages and tissue destruction which "offers a clear demonstration of the fact that [ECT] is followed at times by structural damage of the brain."

Eye Movement Desensitization and Reprocessing Helps Post-Traumatic Stress Disorder

by Irene Barrett

About the author: *Irene Barrett is a pseudonym for a freelance writer and writing instructor who lives in Portland, Oregon.*

In 1991, I suffered an emotional crisis so debilitating that, even after countless hours and thousands of dollars worth of therapy, I was depressed, utterly hopeless—and contemplating suicide.

The crisis that started this ordeal is a story unto itself. Suffering from chronic depression, I'd started to see a psychiatrist in my town for treatment. His "therapy" included sex, and we began an affair that lasted two years. When the relationship soured, he severed all contact, both medical and personal. I contacted the state board of medical examiners for help. I knew that his conduct had been unconscionable, but I didn't know what I could do about it.

They told me to file a complaint, which I did. But when I went to the doctor's house to retrieve some of my belongings, he called the police and accused me of trespassing. As a result, I was arrested. There was a court case—and he won. I was convicted of criminal trespass, sentenced to eighty hours of community service, and placed on two years' probation. Soon thereafter, my complaint against the doctor's behavior was dismissed by the state board because of lack of evidence. I was completely humiliated.

To say that the experience was devastating is to put it mildly. After my conviction, I began treatment with a psychotherapist, a woman in whom I could truly put my trust. But after three years of therapy—and trying everything from meditation, prayer, affirmations, and volunteer work to Western drugs, Eastern drugs, and acupuncture to relieve my pain—I was still in misery. I'd talked to

Reprinted, with permission, from Irene Barrett, "Right Before My Eyes," *Natural Health*, December 1996. For a trial issue of *Natural Health* call 1-800-526-8440.

ministers, psychiatrists, psychics, and astrologers. I'd even been to an exorcist. But I was still reliving the events of that autumn day—when a jury found me guilty of injuring the man who had caused me such agony—over and over and over. Each time I remembered the moment, I cried with the same intensity and felt the same depth of despair as I had when it all happened.

> **"Eye movements help the brain catalyze the information from traumatic experiences and allow it to be translated into a less distressing form."**

At first, I tried to rationalize my way out of my feelings. Injustice happened, I knew. People got over shipwrecks and earthquakes and being taken in by con artists—and worse. So why couldn't I forget about my own experience? Why couldn't I just get over it too? It was just a memory, but it was ruining my life.

One summer evening, I lay propped up in bed, reading. As usual, the story on which I was trying to concentrate was interrupted by the intrusive flashbacks of my own drama, and I began to pound my head against the wall in frustration. If I could beat the memories out, I thought, damage the part of my brain where they were stored and finally get my life back, I would do it.

Out of Hope

I had reached the point where my options seemed to have dwindled to one: suicide. When I told my therapist this, she didn't seem surprised. She said she had to admit that although we had accomplished a lot together, she didn't know what to do next.

But my therapist had one more idea. "I'm taking training next month in a technique called Eye Movement Desensitization and Reprocessing, or EMDR," she told me. "Would you like to try it?" I told her Ed heard something about an eye movement therapy that was being used with Vietnam vets suffering from posttraumatic stress disorder, but that was all; I didn't know anything about EMDR.

The Philosophy Behind EMDR

My therapist explained to me that EMDR was developed by Francine Shapiro, Ph.D., who believes that rapid back-and-forth eye movements (much like those that occur spontaneously during REM—rapid eye movement—sleep, which is the deepest phase of the sleep cycle) can help people deal with traumatic memories. Shapiro had theorized that the eye movements help the brain catalyze the information from traumatic experiences and allow it to be translated into a less distressing form. It defuses the emotional stress attached to a memory without erasing the emotions or the memory itself.

Eye movement therapy, my therapist told me, right now is at about the same place that gravity was before Newtonian physics: It's here, and it works, whether we understand it or not.

But just as with antidepression drugs like Prozac and Zoloft, EMDR won't work for everyone, and there's no real way to predict whom it will or won't help. Apparently, the original theory behind EMDR held that rapid back-and-forth eye movements tap into the same learning and memory mechanisms that are affected during REM sleep. In later studies, other types of rhythmic, sustained interventions, such as repetitive sounds or tapping on a patient's hands, for example, also were shown to help the mind process traumatic events.

Despite my faith in my therapist, once she explained how EMDR worked, I wasn't exactly overwhelmed with optimism. But I felt so desperate for a cure to my depression that I agreed to give it a try.

How EMDR Works

For my first EMDR session I met my therapist in the same cozy, book-lined office where we always met for therapy. To start, she led me through some questions. What was bothering me? What core belief did I hold as a result of my feelings, and on a scale of 1 to 10, how true did I believe it to be?

"Now bring up a memory attached to that," she said. That was easy; scenes from the court case came up in living color, as they had constantly since that awful day. "Now stay with that scene and follow my fingers," she said. I tracked her hand as she waved her fingers rhythmically back and forth like windshield wipers. After a minute or two, she stopped. "What are you seeing?" she asked.

> *"The change that EMDR made in my life was so immediate and dramatic that it felt like a miracle."*

I thought hard, and described the scene: I was a teenager. My mother had caught me smoking marijuana and had called the police. Now I was in court, and my mother was trying to have me committed to an institution. The judge was ruling against her, but I was mortified nonetheless. My distress at that experience came back to me in full force.

"Stay with it," said my therapist. She began waving her hand again. One scene led to another as we repeated the drill for over an hour. I would track her fingers with my eyes and watch a multimedia show of my life, almost the same way people who've had near death experiences describe, complete with sound, color, motion, and emotions. I saw the scene in court with my mother, heard her accusations, and felt shame. It was a trancelike experience for me; I was hardly aware of my surroundings. When the EMDR session was over, I was drained and emotionally wrung out, and had very little to say.

A Revelation

The following week was a revelation to me. While lying in bed one night reading, I paused for a moment and reflected on the crisis and court case of four years earlier. I felt sad about it—a distant sadness, like the tender, bittersweet way we look upon old wounds that have served as big lessons in life. I carried myself into the sadness and found, for the first time, that it was manageable. In the past, every time I had tried to reach into an emotion, to really feel it in order to get beyond it, I had found myself in a black abyss of despair from which I could not escape. Now it was different. So this, I thought, is what it means to "sit with your feelings." Not denying, not repressing, just feeling them and then moving on.

Over the next three weeks, I had two more EMDR sessions; regular therapy in between allowed me to "debrief" (as my therapist put it). That single month turned the corner for me on a period of trauma and depression that had taken more than four years of my life. In each session, the traumatic scene I was fixated upon would quickly give way to a much older trauma that obviously had taken deep root in my psyche. In every case it was something that was easily verifiable, but something I'd strenuously repressed. In high school, for example, I'd laughingly dismissed the powerlessness and humiliation that the episode of drug charges had caused me in my small Ohio town. But my mind had held onto those emotions.

Before my EMDR, I had completely buried the memory. It's hard to believe I had virtually forgotten such a momentous event—it had completely disrupted my high school education—and yet I had. Was it a coincidence that for all of my well-intentioned, virtuous living since high school, I had somehow managed to find my way back into a courtroom again? Both my therapist and I were fascinated by the possible connections.

The Results of EMDR

The change that EMDR made in my life was so immediate and dramatic that it felt like a miracle. Freed from the clutches of my traumatic memories, I could go to a job interview and not start to cry in the middle of it. No longer dwelling on my "victimization" and the injustice done to me, my life became positive again. I was able to turn my energies toward repairing the damage that my depression had done to my career and to my personal and financial life. I looked toward a future of new relationships and opportunities instead of living in the past. I felt as if my mind had been freed.

Of course, I still have my ups and downs, but I am much better able to live in the present tense, and I know that if my mind ever gets caught again in a groove like the broken record that was playing in my head before I began EMDR, there is a way to get out of it. My therapist tells me that some of her clients have been helped as dramatically as I was by this technique; other clients remain virtually unaffected. I don't even know if science is advanced enough to do more than hypothesize about how EMDR works. I only know that it worked for me.

The Effectiveness of Eye Movement Desensitization and Reprocessing Is Unsubstantiated

by Scott O. Lilienfeld

About the author: *Scott O. Lilienfeld is an assistant professor of psychology at Emory University in Atlanta, Georgia.*

"Quick fixes" for emotional maladies have struck a responsive chord in the general public, as biopsychologist B.L. Beyerstein has noted. Because these interventions often hold out the hope of alleviating long-standing and previously intractable problems with a minimum of time and effort, they are understandably appealing to both victims of psychological disorders and their would-be healers.

More often than not, however, the initial enthusiasm generated by such treatments has fizzled as soon as their proponents' claims have been subjected to intensive scrutiny. . . .

In the past few years, a novel and highly controversial treatment known as "eye movement desensitization and reprocessing" (EMDR) has burst onto the psychotherapy scene. EMDR has been proclaimed by its advocates as an extremely effective and efficient treatment for Post-Traumatic Stress Disorder (PTSD) and related anxiety disorders. These assertions warrant close examination because PTSD is a chronic and debilitating condition that tends to respond poorly to most interventions.

What Is Post-Traumatic Stress Disorder?

Although PTSD was not formally recognized as a mental disorder until 1980, descriptions of "shell shock," "battle fatigue," and similar reactions to wartime trauma date back at least to the late nineteenth century. PTSD is defined by the

Excerpted from Scott O. Lilienfeld, "EMDR Treatment: Less Than Meets the Eye?" *Skeptical Inquirer*, January/February 1996. Used by permission of the *Skeptical Inquirer*, PO Box 703, Amherst, NY 14226-0703.

American Psychiatric Association as an anxiety disorder resulting from exposure to "an event . . . that involved actual or threatened death or serious injury, or a threat to the physical integrity of self or others." Among the most frequent precipitants of PTSD are military combat, rape, physical assault, motor vehicle accidents, natural disasters, and the witnessing of a murder or accidental death. The primary symptoms of PTSD fall into three categories: (1) psychological reexperiencing of the traumatic event (e.g., recurrent and disturbing flashbacks and dreams of the event); (2) avoidance of stimuli (e.g., television programs, conversations) that remind the individual of the event; and (3) heightened arousal (e.g., sleep disturbances, increased startle responses).

> *"The ostensible improvement resulting from EMDR in . . . reports may be due to numerous variables other than EMDR itself."*

Although PTSD is difficult to treat, there is accumulating evidence that "exposure treatments," which involve confronting clients with memories and images of the traumatic event, are effective for many cases of PTSD. One of the best known of such interventions is "flooding," in which clients are exposed to trauma-related stimuli for prolonged time periods (often two hours or more) until their anxiety subsides. Flooding can be performed using either real-life stimuli or visual imagery, although the inability to recreate the actual details of the traumatic scene typically means that the treatment must be conducted imaginally. The mechanisms underlying the success of exposure techniques are still a subject of debate, but many psychologists believe that the effective ingredient in such treatments is "extinction"—the process by which a response dissipates when the stimulus triggering this response is presented without the original emotional concomitants.

Despite their advantages, exposure treatments for PTSD tend to provoke extreme anxiety and consume much time. Often 20 sessions are required for maximal efficacy. As a result, many clients with PTSD are reluctant to undergo such treatments, leading some practitioners to search for less stressful and more time-efficient interventions. Enter EMDR.

The Origins of EMDR

Francine Shapiro, the psychologist who originated EMDR, recalls having fortuitously "discovered" this technique when she found that rapid back-and-forth eye movements reduced her own anxiety. Shapiro thereafter applied this procedure to her own clients with anxiety disorders and claims to have met with remarkable success. Since the initial published report of its use in 1989, EMDR has skyrocketed in popularity among practitioners. As of mid-1995, approximately 14,000 therapists were licensed to perform EMDR in the United States and other countries, and this number is growing. EMDR is also attracting international attention. For example, a team of American psychologists recently trained 40 European therapists to administer EMDR to victims of war trauma in Bosnia.

Although EMDR is alleged to be a complicated technique that requires extensive training, the treatment's key elements can be summarized briefly. Clients are first asked to visualize the traumatic event as vividly as possible. While retaining this image in mind, they are told to supply a statement that epitomizes their reaction to it (e.g., "I am about to die"). Clients are then asked to rate their anxiety on a Subjective Units of Distress (SUDs) scale, which ranges from 0 to 10, with 0 being no anxiety and 10 being extreme terror. In addition, they are told to provide a competing positive statement that epitomizes their *desired* reaction to the image (e.g., "I can make it"), and to rate their degree of belief in this statement on a 0 to 8 Validity of Cognition scale.

Following these initial steps, clients are asked to visually track the therapist's finger as it sweeps rhythmically from right to left in sets of 12 to 24 strokes, alternated at a speed of two strokes per second. The finger motion is carried out 12 to 14 inches in front of the clients eyes. Following each set of 12 to 24 strokes, clients are asked to "blank out" the visual image and inhale deeply, and are then asked for a revised SUDs rating. This process is repeated until clients' SUDs ratings fall to 2 or lower and their Validity of Cognition ratings rise to 6 or higher.

Although EMDR technically requires the use of eye movements, Shapiro claimed that she has successfully used the technique with blind clients by substituting auditory tones for movements of the therapist's finger. Recently I attended a presentation on EMDR given by a clinician who reported that, when working with children, he uses alternating hand-taps on the knees in lieu of back-and-forth finger movements.

Since its development, EMDR has been extended to many problems other than PTSD, including phobias, generalized anxiety, paranoid schizophrenia, learning disabilities, eating disorders, substance abuse, and even pathological jealousy. Moreover, Shapiro asserted that "EMDR treatment is equally effective with a variety of 'dysfunctional' emotions such as excessive grief, rage, guilt, etc." The theoretical rationale for EMDR has not been clearly explicated by either Shapiro or others. Indeed, a recent attempt by Shapiro to elaborate on EMDR's mechanism of action may mystify even those familiar with the technique: "The system may become unbalanced due to a trauma or through stress engendered during a developmental window, but once appropriately catalyzed and maintained in a dynamic state by EMDR, it transmutes information to a state of therapeutically appropriate resolution." Shapiro has further conjectured that the eye movements of EMDR are similar to those of rapid eye movement (REM) sleep. Because there is evidence from animal studies that REM sleep is associated with the processing of memories, Shapiro

"Controlled studies provide mixed support for the efficacy of EMDR."

has suggested that the eye movements of EMDR may similarly facilitate the processing of partially "blocked" memories. Because there is no evidence that EMDR produces brain changes resembling those occurring during REM sleep, however, the analogy between the eye movements of EMDR and those of REM sleep may be more superficial than real.

A Therapeutic Breakthrough?

EMDR has been hailed by its advocates as a novel treatment that produces much faster and more dramatic improvements than alternative treatments. Shapiro, for example, asserted that EMDR can successfully treat many or most cases of PTSD in a single 50-minute session, although especially severe cases may require several sessions. Moreover, claims for EMDR's efficacy have not been limited to Shapiro. Psychologist Roger Solomon described EMDR as "a powerful tool that rapidly and effectively reduces the emotional impact of traumatic or anxiety evoking situations." Beere reported "spectacular" results after using EMDR on a client with multiple personality disorder.

Similar reports of EMDR's sensational effectiveness have appeared in the media. On July 29, 1994, ABC's "20/20" news-magazine show aired a segment on EMDR. Host Hugh Downs introduced EMDR as "an exciting breakthrough . . . a way for people to free themselves from destructive memories, and it seems to work even in cases where years of conventional therapy have failed." Downs stated, "No one understands exactly why

> *"There is no convincing evidence that EMDR is more effective for post-traumatic anxiety than standard exposure treatments."*

this method succeeds, only that it does." The program featured an excerpt from an interview with Stephen Silver, a psychologist who averred, "It (EMDR) leads immediately to a decrease in nightmares, intrusive memories, and flashback phenomena. It is one of most powerful tools I've encountered for treating post-traumatic stress."

Although based largely on unsystematic and anecdotal observations, such glowing testimonials merit careful consideration. Are the widespread claims for EMDR's efficacy substantiated by research?

Uncontrolled Case Reports

Many uncontrolled case reports appear to attest to the efficacy of EMDR. All of these case reports utilize a "pre-post design" in which clients are treated with EMDR and subsequently reassessed for indications of improvement. These case reports, although seemingly supportive of EMDR, are for several reasons seriously flawed as persuasive evidence for its effectiveness.

First, case reports, probably even more than large controlled investigations, are susceptible to the "file drawer problem"—the selective tendency for negative findings to remain unpublished. It is impossible to determine the extent to which the published cases of EMDR treatment, which are almost all successful, are representative of all cases treated with this procedure.

Second, in virtually all of the published case reports, EMDR was combined with other interventions, such as relaxation training and real life exposure. As a result, one cannot determine whether the apparent improvement reported in such cases is attributable to EMDR, the ancillary treatments, or both.

> *"The most justified conclusion concerning EMDR's effectiveness is: Not proven."*

Third, and most important, these case reports cannot provide information regarding cause-and-effect relations because they lack a control group of individuals who did not receive EMDR. The ostensible improvement resulting from EMDR in these reports may be due to numerous variables other than EMDR itself, such as placebo effects (improvement resulting from the expectation of improvement), spontaneous remission (natural improvement occurring in the absence of treatment), and regression to the mean (the statistical tendency of extreme scores at an initial testing to become less extreme upon retesting). Consumers of uncontrolled case reports thus must be chary of falling prey to the logical fallacy of *post hoc, ergo propter hoc* (after this, therefore because of this): Only in adequately controlled studies can improvement following EMDR treatment be unequivocally attributed to the treatment itself. . . .

A Look at the Evidence

Because of the paucity of adequately controlled studies on EMDR, it would be premature to proffer any definitive conclusions regarding its effectiveness. Nevertheless, the following assertions are warranted on the basis of the evidence.

1. Although a multitude of uncontrolled case reports seemingly demonstrate that EMDR produces high success rates, these reports are open to numerous alternative explanations and thus do not provide compelling evidence for EMDR's effectiveness.

2. Controlled studies provide mixed support for the efficacy of EMDR. Most of the evidence for EMDR's effectiveness derives from clients' within-session ratings (which in some cases may be influenced by the desire to terminate exposure), but not from more objective measures of improvement. There is no evidence that EMDR eliminates many or most of the symptoms of PTSD in one session.

3. There is no convincing evidence that EMDR is more effective for post-traumatic anxiety than standard exposure treatments. If EMDR works at all, it may be because it contains an exposure component. The proponents of EMDR have yet to demonstrate that EMDR represents a new advance in the treatment of anxiety disorders, or that the eye movements purportedly critical to this technique constitute anything more than pseudoscientific window dressing.

Thus, the most justified conclusion concerning EMDR's effectiveness is: Not proven. Nonetheless, many proponents of EMDR remain convinced that the treatment utility of EMDR will ultimately be demonstrated. Shapiro, for example, opined, "When the efficacy of EMDR is fully established, I would like to see it taught in the universities. When that happens, three-hour workshops on specialized applications of EMDR will undoubtedly be offered. . . ." These statements, which were made after approximately 1,200 licensed therapists had already received formal training in EMDR, raise troubling questions. Should not the efficacy of a therapeutic technique be established *before* it is taught to clinicians for the express purpose of administering it to their clients? Moreover, does not the spirit of open scientific inquiry demand that the proponents of a novel technique remain agnostic regarding its efficacy pending appropriate data, and that the two sentences quoted above should therefore begin with "if" rather than "when?". . .

Because of the limited number of controlled studies on EMDR, both practitioners and scientists should remain open to the possibility of its effectiveness. Nevertheless, the standard of proof required to use a new procedure clinically should be considerably higher than the standard of proof required to conduct research on its efficacy. This is particularly true in the case of such conditions as PTSD, for which existing treatments have already been shown to be effective. The continued widespread use of EMDR for therapeutic purposes in the absence of adequate evidence can be seen as only another example of the human mind's willingness to sacrifice critical thinking for wishful thinking.

Transcranial Magnetic Stimulation Offers Potential for Severe Depression

by Matthew Kirkcaldie and Saxby Pridmore

About the authors: *Matthew Kirkcaldie was a graduate student at the University of Tasmania at the time this viewpoint was written. Saxby Pridmore is the director of Psychological Medicine at Royal Hobart Hospital in Tasmania.*

The brain is elusive: its most interesting qualities appear when it is tucked inside its shell of bone, reading the world through senses and driving the body through the wide range of human behaviour. Anatomists can describe its structure in incredible detail, physiologists can tease out the complex chemistry of its cells, and neuropsychologists have pieced together a broad but incomplete picture of how its functions work together. Despite this enormous body of knowledge, the day-to-day running of the brain's activities—and how to help when they go wrong—is still difficult to comprehend. Our knowledge is based on accidental damage, comparisons made at autopsy, and some difficult imaging techniques, rather than through direct interaction with the brain working inside its enclosure.

Historically, interventions made on the brain have been fairly drastic—from holes bored in the skull by primitive healers, through to the drugs, electrical treatments and psychosurgery of more recent times. Psychiatry, surgery and pharmacology have combined to alleviate or prevent many conditions which were once a death sentence, or meant a life of misery for the sufferer. However, their techniques have often carried enormous risk, or drastic side effects, due to the severity of the interventions used.

A New Potential

One very promising avenue for influencing the living brain has emerged in the last decade, based on the use of pulsed magnetic fields. The skull is a good insulator, and past efforts to alter the electrical activity happening inside it have

Reprinted, with permission, from Matthew Kirkcaldie and Saxby Pridmore, "A Bright Spot on the Horizon: Transcranial Magnetic Stimulation in Psychiatry," *Open Mind*, 1996, at www.musc.edu/ tmsmirror/intro/layintro.html.

required high voltages, with little opportunity for fine control or focus of the effects. Consider instead how easily a magnet under a wooden tabletop can move a pin on the surface—magnetic fields pass almost unaffected through insulators, including the skull.

It is easy in principle to get a magnetic field to produce electrical effects: simply change the field over time, and any charge-carriers (like the ions in the cells of the brain) will be influenced to flow, creating an induced current. However, affecting neurons inside the head requires a lot

> *"[Transcranial magnetic stimulation] is a non-invasive technique, apparently free of serious side effects, capable of modifying the activity of specific brain areas."*

of magnetic force to be changed very quickly, and the technology to do this has only been around for about a decade. The first *transcranial magnetic stimulation* (TMS) machines, capable of delivering a pulse every three seconds, were developed as diagnostic aids for neurologists. For instance, the motor part of the brain can be stimulated, inducing a twitch of the thumb, which tells a neurologist that the intervening nerve pathways are intact. Machines are now available which can give up to 50 stimuli per second (rapid-rate TMS, or rTMS) and their effects are more interesting. Among a wide range of possibilities, it is believed that rTMS may have a place in the treatment of some mental illnesses. It is a non-invasive technique, apparently free of serious side effects, capable of modifying the activity of specific brain areas.

How It Works

The magnetic fields used in TMS are produced by passing current through a hand-held coil, whose shape determines the properties and size of the field. The coil is driven by a machine which switches the large current necessary in a very precise and controlled way, at rates up to 50 cycles per second in rTMS. The coil is held on the scalp—no actual contact is necessary—and the magnetic field passes through the skull and into the brain. Small induced currents can then make brain areas below the coil more or less active, depending on the settings used.

In practice, TMS and rTMS are able to influence many brain functions, including movement, visual perception, memory, reaction time, speech and mood. The effects produced are genuine but temporary, lasting only a short time after actual stimulation has stopped.

Generally, TMS appears to be free from harmful effects. Research using animals and human volunteers has showed little effect on the body in general as a result of stimulation, and examination of brain tissue submitted to thousands of TMS pulses has shown no detectable structural changes. It is possible in unusual circumstances to trigger a seizure in normal patients, but a set of guidelines which virtually eliminate this risk are available. Research continues, but

TMS is certainly free of obvious side effects like those of electro-convulsive therapy (ECT), which still makes quite an impact on patients despite refinements in technique.

TMS/rTMS in the Treatment of Mental Illness

Many mental illnesses can be demonstrated to stem from the abnormal behaviour of particular brain regions, in much the same way that diabetes is the result of malfunctioning cells in the pancreas. It is believed that some mental disorders are the result of nerve cells being over- or under-excitable (in other words, it is too easy or too difficult for them to "fire" and work properly). In this context, successful psychiatric treatment is achieved by modifying these cells' behaviour. The range of effects produced by TMS are a clear indication of its potential to work in this way.

Of course, TMS could only be used to treat diseases whose functional causes are understood. Recent progress in understanding the mechanisms behind depression, obsessive-compulsive disorder, and neurological diseases like Parkinson's and Huntington's, offers some hope in these areas. It must be stressed that most of the excitement about TMS is based on potential rather than proven effectiveness, but research is being conducted around the world. For instance, there is reason to believe that rTMS could replace some ECT treatments currently used for severely depressed patients. Groups in Germany, the United States and Israel have reported positive results from using TMS and rTMS to treat depressed patients. The prospect of replacing ECT with a near-painless treatment, which does not require anaesthesia, would change these people's lives remarkably.

> *"[Transcranial magnetic stimulation is] able to influence many brain functions, including movement, visual perception, memory, reaction time, speech and mood."*

Biofeedback Therapy Improves Mental Conditions

by Jim Robbins

About the author: *Jim Robbins is a freelance writer who lives in Helena, Montana.*

When Mary Obringer and her husband adopted a five-month-old South Korean baby in May of 1987, she knew immediately that something was wrong. "He developed slowly," Obringer says of the infant, whom they named Max. "He had speech disabilities, motor skill problems, social problems. He was hyperactive and had trouble concentrating." As a toddler, Max couldn't be in a large group of people without getting violent—hitting, kicking, and screaming. By the time he started kindergarten, in Jackson, Wyoming, "It was clear right away he wasn't going to be able to stay." Even after doctors diagnosed the boy with attention deficit disorder (ADD) and put him on the drug Ritalin, Max's condition still required that he be in a special-education classroom. The family's frustration level was reaching a peaking point. And then they met psychologist Michael Enright.

Enright, a member of the oversight board of the American Psychological Association, told Obringer he knew of a treatment that might help her son. The treatment was Electroencephalographic (EEG) biofeedback—a promising new approach that teaches patients to consciously recognize and control their own brain-wave patterns.

Obringer was more than willing to give it a try. Twice a week for the next six months, she brought Max to his thirty-minute treatments in Enright's small, darkened EEG room at the Jackson hospital. At the start of each session, Enright would dab globs of conducting paste on Max's scalp and attach two electrodes to amplify his brain waves, which were displayed on a computer screen. A second machine was set up to run a variation of the popular video game Pac-Man.

Instead of using buttons or a joystick, however, Max would play this game with his brain waves alone. Whenever he generated certain patterns associated

Excerpted from Jim Robbins, "Wired for Miracles," *New Age Journal*, March/April 1996. Reprinted by permission of the author.

with alert concentration, the little yellow monster would gobble his way around a maze to reward him. And the more he played, the better his technique became: As the weeks went on, Max became something of a pro at generating those focused brain waves.

Today, Obringer believes that EEG feedback has worked wonders for her son. "We started seeing immediate results," she recalls. "Within a couple of weeks he could sit in a chair and not fidget." The violent outbursts stopped, too—"no kicking, no hitting, no fighting," his mother says

> *"Problems as diverse as closed-head injury, alcoholism, and learning disabilities are being addressed by teaching people to consciously change the rhythms in their own brain."*

with relief. And though he still needs to take Ritalin, Max has begun to spend part of every day in a regular classroom. "He's like every other kid," she concludes, gratefully.

A New, Controversial Treatment

Max is one of a growing number of people turning to EEG biofeedback—a cutting-edge, if controversial, treatment used to relieve a host of health complaints, both mental and physical. Though some forms of EEG biofeedback have been around since the 1970s, today researchers and practitioners are directing the technique toward more than alleviating anxiety and stress. Problems as diverse as closed-head injury, alcoholism, and learning disabilities are being addressed by teaching people to consciously change the rhythms in their own brain.

"The field is just exploding," says Joel Lubar, a professor of psychology at the University of Tennessee and incoming president of the Association for Applied Psychophysiology and Biofeedback (AAPB), the professional association that represents the biofeedback field. Indeed, the Association has seen the number of EEG specialists in its membership grow from a handful a decade ago to a full 500 of its 2,300 members today. Among them are psychologists, nurses, physicians, and educational specialists variously affiliated with hospitals, clinics, university research centers, and doctors' offices. All of them practice a treatment that would seem the ultimate in self-healing: training the brain to fix its own disorders.

Reprogramming the Brain

By broad definition, the term *biofeedback* refers to the process in which subtle information on how a person's body and brain are operating is amplified and shown back to that person. Simple devices measuring muscle tension and body temperature, for example, help people learn to regulate their blood pressure, temperature, and other physical and mental processes not typically under their conscious control. Many forms of biofeedback are now well established as treatments for stress-related conditions such as migraine headaches and chronic pain. Today these types of biofeedback are not only practiced at such bastions of mainstream medicine as the Mayo Clinic, but are increasingly being paid for by insurance companies as well.

The branch of the field known as EEG biofeedback has remained more controversial. Indeed, only in the last few years has this approach attracted widespread research interest or clinical use. Its premise: that many conditions—from learning disabilities to depression to panic attacks—can be helped by teaching patients how to alter their brain-wave patterns.

"No-Hands Nintendo"

In a typical EEG biofeedback session, electrodes are placed on the scalp to pick up brain-wave activity. ("No electricity goes into the brain," one practitioner says reassuringly.) The brain-wave information is then fed into a computer, which translates its patterns into a user-friendly display on the screen—a game showing cars speeding along a highway, say, or small squares whose size and color can be changed. There's only one catch with these computer games: You can't use your hands. Instead, the object is to try to manipulate what happens on the screen by mind power alone.

While this kind of no-hands Nintendo may sound impossible, practitioners say that, through trial and error, users can actually be trained to increase and decrease their brain waves at will. "It's like learning to ride a bicycle: You learn by experimenting," says one. (EEG biofeedback therapy used to induce brain waves associated with relaxation is a simpler process: Electrodes are attached to devices that emit audible tones when the person gets into a relaxed state.) Sessions typically last from forty-five minutes to an hour, and an entire treatment program can take from ten to sixty sessions, depending on the condition being addressed.

> *"Biofeedback users [can], in just a session or two, get into a deeply relaxed state—a state as deep as that reached by people who'd meditated for years."*

Where other forms of biofeedback aim to teach people a skill they can call upon in specific situations—for example, learning to relax deeply to head off an impending migraine headache—EEG biofeedback may have a more enduring goal: to "retrain the brain" so it gets in the habit of producing healthy brain-wave patterns on its own thereafter.

Alpha Waves for Addiction

To appreciate the different ways EEG biofeedback is being applied today, it helps to understand some brain-wave basics. The brain continuously produces combinations of four distinct frequencies, or speeds, of brain waves—delta, theta, alpha, and beta—and our state of consciousness depends on which of these waves is dominant. When we sleep, delta waves take over, with their slow-moving signals traveling at up to 4 cycles per second, or 4 hertz (Hz). Slightly faster are theta waves (4 to 8 Hz), associated with the twilight consciousness on the brink of sleep in which dreamlike mental images can surface. Above theta is alpha (8 to 12 Hz), the calm and mentally unfocused state typically connected with relaxation. In our normal waking state, when our eyes are open and focused on the world, beta waves are in charge. Within beta itself, scientists recognize a range—from low beta, a relaxed but alert state of 12 to 15 Hz, to the excited, anxious state of high beta, which can climb as high as 35 Hz.

Much of the early interest in EEG biofeedback focused on helping people learn to generate waves associated with deep relaxation: alpha and theta. Alpha-theta biofeedback was pioneered in the '70s by Elmer and Alyce Green of the Menninger Clinic in Topeka, Kansas—still a leading center for biofeedback research—and Joe Kamiya, a researcher in San Francisco. The researchers found that if biofeedback users were alerted with an audible tone when they generated sufficient alpha waves, the subjects could, in just a session or two, get into a deeply relaxed state—a state as deep as that reached by people who'd meditated for years. Today, alpha training is commonly practiced to reduce stress and anxiety, and to help manage pain.

Treating Alcoholics

Recently, however, researchers have begun studying some surprising new applications for alpha-theta training. In one provocative, if small-scale, 1989 study, Eugene Peniston, a clinical psychologist then of Fort Lyon Veterans Affairs Medical Center in Fort Lyon, Colorado, gave ten chronic alcoholics thirty sessions of biofeedback training focused on boosting their alpha and theta waves. A second group was given conventional treatment, including participation in a twelve-step program and antidepressant medications. As part of what has since become known as the "Peniston protocol," alcoholics in the first group were coached in basic relaxation techniques, trained to boost their own alpha-theta waves, and led through visualization and imagery exercises (such as scenes in which they saw themselves refusing an offered drink). Counseling was also provided to help subjects work through any images and feelings that might surface.

At the end of a month of treatment, the biofeedback trainees achieved an unprecedented 80 percent abstinence rate, compared to 20 percent in the conventional group. What's more, when the trainees were followed up five years after treatment's end, their recovery rate remained an impressive 70 percent, having declined by only 10 percent.

"[Alcoholics who underwent biofeedback therapy] achieved an unprecedented 80 percent abstinence rate."

What's to account for the dramatic shift? Alcoholics before treatment have trouble reaching and staying in the alpha state, where "self-soothing" neurotransmitters are produced, theorize researchers. Often they turn to alcohol as an artificial means of inducing this state of relaxation. But as biofeedback treatment progresses, and those self-soothing neurotransmitters begin to flow, the craving for a drink may be reduced.

Another possible reason for biofeedback's effectiveness is that it can help subjects stay in a theta, or *hypnogogic,* state for a sustained period of time. While people pass through theta on their way to sleep every night, they quickly move on to delta. "EEG helps people linger in theta," says Dale Walters, of Topeka, Kansas, who conducted biofeedback at the Menninger Clinic and is currently working to set up a six-week outpatient biofeedback program to treat addiction in Kansas City, Missouri. In a theta state, says Walters, childhood memories and buried emotions bubble spontaneously to the surface. With the help of a psychologist, he says, such associations can often be worked through. "Those experiences lead to unblocking of intense emotions," says Walters.

> *"[Biofeedback therapy] is truly a way to integrate body, mind, emotion, and spirit."*

Peniston's treatment is slowly beginning to make inroads into clinical settings. In Topeka, Kansas, the Life Sciences Institute of Mind-Body Health now offers an intensive outpatient program that includes seven weeks of two-and-a-half-hour daily alpha-theta training sessions, coupled with intensive psychotherapy. According to Carol Snarr, a registered nurse and biofeedback therapist at the Institute, the program has so far treated not only alcoholics but also drug addicts, people with eating disorders, even smokers, some of whom have come across the country for treatment. "It is truly a way to integrate body, mind, emotion, and spirit," she says. Over the next few years, the Institute will be following patients' progress as part of a long-term follow-up study on Peniston's findings.

Helping Children Focus

If this dreamy theta state is a boon to alcoholics, it's a bane to children who suffer from attention deficit disorder and attention deficit hyperactivity disorder (ADHD), according to Joel Lubar, a professor of psychology at the University of Tennessee. For more than two decades, Lubar has studied biofeedback's applications with ADD and ADHD children and adults, publishing his findings in such leading medical journals as the *Journal of Pediatrics* and *Pediatric Neurology.* Lubar has found that many children who suffer from ADD and ADHD have brain-wave patterns high in theta and low in beta—the latter waves being associated with alert concentration. As a result of such brain-wave imbalance, these children can go through life prone to daydreaming and unable to focus their attention.

Lubar says he has treated hundreds of children with these two disorders, using a treatment protocol typically aimed at boosting beta waves and decreasing those theta waves. "Once they can control their minds, their native intelligence comes out, and their self-worth increases," he says. Follow-up studies on these children, notes Lubar, show significant increases in academic and behavior scores: Some can leap as much as two and a half years in grade-level achievement and boast IQ increases of as much as 15 points. Thanks in part to such work, treatment of ADD and ADHD is one of the most widely accepted applications for EEG biofeedback, says Francine Butler, executive director of the AAPB. . . .

Epilepsy and Beyond

Those on the cutting edge of this twenty-first-century treatment believe its potential applications may be unlimited. Currently, researchers are studying EEG biofeedback for conditions ranging from premenstrual syndrome to depression to post-traumatic stress disorder in Vietnam vets. At the Sepulveda Veterans Affairs Medical Center in California, Barry Sterman, a professor in the school of medicine at UCLA and a career scientist at the Sepulveda center, has had impressive results using the treatment with epileptics resistant to standard drug treatment. EEG biofeedback, he says, helps his subjects learn to control the excitability that triggers seizures along the brain's motor pathways. Published findings show a 60 percent seizure-reduction rate in a full 70 percent of Sterman's patients.

> *"Some [children] can leap as much as two and a half years in grade-level achievement [after biofeedback therapy]."*

Siegfried Othmer—who founded his Encino, California–based company, EEG Spectrum, after his epileptic son was treated successfully with EEG-biofeedback—brims with an almost evangelical fervor about the therapy's potential. "What's remarkable about this new technique is that we're not stuck with the brain we're born with," he enthuses. Othmer's four California-based clinics have treated some 2,000 patients—not only sufferers of attention deficit disorder and anxiety, but also people with Tourette syndrome, bipolar disorder, premenstrual syndrome, even stutterers. What these disorders have in common, he argues, is that they all can benefit from stabilizing and normalizing brain patterns.

Take the case of Los Angeles writer Margaret Sachs, forty-seven, a patient at one of Othmer's clinics who underwent EEG biofeedback for mood swings associated with menopause. "I was waking up in the middle of the night totally drenched with sweat," she recalls. "I started waking up at three or four in the morning as if I were on speed." But after twenty sessions of EEG biofeedback, designed to teach her to stabilize her brain rhythm, her symptoms vanished. "I felt grounded in a way I never had before," says Sachs.

According to Othmer and other proponents, the promise of EEG biofeedback may not be limited to the sick. Othmer has worked with professional athletes to help them improve their ability to focus. Others bring the benefits home with them: Therapist Michael Enright from time to time pastes the electrodes on his own scalp. "If I had an article that was due and I had to have extended periods of mental activity without distraction, I'd do beta protocol," says Enright. "It's much better than a cup of coffee." And there's nothing that beats a bedtime alpha session, he says, to foster a good night's sleep.

This explosion of interest worries some in the field who believe that solid scientific proof of the effectiveness of EEG biofeedback has not yet kept pace with the promises of some of its practitioners. Indeed, while applications such as ADD and epilepsy do have a growing body of research to back them up, other applications must still be considered experimental. "One of the criticisms of this field is that there needs to be more scientific studies in peer-reviewed journals—and I absolutely agree with that," says researcher and clinician Steven Stockdale, who notes that many such studies are in fact on the way.

Adds Peter Parks, a biofeedback therapist at the Menninger Clinic: "It is being used by reputable clinics, but it's still considered controversial. You'll find doctors who use it and doctors who are skeptical. In our clinical experience, EEG biofeedback seems to be helpful." Certainly, with so many factors unknown, potential subjects should be aware that they're signing up for a therapy that is still unproven—especially if they're anticipating extended treatment.

And in some cases, note experts, EEG biofeedback may actually be harmful. In its published guidelines, the Association for Applied Psychophysiology and Biofeedback warns that patients with a history of seizures should *not* be treated with EEG biofeedback unless they coordinate that treatment with their physician. People suffering from severe mental illnesses—acute psychoses, major affective disorders, histories of dissociation experiences, or borderline personality disorders—also should undertake treatment only in close conjunction with their doctors.

"If a person has a propensity toward mania and you do this training wrong, you can put them into mania," cautions Othmer. "Likewise with depression. In a clinical setting, people know this and redirect the training."

But even if EEG biofeedback must be considered a brave new world, for some it has offered relief where more-established medical practices could not. Ask Mary Obringer. "I can't tell you how important this is to our family," she says of her son Max's experience. "Our family was falling apart because of this. It has turned our lives around."

Phototherapy Alleviates Seasonal Affective Disorder

by the *Harvard Mental Health Letter*

About the author: *The* Harvard Mental Health Letter *is a monthly publication of Harvard College.*

A sunny disposition, by definition, is a happy one, and a wintry atmosphere is cheerless. Many people become somewhat sluggish or gloomy as the days grow short; the annals of the Far North tell repeatedly of cabin fever in winter and elation under the midnight sun. For some the winter mood change is a clinical depression. It was first noticed long ago but had no accepted name until the early 1980s, when researchers at the National Institute of Mental Health in Washington began to call it seasonal affective disorder (SAD).

In its most common form, SAD is a major (serious) depression that recurs each year at the same time, starting in fall or winter and ending in spring. Some of the symptoms are typical of depression—sadness, anxiety, irritability, inability to concentrate, withdrawal into solitude, loss of interest in life. Other symptoms are unusual or atypical—excessive (although restless and unrefreshing) sleep, increased appetite, and weight gain (an average of ten pounds). Lethargy is such an important feature of the disorder that the term "seasonal energy syndrome" has been proposed. The depression is usually unipolar but can also be bipolar, alternating with hypomania or mania (troublesome elation and hyperactivity) for a few months in summer.

A Common Condition

More than three-quarters of the sufferers are women, and most are in their twenties, thirties, and forties. About a third of them have a family member with SAD; high rates of nonseasonal depression and alcoholism are also found in their families. The disorder is more common at high latitudes, where seasonal changes are greater. Judging from telephone interviews and questionnaires, researchers have estimated a prevalence of 1–2% in Florida, 4% in Washington, D.C., and 9% in Fairbanks, Alaska. In Washington untreated winter depression often lasts from October or November to March or April. In Alaska it may start as early as late August. Winter depressions in Australia and New Zealand begin in May.

The discovery of SAD has drawn attention to similar but milder mood changes in the general population. A telephone survey in Maryland revealed that more than 90% of people had some seasonal changes in symptoms typical of SAD—alertness, sleep, mood, and eating habits. More

> *"[One study] revealed that more than 90% of people had some seasonal changes in symptoms typical of [Seasonal Affective Disorder]—alertness, sleep, mood, and eating habits."*

than a quarter thought these changes caused them some problems. As many as one out of four people in Manhattan sleep more and gain weight in winter. The prevalence of some symptoms resembling a mild form of SAD has been estimated at 2% in Florida, 9% in Washington, D.C., and 11% in Fairbanks. According to various studies, 16–38% of people who visit depression clinics have symptoms typical of SAD, and 15% of patients hospitalized for depression become worse in winter.

Although there have been no controlled studies, it is clear that SAD can be effectively treated with antidepressant drugs. But the standard tricyclic antidepressants, imipramine (Tofranil) and its relatives, tend to cause drowsiness and increased appetite, which are obviously unwanted. Fluoxetine (Prozac) is preferable because it does not have these side effects. Another treatment that may be just as effective, with fewer disadvantages, is light therapy (phototherapy).

Light as Therapy

The use of bright light as an antidote to lethargy and gloom has been known for thousands of years but explored systematically only in the last ten or 15. The device most often used today is a bank of white fluorescent lights mounted on a metal reflector and shielded with a plastic screen. The patient sits three feet away, occasionally looking directly at the light, for a couple of hours a day. The standard intensity in most experiments has been 2,500 lux—five to ten times brighter than ordinary indoor light, although much dimmer than summer sunshine (100,000 lux) or even a dark gray natural day (10,000 lux). In controlled studies 40–60% of patients improve under bright light, as compared with 10–20% given an inert alternative (usually light five to ten times dimmer radiated by the same device). The improvement begins in two to four days and is complete within a week or two. Patients usually relapse quickly when the treatment is discontinued. There is some evidence that light therapy and drug treatment in combination are better than either alone.

Some doubt exists about which color or colors (wavelengths) of light are best, how bright the light must be, how long the patient must be exposed to it, and whether the time of day matters. Two hours a day is clearly helpful, but more, at least up to five or six hours, may be even better for some patients. Brighter light may be better as well. Today many people who treat SAD prefer an intensity of 10,000 lux, which apparently works as well as 2,500 lux in a quarter of the time. The full spectrum of natural sunlight is probably not needed. Some experimenters have found that green or white light is better than red (ordinary incandescent bulbs radiate a good deal of red light; fluorescent lamps produce more yellow and green). Ultraviolet light—notoriously damaging to the skin and eyes—is unnecessary and can be filtered out.

There is also somewhat confusing evidence that open eyes and bright lights are not always required. Patients have been found to recover when exposed in their sleep to an artificial dawn in which their surroundings are gradually brightened from pitch dark to merely dim over a period of two hours starting at 4 A.M. Although no one knows exactly how this method works, most authorities believe it is the result of light passing through closed eyelids at a time of day when the retina is unusually sensitive.

The Importance of Timing

Timing, in fact, is the most disputed issue in the treatment of SAD. Most authorities believe that phototherapy works best in the early morning, but studies are not entirely consistent. In a review combining data from many experiments, researchers found that by the broadest criterion of improvement, 69% of patients treated in the early morning recovered, as compared with 50% treated at midday or in the evening. By the strictest standard, 50% recovered under morning light and about a third under evening or midday light. By this criterion, midday and evening light were ineffective, since 20–40% of patients in controlled studies of antidepressant drugs recover when given a placebo.

Some people should not be subjected to phototherapy because they have eye or skin problems affected by bright light or because they are taking drugs that heighten light sensitivity. Otherwise the side effects are minor: eye strain, headaches, and insomnia are each reported by about 25% of patients. But the treatment is time-con-

> *"In controlled studies 40–60% of patients improve under bright light, as compared with 10–20% given an . . . alternative."*

suming and often inconvenient. In 1988 researchers sent a questionnaire to 250 patients who had been treated with light therapy three years before. About half responded, and two-thirds were still using light therapy. But two-thirds also complained of the inconvenience, and some had abandoned morning sessions because of it. Of the minority who had dropped phototherapy entirely, 60% were trying out other approaches, including more exposure to natural light.

Therapists have begun to experiment with less cumbersome ways of providing light. One alternative is a battery-powered device resembling a visor mounted on a helmet. It is not yet clear how effective this is, or even how much light from the visor actually reaches the eye; patients may have a tendency to squint or lower their gaze. For milder winter symptoms, spending time outdoors during the day or arranging homes and workplaces to receive more sunlight may be helpful. One study found that an hour's walk in winter sunlight was as effective as two and a half hours under bright artificial light.

> *"[Depressed] patients have been found to recover when exposed in their sleep to an artificial dawn in which their surroundings are gradually brightened . . . starting at 4 A.M."*

Because of gaps and inconsistencies in the evidence, some still doubt the reality of SAD. In experiments on light therapy, a convincing placebo is difficult to devise, since everyone knows who is sitting under a bright light. Experimenters have tried asking preliminary questions to correct for bias induced by the expectations of patients. But results may also be biased by individual variation in sleep schedules and exposure to natural light. To refute these criticisms, advocates of phototherapy point out that the timing and duration of light exposure influence its effectiveness. They also note that the treatment requires several days to work, and that among depressive symptoms light seems to influence sleep and appetite most, although a placebo might be expected to affect moods and attitudes more.

The Phase Shift Theory

The influence of latitude on SAD and the effectiveness of light therapy strongly suggest that the disorder is caused by changes in the availability of sunlight. Many physiological functions are patterned in circadian (approximately 24-hour) cycles. The length of these cycles is set mainly by internal biological clocks, but they are more precisely adjusted and coordinated by the alternation of darkness and light. In animals sunlight and its absence often stimulate or suppress hormones that influence sleep, eating, body temperature, activity, and reproduction. When people are experimentally isolated from changes in ambient light, their internal circadian cycles usually become longer, gradually diverging from one another and from the solar day.

The sleeping and eating habits and activity levels of many animals change with the seasons as they adapt to changes in temperature and the availability of food. The regular and reliable change in day length serves as a signal for these adaptations. Winter is a time to conserve energy; some patients with SAD say they wish they could hibernate. According to one popular view, the circadian rhythms of people with SAD are slow to adapt when winter arrives and dawn comes later. As a result, their biological cycles are delayed in relation to the sleep-wake cycle, which remains keyed to the 24-hour day. Bright artificial light normalizes and desynchronizes the cycles.

This explanation, known as the phase shift theory, seems plausible, but the evidence for it is uncertain. Light therapy not only shortens sleeping time but improves its quality by increasing the ratio of slow-wave (deep) to REM (dreaming) sleep. The phase shift theory correctly predicts that morning light will be an effective treatment, since it moves circadian cycles forward. But the theory also incorrectly predicts that evening light will make the symptoms worse by further slowing physiological rhythms that are already lagging. In fact, evening light does no harm and in some studies is just as effective as morning light. Finally, it is difficult to show consistently that patients with SAD have delayed circadian cycles (for example, in hormone production and body temperature) or that these rhythms are normalized by phototherapy. To account for the inconsistencies, researchers have suggested various modifications, and the theory may turn out to be applicable in at least some cases.

Another Theory

Another theory is that the physiological cycles of patients with SAD are flattened out instead of lengthened, and bright light brings them up to normal amplitude. This idea has not been adequately tested, but a few studies suggest that the daily body temperature fluctuation of SAD patients is not abnormally low in winter.

One body function governed by a circadian rhythm is the release of the hormone melatonin by the pineal gland. This process, which is stimulated by darkness and suppressed by light, serves as a cue for seasonal changes in many animals. It influences the sleep-wake cycle and may help to synchronize other circadian rhythms. The pineal gland is controlled in part through nerve pathways from the retina using the neurotransmitters dopamine and serotonin. The release of these chemicals is affected by antidepressant drugs and perhaps stimulated by bright light. Some researchers have suggested that people with SAD are hypersensitive to melatonin, produce too much of it, or release it at the wrong times.

The evidence for this theory is also questionable. On average, winter melatonin secretion in SAD patients begins later and reaches lower levels than it does in most people, but the differences are small. The beta-adrenergic drug atenolol has no therapeutic effect on SAD in the majority of patients, although it suppresses melatonin secretion (probably by affecting the release of dopamine in the retina and pineal gland). Phototherapy is effective in the daytime, when it does not influence melatonin production. An extra dose of melatonin in the evening only partially reverses the therapeutic ef-

> *"One study found that an hour's walk in winter sunlight was as effective as two and a half hours under bright artificial light."*

fect of bright light. But melatonin does sometimes increase weight, sleeping time, and carbohydrate craving; and atenolol may be helpful for a few patients with SAD.

Variations on a Theme

The study of SAD has recently been complicated and enriched by the discovery that there are summer as well as winter depressions. One survey found that summer depression affects 0.7% of the population in the Washington, D.C., area. It seems to be more common and more serious at lower latitudes, and it may be influenced by heat and humidity as well as sunlight. In its physical symptoms, which include insomnia and loss of appetite, it resembles typical (endogenous or melancholic) depression rather than winter depression. Summer SAD might partly explain why the number of hospital admissions for depression rises not only in fall but also in spring.

Aside from SAD itself, the psychiatric disorder with the most striking seasonal pattern is bulimia nervosa. People with bulimia and patients with SAD often show the same changes in energy, appetite, sleep, and social activity. Both disorders occur mainly in young women, both are associated with premenstrual symptoms, and both can be treated with antidepressant drugs. In one study the drug fenfluramine, which enhances serotonin activity and reduces appetite, prevented weight gain and excessive sleep in women with SAD. Light therapy has not been tested in eating disorders, but some studies suggest that it may improve premenstrual symptoms when administered in the middle of the menstrual cycle.

This relationship between SAD, eating disorders, and premenstrual symptoms demands further research. Different combinations of antidepressant medication and phototherapy must be studied. A better understanding of SAD (including summer depression) will also teach us a great deal about the complex effects of lighting on human emotional and physical functions. Bright light has already proved useful in preventing jet lag and improving the quality of night work. The study of seasonal disorders may eventually provide insight into many other problems associated with disrupted physiological cycles.

Exercise Helps Maintain Mental Health

by Depression.com

About the author: *Depression.com is a website that provides information on depression and mental health treatments.*

Exercise helps treat depression in four ways:
1. It releases endorphins, the body's own mood-elevating, pain-relieving compounds.
2. It reduces levels of the stress-depression hormone, cortisol, in the blood.
3. It helps provide perspective on life.
4. It provides a feeling of accomplishment, which enhances self-esteem.

Many, many studies demonstrate that exercise helps treat depression. Here are summaries of just a few:

Exercise and Depression

At the University of Illinois, researchers surveyed 401 adults about their health, mental health, and lifestyle. The more time the respondents spent in strenuous exercise, the less depression, anxiety, and insomnia they reported.

At Harvard University, researchers divided 32 mildly-to-moderately depressed individuals over age 60 into two groups. Half continued to live as they had. The other half enrolled in a weight-lifting class. At the end of 10 weeks, everyone in the control group was still mildly-to-moderately depressed. But among the exercisers only two of 16 still were.

Mental Health and Lifestyle

At the University of California, at Berkeley, School of Public Health, researchers have been periodically assessing the health, mental health, and lifestyle of 6,000 residents of the San Francisco Bay Area since 1965. The ongoing survey clearly shows a strong association between a sedentary lifestyle and depression, and an equally strong association between becoming physically active and relief from depression.

Reprinted from "Exercise as Therapy," at www.depression.com/anti/anti_23_exercise.htm, (May 8, 1998) by permission. Depression.com is created and published by NetHealth, a division of Epicenter Communications.

University of Nebraska researchers tested 180 college students for depression and then divided them into three groups. A control group continued to live their lives as they had. One test group enrolled in a swimming class that met twice a week for an hour. The other test group enrolled in an hour-long weight-training class that met twice a week. Seven weeks later, the researchers re-tested all the students for depression. Compared with the controls, both exercise groups were significantly less depressed, and showed improved self-esteem.

> *"[An] ongoing survey clearly shows a . . . strong association between becoming physically active and relief from depression."*

At LaTrobe University in Bundoora, Australia, researchers tested 33 people's mental health, and then enrolled them in a two-month tai chi class. Tai chi is a gentle, non-strenuous, dance-like, Chinese exercise program. After the class, the people were tested again. They were less depressed, anxious, tense, and fearful.

Other studies have shown that for mild-to-moderate depression, regular aerobic exercise helps about as much as talk-based psychotherapy.

Which kind of exercise is best? Whatever you like. Do something that appeals to you personally. It doesn't matter what you do as long as you do something physical for a half hour or so three or more times a week, ideally every day: take walks, ride a bike, swim, play volleyball, garden, go bowling, play golf—anything. Just do something. If no physical activity appeals to you, think back to when you were a kid. What kind of physical play did you enjoy? Bicycling? Roller skating? Jumping rope? Try your childhood favorites again. You might still enjoy them.

The most accessible exercise program is walking. You already know how to do it, and there's no outfit or equipment to buy, no gym to join. Just open your front door and put one foot in front of the other. In recent years, walking has become Americans' most popular form of exercise.

It takes about a month of regular exercise to notice a significant mood-elevating effect. Be patient. Stick with it, and you'll feel better.

Chapter 4

How Should the Legal System Respond to the Mentally Ill?

CURRENT CONTROVERSIES

Chapter Preface

One of the most contentious issues surrounding mental illness is the debate over how the legal system should deal with the mentally ill who commit crimes. The insanity defense was adopted so that mentally ill criminals could receive psychiatric treatment instead of being sent to jail. However, debate flourishes over whether the defense is a loophole for criminals or a way to provide help to defendants who cannot distinguish between right and wrong.

Even trickier is the question of how to determine the criminal responsibility of defendants who suffer from multiple personality disorder (MPD)—a disorder in which a person demonstrates one or more "alter" personalities. In one such case, Thomas Huskey was accused of murdering four women in Knox County, Tennessee. While Huskey declares to have no memory of committing the crimes, his alter Kyle has admitted responsibility. The courts must decide if Huskey is culpable for the criminal acts committed by his alter.

Some legal experts assert that multiples should always be held responsible for the actions of their alters. Stephen Behnke, a lawyer and psychologist at the Massachusetts Mental Health Center in Boston, claims that in cases like Huskey's, "[An MPD defendant] may have been experiencing a certain state of mind, but a personality doesn't commit a murder. A person commits a murder."

Other analysts disagree. They maintain that MPD sufferers cannot control the actions of an alter; in fact, the "host" personality often experiences amnesia during the episodes when an alter takes over. Therefore, some commentators claim, it is unjust to hold people with MPD responsible for crimes committed by an alter.

The issue of MPD defendants illustrates the dilemma of whether or not mental illness absolves people from liability for their crimes. Many social critics are angry at what they perceive as the legal system's failure to hold people accountable for their actions. Mental health advocates, on the other hand, contend that the mentally ill should receive treatment, not punishment, for their illnesses. The following chapter presents opposing views on the validity of the insanity defense and other issues related to how the legal system should deal with the mentally ill.

The Insanity Defense Is Legitimate

by Stephen Lally

About the author: *Stephen Lally is a clinical psychologist and serves on the faculty of the American School of Professional Psychology in Rosslyn, Virginia.*

As a forensic psychologist, I am often asked to evaluate men and women accused of committing crimes in order to assess their competency and whether they can be held criminally responsible for their acts. The law sets fairly straightforward standards for criminal responsibility, and usually I have little difficulty in deciding whether an accused individual qualifies for the insanity defense.

Thus, I'm often struck by the public outcry accompanying a high-profile trial that raises the question of whether the defendant was legally sane when he or she committed the crime. Each time, there is the same focus on the possibility that the perpetrator might be "let off," often accompanied by a hue and cry about a criminal justice system that would permit such a thing to happen.

Myths About the Insanity Defense

In fact, very few defendants actually succeed with the insanity defense. (It is raised in approximately about 1 percent of felony cases and is successful only about one-quarter of the time.) Among those who are found not guilty by reason of insanity, virtually none are "let off"—in the sense that they remain free. Indeed, some of those found not guilty by reason of insanity spend more time confined in a locked mental hospital than those sane criminals who are convicted of similar acts and imprisoned for them. People are "let off" in the sense that they escape being formally condemned as "responsible" for their acts, but that is small comfort, I suspect, to a defendant in his 10th or 15th year at St. Elizabeths Hospital, where I used to work. That sort of escape brings to the fore issues of moral responsibility and personal responsibility that are very different—and much vaguer—matters, than criminal responsibility. . . .

During the seven years that I worked at St. Elizabeths, many of the cases I

Excerpted from Stephen Lally, "Drawing a Clear Line Between Criminals and the Criminally Insane," *The Washington Post*, November 23, 1997, p. C2. Reprinted with permission.

saw were straightforward in terms of criminal responsibility. Take the homeless man I evaluated several years ago. In a delusional rage, he had attacked a stranger in broad daylight. He was within a stone's throw of half a dozen police officers. From what I could tell, he had never seen his victim before, but he was convinced that she had been persecuting him for many years. Even the presence of police officers did not inhibit his actions (although it did prevent the victim from being seriously injured).

Who Succeeds with the Insanity Defense?

This homeless man is typical of those who are found to be not guilty by reason of insanity. According to the courts, to qualify for the insanity defense, defendants must suffer from a "serious mental disease or defect" that interferes with their understanding of what they did or impairs their controls. The homeless man I evaluated had been suffering from schizophrenia for years. His mental condition clearly interfered with his understanding of the situation (believing that his victim represented a threat to him). Oddly enough, the shorthand often used by experts to assess whether an individual's control is impaired is to ask whether he would commit the act with a policeman at his elbow. The homeless man did just that. He was, quite appropriately, found not guilty by reason of insanity and committed to hospital.

"Very few defendants actually succeed with the insanity defense."

In this case, as in about 70 percent of insanity adjudications, the decision to commit this man was made by plea bargain, in which both prosecution and the defense agree to the plea and there is no trial.

But, like John Hinckley [who was acquitted of shooting President Ronald Reagan by reason of insanity], the homeless man did not "get off." He is indefinitely confined to a locked psychiatric hospital. He will be released only when a judge is persuaded that he is no longer mentally ill and dangerous. The average length of stay at St. Elizabeths is eight years. Some individuals remain confined for decades, if not for their entire lives.

Defining Criminal Responsibility

In this way, courts have drawn a clear—if somewhat arbitrary—line to define criminal responsibility. If you meet the criteria for insanity, like the homeless man, you are viewed as not being criminally responsible: In other words, your thinking was too disordered or your actions too impaired to have formed the intention to commit a criminal act, and so it is unfair to inflict punishment on you. This singular exception justifies treating all other defendants as competent and criminally responsible: They rationally chose to commit a crime and should be punished for their actions.

There are, of course, many criminals who have some degree of mental illness but are clearly not eligible for the insanity defense. As surveys of prison populations have shown, there are higher rates of mental illness, mental retardation, brain damage and substance abuse among prison inmates than in the general population. Despite these conditions, the law views all these people as equally criminally responsible: Their mental state did not interfere with their understanding of what they did, nor did it impair their controls. A fine example of somebody whom many would consider sick but who was fully criminally responsible was Jeffrey Dahmer, who murdered, dismembered and cannibalized 15 men in Milwaukee. He did not meet the threshold of having a serious mental illness; he hid his victims' bodies, showing that he was aware his behavior was wrong; when a police officer confronted him, he was able to control his actions. Dahmer pleaded not guilty by reason of insanity, but he was found guilty and sentenced to 15 consecutive life sentences.

> *"Some [defendants] found not guilty by reason of insanity spend more time confined . . . [than] sane criminals who are convicted of similar acts."*

The Role of Moral Responsibility

While the legal system does provide clear guidelines for assessing criminal responsibility, mental health professionals are often left to wrestle with the vaguer questions of assessing an individual's moral responsibility. I once evaluated a man, accused of brutally murdering a woman, to determine whether he qualified for the insanity defense. My opinion was that he was not criminally responsible. I was convinced by his pattern of behavior that he was seriously ill. At the time of the crime, he was hearing voices that told him to kill the victim—and were threatening to kill him if he did not comply. His condition was severe and there was a clear link between his illness and his crime.

He was found not guilty by reason of insanity and indefinitely committed to the hospital until he could show that he was no longer mentally ill and dangerous.

Much later at the hospital, I saw the same man in therapy, and the focus of our sessions was this issue of responsibility—whether he was in some way morally responsible for his actions. What would have happened, I asked him, if the voices had told him to kill his brother? That he would never do, he told me. He would have killed himself first. In other words, his attachment to his brother would have controlled his actions. But he felt no such attachment or empathy for the women he had killed. It is only by developing that sense of moral responsibility that he could ever hope to be released. No such requirements are made of inmates before their release from prison.

The Legal System Should Not Allow Psychiatric Testimony

by Bruce Wiseman

About the author: *Bruce Wiseman is the national president of the Citizens Commission on Human Rights, an organization that advocates the abolition of psychiatry. He is also the author of* Psychiatry—The Ultimate Betrayal.

During the 1995 New Mexico legislative session, State Sen. Duncan Scott proposed an amendment to a bill stating: "When a psychologist or psychiatrist testifies during a defendant's competency hearing, the psychologist or psychiatrist shall wear a cone-shaped hat that is not less than 2 feet tall. The surface of the hat shall be imprinted with stars and lightning bolts. . . ."

While the New Mexico State Senate was voting in favor of the "Wizard's hat" amendment, a Florida columnist proposed another solution. He recommended that the confusion created by psychiatric "experts" be reduced by placing a red light and a digital display above the witness stand indicating the price paid for the testimony.

The New Mexico bill was not signed into law, and digital displays and red lights have not been installed. Both solutions might have reminded judges and juries of the actual value of "expert" psychiatric and psychological testimony.

Psychiatric Testimony Obstructs Justice

Justice is based on the concept that each man is responsible for what he does and accountable for his actions. However, psychiatry has pushed society to a state of chaos wherein no one is responsible for anything. A wife can mutilate her husband; children can kill their parents; and a man can shoot the President—yet, psychiatrists claim the perpetrators are themselves the victims, and therefore not guilty. Psychiatric testimony often serves to occlude the fact that a crime has been committed, prolong litigation, and drive the cost of justice even higher.

Excerpted from Bruce Wiseman, "Confronting the Breakdown of Law and Order," *USA Today* magazine, January 1997, by permission of the Society for the Advancement of Education, ©1997.

Psychiatrists' inability to assess and predict human behavior is a well-documented fact. In one typical study, two "skilled psychiatrists" each chose six of 20 patients as being depressed—but they were not the *same* six.

Psychiatric testimony is valueless in adjudicating criminal intent. In 1988, psychologist Jay Ziskin indicated: "Studies show that professional clinicians do not in fact make more accurate clinical judgments than lay persons." Defense attorneys

> *"Psychiatry has pushed society to a state of chaos wherein no one is responsible for anything."*

are aware of this and have been known to "shop around" for a psychiatric report that will serve their purposes. Hence, the red light to expose the nature of the witness and the digital display to advise the jury at what price the criminal's "illness" was manufactured.

"What amazes me is that, in any trial I've ever heard of, the defense psychiatrist always says the accused is insane, and the prosecuting psychiatrist always says he's sane," Jeffery Harris, executive director of the Attorney General's Task Force on Violent Crime, points out. "This happened invariably, in 100% of the cases, thus far exceeding the laws of chance. You have to ask yourself, 'What is going on here?'"

Destroying Faith in Justice

Even when courts do not accept the psychobabble, its introduction into the legal process has come close to destroying Americans' faith in justice. Examples include the "Twinkie" defense, blaming the sugar in the snack cake for driving the accused to crime, and the murder trial in which a psychiatrist testified that a man murdered his wife because of the movie (which made its debut one month after the crime), *Crocodile Dundee.*

Psychiatrists even have given Americans another reason to stay indoors during the winter's cold. According to psychiatrist Marc Sageman, murders committed during cold weather are not a crime. In 1995, he testified that Joseph Harris killed his ex-supervisor, her boyfriend, and two former co-workers because he "hated the onset of winter."

The justice system has been subverted so thoroughly that gross injustices such as in the New York trial of April Dell'Olio are common. Dell'Olio was acquitted of murder by reason of insanity and, because two psychiatrists testified she did not pose a danger to society, was released with no incarceration whatsoever. Presiding Judge Kevin Dowd said the insanity defense laws forced him to treat the killing "with the psychiatric equivalent that April had a 'bad hair day' on Oct. 20, 1992."

These two psychiatrists provided "expert" testimony on a matter they knew themselves unqualified to adjudicate. In 1979, an American Psychiatric Association task force admitted to the U.S. Supreme Court that "psychiatric expertise in the prediction of 'dangerousness' is not established and clinicians should avoid 'conclusionary judgments in this regard.'"

The Supreme Court concurred, stating that "professional literature uniformly established that such predictions are fundamentally of very low reliability, and that psychiatric testimony and expertise are irrelevant to such predictions. In view of these findings, psychiatric testimony on the issue of future criminal behavior only distorts the fact finding process."

It was not always this way. Once, there was no set definition of insanity, and the courts had difficulty in determining who was or was not conscious of what they were doing.

History of the Insanity Plea

That changed in 1843, when Daniel M. Naughten shot the British Prime Minister's secretary and was acquitted on the grounds of insanity. Fearing the ruling would establish a precedent making it easier to excuse criminal behavior, the English Parliament passed a measure known as the "right-wrong" test. As this legislation contained the words "at the time of committing the act," it opened the door to the "temporary insanity" plea.

This concept reached the U.S. in 1859. Congressman Daniel Sickles shot and killed Phillip Barton Key, the U.S. Attorney for the District of Columbia, over an affair he had been having with Sickles' wife. Sickles was acquitted, becoming the first American beneficiary of the temporary insanity plea.

In 1929, the Court of Appeals for the District of Columbia adopted the "irresistible impulse" rule. Such an impulse could "override the reason and judgment and obliterate the sense of right and wrong." The British Royal Commission on Capital Punishment expanded this defense in 1953 to excuse a criminal who systematically planned out a crime, stating that "The criminal act may be the reverse of impulsive. It may be coolly and carefully prepared; yet it is still the act of a madman." The insanity, it said, lay in "psychosis due to disease of the brain."

> *"Psychiatric testimony on the issue of future criminal behavior only distorts the fact finding process."*

Not a Justification for Murder

Almost half a century and billions of research dollars later, psychiatry still hopes to prove one day that this "disease" has a biological or organic cause. Even if its comparison to a medical illness were supported by scientific research, the theory remains flawed. While cancer and other medical conditions may cause tremendous pain and mental anguish, they are not used as a justification for murder.

Despite the faulty logic, the U.S. Court of Appeals in Washington, D.C., adopted this standard in 1954. Judge David Bazelon ruled that an accused is blameless if the crime was "the product of a mental disease or mental defect." This became known as the "Durham Rule."

Abe Fortas, the court-appointed defense attorney in *Durham v. United States*, assessed the impact of the decision: "What then is the basic significance of the Durham case? It is, I suggest, that the law has recognized modern psychiatry. . . . Its importance is that it is a charter, a bill of rights, for psychiatry and an offer of limited partnership between criminal law and psychiatry." Psychiatry had arrived. . . .

Why Is the Insanity Defense So Attractive?

The appeal of "insanity" and "diminished capacity" defenses once was limited by the fact that, while the criminal could escape prison, he risked indefinite incarceration in a state mental hospital. This changed when psychiatric lobbyists pressed Congress to pass the Community Mental Health Centers Act in 1963.

Following passage, it became the practice to send patients home with their "medications," and the insanity defense became very attractive indeed. One study of 55 murderers found not guilty by reason of insanity and placed in mental institutions between 1965 and 1976 revealed that the average time served in the hospital was 500 days.

As for the killers psychiatry sees fit to unleash upon society, many go on and kill again. Edward Kemper was discharged from a California state hospital five years after murdering his grandparents. He then killed and decapitated two women and a 15-year-old girl. Shortly afterward, two court psychiatrists testified that there was no "reason to consider him to be of any danger to himself or any other member of society." In the following two months, Kemper brutally murdered five more women.

Psychiatry's contribution to the breakdown of law and order is not limited to the courts. It is the driving force behind the destruction of personal responsibility in all sectors of society. As such, it is eroding the very fabric of civilization. . . .

Every human emotion and activity—criminal or not—is classified as a reason for psychiatric care. Criminal "disorders" include "Pyromania Disorder," "Kleptomania Disorder," and "Pedophilia Disorder." Life "disorders" include "Oppositional Defiance Disorder," "Attention Deficit Hyperactivity Disorder," "Obsessive Compulsive Disorder," and "Unspecified Mental Disorder." There even are psychiatric labels for those who drink too much coffee, eat junk food, or are happy.

> *"One study of 55 murderers found not guilty by reason of insanity . . . revealed that the average time served in the hospital was 500 days."*

As these "disorders" are promoted, more and more Americans become convinced they are but "victims" of a "mental illness." They now have an alibi for any shortcomings in life, and it is difficult to bring them back into the fold of personal accountability.

Chapter 4

The Corruption of Responsibility

It is as professor of psychiatry emeritus Thomas Szasz warned: "We have to restore the idea of responsibility, which is corrupted and confused by psychiatry, by the idea that something happened to you when you were a child and therefore you are not responsible 30 years later."

While psychiatry masquerades as a science, it is an ideology that does not have society's best interests at heart. Some legislation and court rulings have sought to limit the insanity defense, but these measures are not enough. Psychiatrists will testify as long as attorneys will pay, and attorneys will pay as long as psychiatrists prostitute themselves.

What is painfully clear is that psychiatry and its kindred "sciences" must be thrown out of every sector of the courts and society. Contrary to psychiatric ideology, man is not just another helpless creature, without will or conscience, to be manipulated according to someone else's design. Underneath whatever confusions he may have, he knows he has the courage to confront and solve his problems, as well as the ability to discern between what is right and what is wrong. Underneath it all, he knows that the ultimate betrayal is to try to persuade him otherwise.

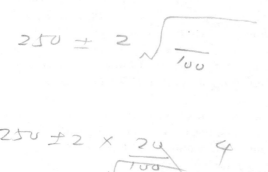

The Legal System Should Allow for a Verdict of Guilty but Mentally Ill

by *Newsday*

About the author: Newsday *is a daily newspaper based in Long Island, New York.*

The stories are the stuff of slasher movies: Empty-eyed madmen indiscriminately butchering innocents unlucky enough to wander into their blood-soaked fantasies. Followed, of course, by a celluloid nightmare of a sequel. But the criminally insane are real. And so is the dilemma of what to do with them.

People like Albert Fentress, now in the Kings Park psychiatric facility—a trim history teacher who in 1979 tied up a young man, mutilated and shot him and then cooked and ate parts of his body. And Daniel Alvarez, a hulking man who, 10 years after stabbing a homeless man to death, walked out of a state psychiatric hospital in Brooklyn only to return 12 hours later and bury a knife in a fellow patient.

People like that scare us. And so does the verdict "not guilty by reason of insanity" that lands them in mental hospitals rather than prisons. The desire to be protected from, and to punish, the criminally insane is valid. Fifteen states have responded by authorizing a middle ground between conviction and acquittal: a verdict of guilty but mentally ill. New York should do the same.

We've all heard the myth of sharp defense lawyers using gullible experts to dupe jurors into letting hordes of cold-blooded killers get away with all-too-short hospital stays. Nothing could be further from the truth.

Current law allows acquittal by reason of insanity if people either didn't know their criminal behavior was wrong or were unable to stop themselves. Such defendants are considered not responsible for their actions and in need of

Reprinted, with permission, from "Update NY's Insanity Plea," *Newsday*, November 27, 1994; © Newsday, Inc. 1994.

treatment, not punishment.

That doesn't mean they go free. In New York, they go into secure psychiatric hospitals and then are integrated over the years into less restrictive settings as their mental condition improves. On average they spend more time in mental institutions than they would have spent in prison if convicted. And the numbers are small. Nationally the insanity defense is raised in fewer than 1 percent of criminal cases. And only one in four times does a defendant win acquittal—130 people in New York between 1991 and 1993.

New York's mental health officials have a fairly good record of treating insanity-defense patients. Only about 8 percent of them have been rearrested for serious offenses in the seven years following their release—a better recidivism record by far than the state's prisons. So responsibility for the custody and care of the criminally insane should remain with the Department of Mental Health.

> *"Guilty but mentally ill . . . offers the advantage of mandating psychiatric care while refusing to absolve a defendant of responsibility for his actions."*

The problem arises when doctors agree that such a patient is ready to be released—a recommendation most mental health professionals make very cautiously. Only a judge can order a defendant released. But the state has no right to hold a psychiatric patient who is no longer ill, a reality that often puts judges at odds with citizens, many of whom would just as soon throw away the key.

Guilty but mentally ill—a finding that a defendant is guilty of a crime and is mentally ill, but not legally insane—offers the advantage of mandating psychiatric care while refusing to absolve a defendant of responsibility for his actions. As a practical matter, if such a person's psychiatric condition improved before his or her prison sentence was up, the mental ward would be traded for a prison tier. A parole board would decide when the inmate should be freed.

The rub is that, in some states, people judged guilty but mentally ill are dumped immediately into regular prison populations where they receive little if any psychiatric treatment—making the verdict a mere feel-good expedient for jurors who recognize defendants are ill but don't want to render them blameless.

Assigning blame and inflicting punishment are the essence of what the criminal justice system does. But in the case of the mentally ill, treatment is critical if the public is to be protected from killer sequels.

The Legal System Should Not Allow for a Verdict of Guilty but Mentally Ill

by William F. Woo

About the author: *William F. Woo, former executive editor of the* St. Louis Post-Dispatch *in Missouri, teaches journalism at Stanford University and the University of California at Berkeley.*

In June, 1969, a man named James Edward Drope went on trial in St. Louis County on charges of raping his wife. A quarter century ago, spousal rape was not the issue it is today, but this was—and would become even more so—an unusual case.

On the night of the crime, Drope and his buddies had been out drinking. Afterward they came to his house, where they all took turns raping his wife.

Drope had been seeing a psychiatrist. He persuaded Drope's wife that it would be good for him and their children if she stayed with him. In fact, it was not until close to the trial that she decided to cooperate fully with prosecutors. This time, he had choked her and threatened to kill her.

On the second day of the trial, Drope shot himself. Despite his attorney's pleas, the trial proceeded. Indeed, the judge—as if speaking from the pages of *Catch-22*—declared that instead of suggesting mental incapacity, by shooting himself Drope showed he knew exactly what to do to avoid the trial.

He was found guilty, but the verdict was overturned by the U.S. Supreme Court. The defendant was entitled to a psychiatric evaluation, the court held.

Then as now Missouri statute 552.020 states:

> No person who as a result of mental disease or defect lacks capacity to understand the proceedings against him or to assist in his own defense shall be tried, convicted or sentenced for the commission of an offense so long as the incapacity endures.

That language reflects the nearly universal belief that the criminal law should distinguish between the sane and the insane. Although the word insane rarely is used in medicine these days, it has force in law, meaning a condition in which people either cannot understand right from wrong or suffer from disorders that compel them to commit criminal acts even though they know them to be wrong.

The Case of Kenneth M. Baumruk

Now, as a result of a more recent attack upon a spouse in St. Louis County, sentiment is growing for a fundamental change in Missouri's criminal laws involving mental illness. This was the case of Kenneth M. Baumruk, who in 1992 went on a shooting rampage in the county courthouse, where proceedings were under way in a divorce action brought by his wife.

Baumruk fatally shot her and wounded four other people before he was shot by sheriff's deputies. His wounds appear to have resulted in a permanent amnesia, and a court recently ruled that he is incompetent to stand trial. Baumruk remains at the state mental hospital in Fulton, Missouri.

The resulting indignation has prompted support to change the laws to include a plea or verdict of guilty but mentally ill. This would permit judges to confer definite sentences, which the defendant would have to serve either in a mental institution, or, if successfully treated, in prison. Proponents say it would eliminate the possibility that someone acquitted because of insanity could quickly be set free upon a finding that the condition was cured.

Moreover, some proponents note, the insanity defense is infrequently used. Hence, many convicted defendants who need mental treatment do not receive it, since they go directly into the regular prison system. Under the guilty but mentally ill arrangement, they would get help.

This assumption may be overly optimistic. A federal commission convened after the successful insanity plea by President Ronald Reagan's assailant, John F. Hinckley Jr., found that in the first 13 months of Illinois' adopting the guilty but mentally ill provision, not one of the 44 defendants so convicted had received treatment.

> *"The term guilty but mentally ill is a contradiction."*

Would taxpayers pay the bill? When the provision was debated in Missouri in 1982, it was estimated that the cost simply to build a facility to treat this new category of inmates would cost $45 million to $60 million.

Myths About the Insanity Plea

There are other reasons for seeking a change in the law. The perception remains that an insanity plea is an easy way of avoiding punishment.

Actually, juries rarely are swayed by the defense. As a result, it is used in less than 1 percent of all criminal cases; and in instances when it is employed only one out of 10 trials ends with a finding of innocent by reason of insanity.

Beyond this, in Missouri the burden is not on the prosecution but the defense to prove insanity beyond a reasonable doubt. And once defendants are committed, it also rests with them to prove at a hearing, presided over by a judge, that they are well enough to be released.

It also is widely believed that the mentally ill are dangerous and that those involved with crimes should be locked up. In fact, the vast majority of the many millions of Americans with mental illnesses are harmless to themselves and others.

> *"The concept of guilty but mentally ill estranges us from a most basic idea, which is that morality and justice are joined inseparably."*

The media must share the blame for this misapprehension. The Hinckley Commission found that in prime time television, the percentage of violent mentally ill characters outnumbered violent normal characters by nearly two-to-one.

For many people a verdict of innocence or the avoidance of trial is outrageous when someone such as Baumruk commits a heinous crime in a public place and is apprehended on the spot. The visible act itself certifies "guilt" beyond any doubt.

Guilt and Free Will

Yet throughout Western history, the notion of guilt has rested solidly upon a moral assumption, namely, that the culprit is a creature of free will who self-consciously embarks upon a course of evil. When the laws are deliberately violated, society must bring the guilty to account and punish him.

But the term guilty but mentally ill is a contradiction. By fact and by definition, the mentally ill are people for whom free will has no meaning.

Overwhelmingly they cannot distinguish between right and wrong. If and when they can, their condition prevents them from choosing good over evil. The concept of guilty but mentally ill estranges us from a most basic idea, which is that morality and justice are joined inseparably.

Involuntary Commitment Laws Are Necessary

by Rael Jean Isaac and D.J. Jaffe

About the author: *Rael Jean Isaac is the coauthor of* Madness in the Streets: How Psychiatry and the Law Abandoned the Mentally Ill. *D.J. Jaffe is on the board of the National Alliance for the Mentally Ill.*

When a bundled-up middle-aged homeless woman named Yetta Adams was found dead at a bus stop opposite the Department of Housing and Urban Development in November 1994, it was front-page news in papers from coast to coast. In the stories Miss Adams was cast as a victim of the nation's callous housing policies—a martyr to affluent America's indifference to the homeless. In the hours after her body was carted away, HUD Secretary Henry Cisneros held a press conference to propose raising spending on homeless programs from $823 million to $1.5 billion a year.

But as James Glassman pointed out in *Forbes Media Critic*, Yetta Adams did not die from lack of housing. She died from lack of treatment. She suffered from schizophrenia, a neurobiological disorder so profound that people who suffer from it—even as they talk back to voices only they can hear—often fail to recognize they are ill and therefore reject treatment. As a result, Miss Adams bounced from shelter to hospital to shelter. In her disorientation she forgot to take the insulin she needed for her diabetes—and there was no way for social workers, judges, or family members to force her to take the medicine that would have kept her alive. At bottom, she was a victim of laws that make it impossible to treat brain-disordered individuals against their will without proof that they are dangerous to themselves or others—at which point they may be dead.

While Cisneros was lamenting Yetta Adams's fate, federally funded lawyers were working to make sure there would be many more victims like her. In each state Congress funds Protection and Advocacy programs (P&As) whose mandate is to prevent abuse and neglect of individuals with mental illness. But many are staffed by civil-libertarian lawyers and radical ex-patients who view

From Rael Jean Isaac and D.J. Jaffe, "Committed to Help," *National Review*, January 29, 1996. ©1996 by National Review, Inc., 215 Lexington Ave., New York, NY 10016. Reprinted by permission.

schizophrenia as an alternative lifestyle and consider treatments that alleviate it a form of abuse. These people are caught in a time warp, impervious to the scientific consensus that major mental illnesses, notably schizophrenia, manic-depressive psychosis, and clinical depression, are brain diseases—and, like other diseases, they *can* be treated.

Mental Illness Is Treatable

During the last two decades there has been a revolution in the neurosciences which has produced new ways of studying the brain through neuro-imaging techniques like MRI (magnetic resonance imaging), CT (computerized tomography), and PET (positron emission tomography). Particularly important are ongoing studies, conducted by the National Institute of Mental Health's Neurosciences Center, of identical twins only one of whom has schizophrenia. (In a high proportion of cases, if one identical twin has schizophrenia, the other is also afflicted, pointing to a strong genetic component in the disease.) MRI scans show striking differences between the sick and well twins, among them larger ventricles in those with schizophrenia (implying that missing tissue has been replaced by cerebrospinal fluid), wider cortical sulci, spaces in the foldings at the surface of the cortex (suggesting atrophy or failure of brain cells to develop), and reduction in the size of the left temporal lobe and the front part of the hippocampus.

As researcher Dr. Fuller Torrey puts it: "Based on studies of gross pathology, neurochemistry, cerebral blood flow, and metabolism, as well as electrical, neurological, and neuropsychological measures, schizophrenia has been clearly established to be a brain disease just as surely as multiple sclerosis, Parkinson's disease, and Alzheimer's disease are established as real brain diseases."

Destructive Ideas About Mental Illness

Unfortunately, our laws and public policy are founded not on this scientific consensus but on destructive ideas—from the Left and the Right—that became fashionable in the militantly anti-institutional climate of the 1960s. British psychiatrist Ronald Laing, a countercultural guru, popularized the notion of schizophrenia as analogous to an LSD trip, a "voyage of discovery" leading to higher forms of perception and "a natural way of healing our own appalling state of alienation called normality." From the libertarian Right came Dr. Thomas Szasz, who disposed of mental illness by verbal sleight of hand. "Mental illnesses do not exist;

> *"Major mental illnesses, notably schizophrenia, manic-depressive psychosis, and clinical depression . . . can be treated."*

indeed they cannot exist, because the mind is not a bodily part or bodily organ."

A number of sociological studies—Erving Goffman's *Asylums* was the most famous—supported these notions by falsely suggesting that the symptoms of mental illness were to a large extent produced by institutions that were meant to cure it. They suggested that mental patients needed lawyers, not doctors. And in the late 1960s and early 1970s, a group of public-interest lawyers created an informal mental-health bar. Bruce Ennis, widely regarded as the father of that bar, spoke candidly of his target. "My personal goal is either to abolish involuntary commitment or to set up so many procedural roadblocks and hurdles that it will be difficult, if not impossible, for the state to commit people against their will."

Reform Gone Awry

To be fair to Szasz and those he inspired, in the 1960s the mental-health system badly needed reform. Vaguely worded commitment laws lent themselves to abuse. Huge numbers of people were warehoused for life in understaffed and badly run state hospitals. State budgets were overwhelmed by the expense, and legislators were looking for a way out.

Unfortunately, instead of rational reform, the way out turned out to be wholesale patient-dumping. California led the way with the revolutionary Lanterman-Petris-Short Act of 1967, which set an arbitrary maximum of 17 days that a patient could be held involuntarily (or up to 90 days if he continued to be "dangerous"). There were no medical grounds to justify these time limits; there had been no pilot program; no one had any idea how the law would work. Yet the California legislature passed the LPS Act unanimously.

> *"Jails have become society's institution of choice for people with brain diseases."*

Fiscal conservatives and civil libertarians made an unbeatable combination, holding out the prospect of saving money by doing good.

Other states followed suit. Part of the strategy of the mental-health bar in the 1970s was to sue to force expensive improvements in state hospitals in the correct expectation that state governments would close them down or radically reduce their size rather than meet court-imposed standards. In 1974, an attorney in a "Mental Health Project" established by a federally funded legal-services program at Mississippi State Hospital boasted of cutting the population there by a third in a single year.

By 1990, state-hospital beds were down to 98,000, roughly a sixth of what they had been forty years earlier. The number of psychiatric beds in general hospitals increased in this period, but in both cases there was no way to keep people who needed treatment inside.

All too many of these people spiral downward to the streets, where they learn to abuse drugs and alcohol. Judy Pritchett, former clinical director for Project Reachout in New York City, says: "Every day we are seeing more and more people with addictions to crack cocaine, alcohol, and other substances. It's a dramatic increase. And the presence of these problems makes it harder and harder to reach these people."

Increasingly, jails have become society's institution of choice for people with brain diseases. A recent study sponsored by the National Alliance for the Mentally Ill and Public Citizen found that 7.2 per cent of the jail population has a mental illness. Put another way, every day more than 30,000 individuals are serving time in jail, most for misdemeanors directly stemming from their illness. Fuller Torrey, the study's lead author, says: "The police have their hands tied by the dangerousness standard, so they are undertaking 'mercy bookings,' charging individuals with small crimes just to get them into jail and treatment. Unfortunately in many cases they are victimized in jail by the regular inmates and get no treatment."

> *"On the street, the untreated may become truly dangerous, especially when they abuse drugs."*

On the street, the untreated may become truly dangerous, especially when they abuse drugs. While old studies are still quoted that claim mentally ill people are less violent than the general population, they were conducted at a time when the most seriously ill were in hospitals. John Monahan of the University of Virginia Law School writes: "The data that have recently become available, fairly read, suggest the one conclusion I did not want to reach. . . . Mental disorder may be a robust and significant risk factor for the occurrence of violence."

The widespread notion that the primary cause of homelessness is lack of housing prompted Alice Baum and Donald Birnes, outreach workers to the homeless in Washington, D.C., to write a book called *A Nation in Denial.* They point out that somewhere between 65 and 85 per cent of the homeless population suffers from chronic alcoholism, drug addiction, severe psychiatric disorders, or a combination of the three. Most researchers agree, they write, "that at least one-third of the homeless suffer from severe and persistent chronic psychiatric disorders such as schizophrenia and manic depression; the proportion may be as high as one-half."

A Change in Commitment Laws

But the denial is starting to break down. A number of states have changed their commitment laws, supplementing the usual standard requiring the patient to be dangerous or "gravely disabled" with a "need for treatment" standard, which permits treatment if the person has a severe mental disorder that will predictably result in his deterioration and lacks the capacity to make informed decisions on treatment as a result of his illness. However, this does *not* mean a return to the bad old days when mental illness was vaguely defined and patients could be confined in mental hospitals indefinitely. Today's existing strict procedural safeguards—including the patient's right to an attorney, prompt judicial hearings, and periodic judicial review—remain in place, ensuring that no one is heedlessly abandoned to a hospital's back wards.

Efforts to reform the law typically start with statewide family/patient groups, many of them affiliated with the National Alliance for the Mentally Ill, in Arlington, Virginia. One of those leading the effort to change the law in California is Carla Jacobs, whose mentally ill sister-in-law Victoria Jacobs Madeira dressed her 11-year-old son in girl's clothes, drove with him seventy miles to her parents' home, and stabbed and shot to death her 78-year-old mother. The family had repeatedly sought to have Mrs. Madeira, who lived in a parking lot with her son and rummaged through dumpsters for food, committed for treatment, but mental-health authorities ruled she was not dangerous.

Civil-libertarian lawyers have successfully opposed reform efforts in many states, but reformers may be gaining a new ally in the judiciary. In September 1994, Justice Salvador Collazo of the New York State Supreme Court ruled that the family of John Winter—a 77-year-old usher at St. Patrick's Cathedral, who had been bludgeoned to death by Jorge Delgado, a mentally ill man—could sue Bellevue Hospital, which had repeatedly treated and released Delgado. Judge Collazo acknowledged that he was flying in the face of established case law. Nonetheless, he ruled: "The cyclical pattern exemplified here of admittance—drug treatment—release—psychosis—readmittance—drug treatment—release, etc., although widely accepted as the modern approach to rehabilitating mentally ill persons, is unreasonable, since released mental patients (without medication and/or supervision) do violence to themselves and to others. Unsupervised and unmedicated, Mr. Delgado was a tragedy waiting to happen."

The Importance of Outpatient Commitment

A particularly important innovation is outpatient commitment. Most patients do not need long-term institutional care. The problem is that many of those who respond to medications stop taking them once they are out of the hospital, and relapse. Requiring these people to take medication as a condition for remaining in the community is the obvious answer.

All states (New York was the last holdout) now make outpatient commitment possible. However, a problem with these programs has been the absence of legal means for enforcement. The judge orders a patient to take medication, but if he subsequently refuses, he can be compelled to do so only if he meets the commitment standard—in most states, that he be a danger to himself or others. But this defeats the whole purpose of outpatient commitment, which is to prevent the individual from deteriorating to that point.

"At least one-third of the homeless suffer from severe and persistent chronic psychiatric disorders such as schizophrenia and manic depression."

Dane County, Wisconsin, has developed a program called "limited guardianship" for patients who cycled in and out of hospitals. An outpatient court-ordered to take medication can be put in the hospital if he fails to comply.

David LeCount, Mental Health Coordinator for Dane County, says that this program, in combination with other forms of outreach, cut the number of days patients spent in hospitals by 75 per cent over three years.

There is a precedent for forced treatment in the community: TB patients. Dr. Torrey observes: "For an individual with tuberculosis and schizophrenia, in some states the individual may be involuntarily treated for the tuberculosis but not for the schizophrenia."

Issues of Constitutionality

Unfortunately, many of the states which have need-for-treatment standards in practice continue to insist on dangerousness for commitment—because those who implement these new laws fear they are unconstitutional. But are they? The mental-health bar has argued that only the dangerousness standard is constitutional, generally citing a 1975 decision, *O'Connor v. Donaldson.* But Donaldson, who sued to be released from Florida State Hospital, was a well-functioning individual with a high degree of motivation, persistence, and intelligence. There were repeated offers, both from a halfway house and a friend of Donaldson's, to provide a home and supervision for him. Paul Stavis, legal counsel to the Commission on Quality of Care for the State of New York, says that the mental-health bar misreads the *Donaldson* decision. Says Stavis: "In its decision, the Supreme Court specifically spoke of someone who could 'live safely in freedom.' The Justices weren't thinking of malnourished individuals lost in delusions lying on park benches in their own waste. I believe a well-crafted need-for-treatment standard would be judged constitutional by this Supreme Court."

> *"A rational system [of involuntary commitment] will improve life for those who suffer from mental illness, not perpetuate their degradation as we do at present."*

Let us hope he is right. Such a rational system will improve life for those who suffer from mental illness, not perpetuate their degradation as we do at present.

Herschel Hardin was director of the British Columbia Civil Liberties Association for nine years. But having a son with schizophrenia, he learned that it was a grotesque distortion to justify abandoning people to the ravages of this disease in the name of civil liberties. Today Hardin says: "The opposition to involuntary committal and treatment betrays a profound misunderstanding of the principle of civil liberties. Medication can free victims from their illness—free them from the Bastille of their psychoses—and restore their dignity, their free will, and the meaningful exercise of their liberties." Exactly.

Involuntary Commitment Is Unconstitutional

by Thomas S. Szasz

About the author: *Thomas S. Szasz is a psychiatrist and the author of a number of books, including* Law, Liberty, and Psychiatry; Psychiatric Justice; Insanity: The Idea and Its Consequences; *and* Psychiatric Slavery.

Psychiatric slavery—that is, confining individuals in madhouses—began in the seventeenth century, grew in the eighteenth, and became an accepted social custom in the nineteenth century. Because the practice entails depriving individuals innocent of lawbreaking of liberty, it requires appropriate moral and legal justification. The history of psychiatry—especially in its relation to law—is largely the story of changing justifications for psychiatric incarceration. The metamorphosis of one criterion for commitment into another is typically called "psychiatric reform." It is nothing of the kind. The bottom line of the psychiatric balance sheet is fixed: Individuals deemed insane are incarcerated because they are "mentally ill and dangerous to themselves and/or others." For more than forty years, I have maintained that psychiatric reforms are exercises in prettifying plantations. Slavery cannot be reformed, it can only be abolished. So long as the idea of mental illness imparts legitimacy to the exercise of psychiatric power, psychiatric slavery cannot be abolished. . . .

The main source of psychiatric power is coercive domination, exemplified by the imposition of an ostensibly diagnostic or therapeutic intervention on a subject against his will. Its other source is dependency, exemplified by individuals defining themselves as unable to control their own behavior and seeking psychiatric controls. Involuntary psychiatric interventions rest on force, voluntary psychiatric relations on dependency. Equating them is as absurd as equating rape with consensual sex. . . .

We Withhold These Truths

In the modern West, slavery qua slavery is of course as dead as the proverbial dodo. Reviewing a book about Thomas Jefferson, Brent Staples declares: "Slav-

Excerpted from Thomas S. Szasz, Preface to *Psychiatric Slavery*, 2nd ed. (Syracuse, NY: Syracuse University Press, 1998). Reprinted by permission of the publisher.

ery and the Declaration of Independence can in no way be reconciled. . . . The natural rights section of the Declaration—the most famous words in American history—reflected the belief that personal freedom was guaranteed by God Himself."

Alas, if only it were that simple. The words "freedom-slavery," like the words "right-wrong," are by definition antithetical. Hence, asserting that they cannot be reconciled is a pleonasm [a redundancy]. But it is a pleonasm only in principle. In practice it is a temptation—a challenge to people's ingenuity to reconcile irreconcilables—to which many yearn to yield. All that is needed to accomplish the task is hypocrisy and demagoguery: Would-be dominators can then "discover" that the persons they seek to enslave are child-like, the victims of one or another calamity from which they need to be protected. This formula explains why chattel slavery and the Declaration of Independence could coexist for nearly a century; why racial and gender slavery and the Declaration of Independence could coexist well into the twentieth century; and why psychiatric slavery and the Declaration of Independence can now coexist in perfect harmony.

Coercive Paternalism

Although modern governments repudiate slavery as the grossest violation of "universal human rights," they continue to exert far-reaching controls over personal conduct, typically justifying coercive paternalism as *the protection of victims from themselves.* Today, the mental patient does not lose his liberty because the state deprives him of it; he loses it because the state declares him to be the beneficiary of a new "constitutional right." In *O'Connor v. Donaldson,* the justices of the Supreme Court discovered such a new right, heretofore hidden in the Constitution. They declared: "[A] State cannot constitutionally confine [in a mental hospital] *without more* a nondangerous individual . . ." [sic]. Psychiatrists lost no time dubbing this "[something] more" the "mental patient's right to treatment." It is important to emphasize that the "treatment" the court had in mind was, by definition, involuntary: It applied *only* to *involuntary mental patients.*

Who was Kenneth Donaldson and how did he become entangled with the psychiatric system? Briefly, he was an unemployed and unwanted guest in his father's house. When Donaldson refused to remove himself, his father turned to the psychiatric system to remove him. Thus did Kenneth Donaldson become a "guest" of the psychiatric hospital system, officially called a "patient." Ensconced in his new home, Donaldson refused "treatment": He insisted that he was not mentally ill and claimed he was a Christian Scientist. Notwithstanding the internally contradictory character of Donaldson's subsequent complaint—that his psychiatrists failed to treat his illness—the

> *"The main source of psychiatric power is coercive domination."*

Supreme Court accepted the case, presumably as an opportunity to reinforce the legitimacy of psychiatric slavery. To be sure, the "complaint" was not really Donaldson's: The real protagonists were his handlers, self-anointed reformers of mental health policy, who fabricated an absurdly hypocritical strategy to advance their own misguided agenda. Donaldson was merely their foil.

Why did the Donaldson case arouse so much professional and popular interest? Partly because it reopened—in the context of the new psychopharmacological treatment of mental illness—the question of what constitutes proper ground for civil commitment; and partly because Donaldson's malpractice suit reached the Supreme Court. Today, the case is an arcanum in the history of psychiatric reform. The issues it raised are, however, of continuing interest and importance.

The Deprivation of Liberty

Although the long-term confinement of mental patients in buildings called "mental hospitals"—as Donaldson had been confined—is no longer fashionable, this does not mean that the uses of coercive psychiatry have diminished. On the contrary. While most mental patients are now housed in buildings *not*

called "hospitals," they are skill deprived of liberty, typically by court-ordered "outpatient commitment" and "drug treatment," euphemisms that disguise their true status more effectively than ever. Since the Donaldson ruling, psychiatrists routinely invoke claims such as that patients'

> *"The mental patient . . . loses [his liberty] because the state declares him to be the beneficiary of a new 'constitutional right.'"*

"rejection of treatment is itself a symptom of their illness"; that, according to Jon Rubinstein, the "cause [of the 'revolving door syndrome'] may be the result of efforts to protect patients' civil rights—sometimes at the cost of their 'treatment rights'"; and that, according to the American Psychiatric Association, a "180-day outpatient commitment" policy should be widely adopted because a person who "is suffering from a severe mental disorder . . . lacks the capacity to make an informed decision concerning his need for treatment."

The importance of the Donaldson ruling lay in the fact that it ratified psychiatry's latest medical and therapeutic pretensions. By recognizing the administration of psychoactive drugs to mental patients as bona fide medical treatment, the Supreme Court once again lent the weight of its authority to literalizing the metaphors of mental illness and mental treatment. In addition, by defining involuntary psychiatric interventions—epitomized by involuntary drugging—as bona fide medical treatments, the court redefined involuntary psychiatric interventions from serving the needs of the public to serving the needs of the denominated patient.

The catastrophic implications of these ideas have not yet begun to dawn on American lawmakers, much less on the American people. The "new Nero," C.S.

Lewis warned, "will approach us with the silky manners of a doctor." Today, almost a quarter of a century after the Donaldson decision, the Supreme Court is considering whether a terminally ill patient has a constitutional right to physician-assisted suicide. Never mind that the term "terminally ill" is dangerously elastic; that suicide is illegal, prohibited by the *mental health law* of every one of the fifty states; or that because suicide is illegal, it cannot be "assisted," it can only be "ac-

> *"Psychiatrists routinely invoke claims such as that patients' 'rejection of treatment is itself a symptom of their illness.'"*

compliced." These are but minor roadblocks retarding our triumphant march toward the full realization of the Therapeutic State. "Even if the treatment is painful, even if it is life-long, even if it is fatal, that"—mocked Lewis—"will be only a regrettable accident; the intention was purely therapeutic."

Psychiatric slavery rests on civil commitment and the insanity defense. Each intervention is a paradigm of the perversion of power. If the person called "patient" breaks no law, he has a right to liberty. And if he breaks the law, he ought to be adjudicated and punished in the criminal justice system. It is as simple as that. Nevertheless, so long as conventional wisdom decrees that the mental patient must be protected from himself, that society must be protected from the mental patient, and that both tasks rightfully belong to a psychiatry wielding powers appropriate to the performance of these dues, psychiatric power will remain unreformable.

Some people do threaten society: they commit crimes—that is, acts that deprive others of life, liberty, or property. Society needs protection from such aggressors. What does psychiatry contribute to their management? Civil commitment, inculpating the innocent, and the insanity defense, exculpating the guilty. Both interventions authenticate as "real" the socially useful fictions of mental illness and psychiatric expertise. Both create and confirm the illusion that we are coping wisely and well with vexing social problems, when in fact we are obfuscating and aggravating them. Psychiatric power thus corrupts not only the psychiatrists who wield it and the patients who are subjected to it, but the community that supports it as well. As George Orwell's nightmarish vision of *Nineteen Eighty-Four* nears its climax, O'Brien explains the functional anatomy of power to Winston thus:

> [N]o one seizes power with the intention of relinquishing it. Power is not a means; it is an end. One does not establish a dictatorship in order to safeguard a revolution; one makes the revolution in order to establish the dictatorship. The object of persecution is persecution. The object of torture is torture. The object of power is power. Now do you begin to understand me?

The empire of psychiatric slavery is more than three hundred years old and grows daily more all-encompassing. But we have not yet begun to acknowledge its existence, much less to understand its role in our society.

Chapter 5

How Should Society Deal with the Mentally Ill?

Society's Response to the Mentally Ill: A Historical Overview

by Gerald N. Grob

About the author: *Gerald N. Grob is the Henry Sigerest Professor of History of Medicine at Rutgers University. He is the author of many books on mental illness, including* The State and the Mentally Ill, Mental Institutions in America, Mental Illness and American Society, From Asylum to Community, *and* The Mad Among Us.

In mid-nineteenth-century America, the asylum was widely regarded as the symbol of an enlightened and progressive nation that no longer ignored or mistreated its insane citizens. The justification for asylums appeared self-evident: they benefited the community, the family, and the individual by offering effective psychological and medical treatment for acute cases and humane custodial care for chronic cases. In providing for the mentally ill, the state met its ethical and moral responsibilities and, at the same time, contributed to the general welfare by limiting, if not eliminating, the spread of disease and dependency.

After World War II, by contrast, the mental hospital began to be perceived as the vestigial remnant of a bygone age. Increasingly, the emphasis was on prevention and the provision of care and treatment in the community. Indeed, the prevailing assumption was that traditional mental hospitals would disappear as community alternatives and institutions came into existence. Immediately following the end of the war, a broad coalition of psychiatric and lay activists began a campaign to transform mental health policy. The initial success came in 1946 with the enactment of the National Mental Health Act. This novel law made the federal government an important participant in an arena traditionally reserved for the states. The passage of the Community Mental Health Centers Act in late 1963 (signed into law by President John F. Kennedy just prior to his death) culminated two decades of agitation. The legislation provided federal subsidies for the construction of community mental health centers (CMHCs) that were intended to be the cornerstone of a radically new policy. In short, these centers were supposed to facilitate early identification of symptoms, offer preventive treatments that would both diminish the incidence of mental disorders and prevent long-term hospitalization, and provide integrated and continuous services to severely mentally ill people in the community. Ultimately, such centers would render traditional mental hospitals obsolete.

> *"The expansion of federal entitlement programs hastened the discharge of large numbers of institutionalized patients during and after the 1970s."*

Hailed as the harbingers of a new era, CMHCs failed to live up to their promise. Admittedly, appropriations fell far below expectations because of the budgetary pressures engendered by the Vietnam War. More important, CMHCs served a population different from the one originally intended. Most centers made little effort to provide coordinated aftercare services and continuing assistance to severely and persistently mentally ill persons. They preferred to emphasize psychotherapy, an intervention especially adapted to individuals with emotional and personal problems and one that appealed to a professional constituency. Even psychiatrists in community settings tended to deal with more affluent neurotic patients rather than with severely mentally ill persons. . . .

The Origins of Deinstitutionalization

During and after the 1970s the states accelerated the discharge of large numbers of severely and persistently mentally ill persons from public mental hospitals. The origins of "deinstitutionalization"—a term that is both imprecise and misleading—are complex. Prior to World War II, responsibility for care and treatment had been centralized in public asylums. Under the policies adopted during and after the 1960s, however, responsibility was spread among a number of different programs and systems. The failure of CMHCs to assume the burdens previously shouldered by state hospitals, for example, magnified the significance of the medical care and entitlement systems. General hospitals with and without psychiatric wards began to play an increasingly important role in treating the mentally ill. Because such persons tended to be unemployed and thus lacked either private resources or health insurance, their psychiatric treatment was often financed by Medicaid. Similarly, responsibility for care (that is, for food, clothing, and shelter) was slowly subsumed under the jurisdiction of federal entitlement programs. A paradoxical result followed. The fragmentation of what had once been a unified approach to mental illnesses was accompanied by an expansion of resources to enable seriously mentally ill persons to reside in the community.

During and after the 1960s, deinstitutionalization was indirectly sanctioned by the judiciary when federal and state courts began to take up long-standing

legal issues relating to the mentally ill. The identification of these new legal issues had significant consequences for psychiatrists and the mentally ill. The traditional preoccupation with professional needs was supplemented by a new
concern with patient rights. Courts defined a right to treatment in a least-
restrictive environment, shortened the duration of all forms of commitment and
placed restraints on its application, undermined the sole right of psychiatrists to
make purely medical judgments about the necessity of commitment, accepted
the right of patients to litigate both before and after admission to a mental institution, and even defined a right of a patient to refuse treatment under certain
circumstances. The emergence of mental health law advocates tended to
weaken the authority of both psychiatrists and mental hospitals and conferred
added legitimacy on the belief that protracted hospitalization was somehow
counterproductive and that community care and treatment represented a more
desirable policy choice.

The Expansion of Federal Entitlement Programs

Judicial decisions, however significant, merely confirmed existing trends by
providing a legal sanction for deinstitutionalization. Some knowledgeable figures recognized the danger and voiced concern. Nevertheless, the pattern of dis-
charging patients from mental hospitals after relatively brief stays accelerated
after 1970 because of the expansion of federal entitlement programs having no
direct relationship with mental health
policy. States began to take advantage
of a series of relatively new federal
initiatives that were designed to provide assistance for a variety of disabled groups and thus facilitate their
maintenance in the community. . . .

> *"Deinstitutionalization had
> positive consequences for a
> large part of the nation's
> severely and persistently
> mentally ill population."*

The expansion of federal entitle-
ment programs hastened the discharge of large numbers of institutionalized patients during and after the 1970s. This trend was reflected in the changing pattern of mental hospital populations. In the decade following 1955, the inpatient
population declined modestly, falling from 559,000 to 475,000. The decreases
after 1965 were dramatic. Between 1970 and 1986 the number of inpatient beds
in state and county institutions declined from 413,000 to 119,000. Length-of-
stays dropped correspondingly. Yet state hospitals remained the largest provider
of total inpatient days of psychiatric care; their clients were disproportionately
drawn from the ranks of the most difficult, troubled, and violence-prone. . . .

How Mental Health Policy Changed After 1965

In retrospect, mental health policy changed dramatically after 1965, but not in
the manner envisaged by those active in its formulation. After World War II,
there was a decided effort to substitute an integrated community system of ser-

vices for traditional mental hospitals. The system that emerged in the 1970s and 1980s, however, was quite different. First, mental hospitals did not become obsolete, even though they lost their central position. They continued to provide both care and treatment for the most severely disabled part of the population. Second, community mental health programs expanded dramatically, and inpatient and outpatient psychiatric services became available both in general hospitals and through CMHCs. A significant proportion of their clients, however, represented new populations that did not fall within the seriously mentally ill categories. Finally, a large part of the burden of supporting severely mentally ill persons in the community fell to a variety of federal entitlement programs that existed quite apart from the mental health care system. Since the 1970s, therefore, severely and persistently mentally ill persons have come under the jurisdiction of two quite distinct systems—entitlements and mental health—that often lacked any formal programmatic or institutional linkages.

Whatever its contradictory and tangled origins, deinstitutionalization had positive consequences for a large part of the nation's severely and persistently mentally ill population. Data from the Vermont Longitudinal Research Project offered some dramatic evidence that individuals with severe mental illness who were provided with a range of comprehensive services could live in the community. Between 1955 and 1960, a multidisciplinary team initiated a program of comprehensive rehabilitation and community placement for 269 back-ward patients who were considered to be among the most severely disabled and chronically mentally ill in the Vermont State Hospital. Middle-aged, poorly educated, and lower class, they had histories of illness that averaged sixteen years, had been hospitalized between one and ten times, and as a group, averaged six years of continuous institutionalization. More than 80 percent were single, divorced, separated, or widowed, and they were rarely visited by friends or relatives. Their disabilities were those characteristic of schizophrenics.

Initially the multidisciplinary team constructed a new inpatient program that consisted of "drug treatment, open-ward care in homelike conditions, group therapy, graded privileges, activity therapy, industrial therapy, vocational counseling, and self-help groups." In the community treatment component, the same clinical team established halfway houses and outpatient clin-

> *"Individuals with severe mental disorders prefer and do better in community settings."*

ics, located and placed individuals in jobs, and linked patients to support networks. Periodic follow-up evaluations were conducted over the next twenty-five years. The results indicated that two-thirds "could be maintained in the community if sufficient transitional facilities and adequate aftercare was provided." These results were confirmed by similar longitudinal studies in the United States, Switzerland, and Germany. A variety of other experiments have confirmed that individuals with severe mental disorders prefer and do better in community settings that dispense economic resources (particularly vocational rehabilitation) and a kind of empowerment that provides a feeling of mastery rather than a sense of dependency.

Under the best of circumstances, deinstitutionalization would have been difficult to implement. The proliferation of programs and absence of formal integrated linkages, however, complicated the task of both clients and those responsible for providing care and treatment. Moreover, the decades of the 1970s and 1980s were hardly propitious for the development and elaboration of programs to serve disadvantaged populations such as the severely and persistently mentally ill. The dislocations and tensions engendered by the Vietnam War, the rise of antigovernment ideologies, and an economic system that no longer held out as great a promise of mobility and affluence combined to create a context that made experimentation and innovation more difficult. The founding of the National Alliance for the Mentally Ill (NAMI) in 1979 helped in part to redress the balance. It brought together families of the mentally ill in an advocacy organization that began to play an increasingly important role in the politics of mental health during and after the 1980s.

> *"A subgroup of the severely mentally ill—composed largely of young adults—were adversely affected by the changes in the mental health service system."*

As a policy, deinstitutionalization was based on the premise that the population found in mental hospitals was relatively homogeneous. The first major wave of discharges occurred after 1965 among a group of individuals who had either been institutionalized for relatively long periods of time or who had been admitted later in their lives. This phase was not controversial, nor did it create difficulties, since few of these individuals seemed to pose a threat to others.

The Dilemma of Young Adult Chronic Patients

After 1970, a quite different situation prevailed because of basic demographic trends in the population as a whole and changes in the mental health service system. Following World War II and peaking in the 1960s, there was a sharp rise in the number of births. Between 1946 and 1960, more than fifty-nine million births were recorded. The disproportionately large size of this age cohort meant that the number of persons at risk from developing severe mental disorders was very high. Moreover, younger people tended to be highly mobile. Whereas 40 percent of the general population moved between 1975 and 1979, between 62 and 72 percent of individuals in their twenties changed residences. Like others in their age cohort, large numbers of young adult severely and persistently mentally ill persons also moved frequently both within and between cities and in and out of rural areas.

At the same time that the cohort born after 1945 was reaching their twenties and thirties, the mental health service system was undergoing fundamental changes. Prior to 1970, persons with severe and persistent mental disorders were generally cared for in state hospitals. If admitted in their youth, they often remained institutionalized for decades or were discharged and readmitted. Hence their care and treatment was centralized within a specific institutional context, and in general they were not visible in the community at large. Although chronically mentally ill persons were always found in the community, their relatively small numbers posed few difficulties and in general did not arouse public concern.

After 1970, however, a subgroup of the severely mentally ill—composed largely of young adults—were adversely affected by the changes in the mental health service system. Young chronically mentally ill persons were rarely confined for extended periods within mental hospitals. Restless and mobile, they were the first generation of psychiatric patients to reach adulthood within the community. Although their disorders were not fundamentally different from those of their predecessors, they behaved in quite different ways. They tended to emulate the behavior of their age peers, who were often hostile toward conventions and authority. The young adult mentally ill exhibited aggressiveness and volatility

> *"Virtually every community experienced the presence of . . . young adult chronically ill individuals on their streets."*

and were noncompliant. They generally fell into the schizophrenic category, although affective disorders and borderline personalities were also present. Above all, they lacked functional and adaptive skills.

Complicating Factors

Complicating the clinical picture were high rates of alcoholism and drug abuse among these young adult chronically mentally ill patients, which only exacerbated their volatile and noncompliant behavior. Their mobility and lack of coping skills also resulted in high rates of homelessness. Many of them traveled and lived together on the streets, thereby reinforcing each other's pathology. Virtually every community experienced the presence of these young adult chronically ill individuals on their streets, in emergency medical facilities, and in correctional institutions. Recent estimates have suggested that perhaps a quarter to a third of the single adult homeless population have a severe mental disorder. Many have a dual diagnosis of severe mental illness and substance abuse. Studies of these individuals have found that they experienced extremely harsh living conditions, were demoralized, granted "sexual favors for food and money," and were often caught up in the criminal justice system. They had few contacts with their families, were often victimized and socially isolated, mistrusted people and institutions, and were resistant to accepting assistance. Such patients tended to arouse negative reactions from mental health professionals, if only because chronicity and substance abuse contradicted the medical dream of cure.

Deinstitutionalization was largely irrelevant to many of the young patients who were highly visible after 1970. They had little or no experiences with prolonged institutionalization and hence had not internalized the behavioral norms of a hospital community. To be sure, many of the norms of patienthood in institutions were objectionable, but at the very least they provided individuals with some kind of structure. Lacking such guidance, many young chronically mentally ill patients—especially those with a dual diagnosis—developed a common cultural identity quite at variance with the society in which they lived. The mobility of such individuals, the absence of a family support system, and programmatic shortcomings complicated their access to such basic necessities as adequate housing and social support networks. The dearth of many basic necessities of life further exacerbated their severe mental disorders. Ironically, at the very time that unified, coordinated, and integrated medical and social services were needed to deal with a new patient population, the policy of deinstitutionalization created a decentralized system that often lacked any clear focus and diffused responsibility and authority.

The Mentally Ill in the Community

A superficial analysis of the mental health scene in the recent past can easily lead to depressing conclusions. The combined presence of large numbers of young adult chronically ill individuals as well as larger numbers of homeless people undoubtedly reinforced the public's feelings of apprehension and professionals' feelings of impotence. Indeed, the popular image of mental illnesses and the mental health service system was often shaped by spectacular exposés in the media—broadcast and printed—that seemed to reveal sharp and perhaps irreconcilable tensions. In these exposés could be seen the conflict between absolutist definitions of freedom and other humanitarian and ethical principles, as well as concern that the well-being, if not the very safety, of the community seemed endangered.

The image of deinstitutionalization so often portrayed in the press and on television, nevertheless, represented a gross simplification that ignored a far more complex reality. The popular image of severely and persistently mentally ill adults, using drugs, wandering the streets of virtually every urban area, threatening residents, and resisting treatment and hospitalization, was true but represented only a portion of a much larger problem. Often overlooked were innovative programs that were specifically designed to deal with the rest of the severely and chronically mentally ill in the 1970s and 1980s.

> *"Larger numbers of homeless people undoubtedly reinforced the public's feelings of apprehension and professionals' feelings of impotence."*

Some of the initial results in the early 1980s with community support systems programs were encouraging. They served a chronically ill population, and those with the greatest needs were the beneficiaries. Outward appearances to the contrary, the condition of many severely and persistently ill persons improved during the remainder of the decade, as many states attempted to integrate such federal entitlement programs as Social Security Disability Insurance (SSDI), Supplemental Security Income (SSI), Medicaid, and Medicare

> *"A large proportion of severely and persistently mentally ill persons have made a more or less successful transition to community life."*

with community mental health services. Nevertheless, the impact of these developments was often overshadowed by the massive problems posed by homelessness, the presence of individuals who were both severely mentally ill and substance abusers, and an angry and sometimes alienated public fearful that their security was being endangered. . . .

The persistence of problems, however, should not be permitted to conceal the more important fact that a large proportion of severely and persistently mentally ill persons have made a more or less successful transition to community life as a result of the expansion of federal disability and entitlement programs. To be sure, the media and the public are prone to focus on a subgroup of young adults who have a dual diagnosis of mental illness and substance abuse and who tend to be homeless. Their visibility on the streets often overshadows the inadvertent success of deinstitutionalization. "In fact," two authorities have recently written, "the situation is indeed much better for many people, and overall it is much better than it might have been. . . . While many people still do not have adequate incomes or access to the services theoretically provided through Medicaid and Medicare, the fact that the structure exists within these federal programs to meet the needs of these individuals represents a major step forward.". . .

"Lessons" of History

The history of the care and treatment of the mentally ill in the United States for almost four centuries offers a sobering example of a cyclical pattern that has alternated between enthusiastic optimism and fatalistic pessimism. In the nineteenth century, an affinity for institutional solutions led to the creation of the asylum, an institution designed to promote recovery and to enable individuals to return to their communities. When early hospitals seemed to enjoy a measure of success, institutional care and treatment became the basis of public policy. States invested large sums in creating a public hospital system that integrated care with treatment. The adoption of this new policy reflected a widespread faith that insanity was a treatable and curable malady and that chronicity would only follow the failure to provide effective hospital treatment.

No institution ever lives up to the claims of its promoters, and the mental hospital was no exception. Plagued by a variety of problems, its reputation and image were slowly tarnished. When it became clear that hospitals were caring for large numbers of chronically ill patients, the stage was set for an attack on its legitimacy after World War II. Its detractors insisted that a community-based policy could succeed where an institutional policy had failed and that it was possible to identify mental illnesses in the early stages, at which time treatment would prevent the advent of chronicity. Between the 1940s and 1960s, there was a sustained attack on institutional care. This assault finally succeeded when Congress enacted legislation that shifted the locus of care and treatment back to the community. But the community mental health policy proved no less problematic than its institutional predecessor. Indeed, the emergence of a new group of young chronically mentally ill persons in the 1970s and 1980s created entirely new problems, for the individuals who constituted this group proved difficult to treat and to care for under any circumstances. Yet unforeseen developments—notably the expansion of federal disability and entitlement programs—made it possible for many severely and chronically mentally ill people to live in the community.

Each of these stages was marked by unrealistic expectations and rhetorical claims that had little basis in fact. In their quest to build public support and legitimate their cherished policy, psychiatric activists invariably insisted they possessed the means to prevent and cure severe mental disorders. When such expectations proved unrealistic, they blamed either callous governments, an uninformed public, or an obsolete system that failed to incorporate the findings of medical science.

How Society Should Deal with the Seriously Mentally Ill

If U.S. society is to deal effectively, compassionately, and humanely with the seriously mentally ill, we must acknowledge that this group includes individuals with quite different disorders, prognoses, and needs, the outcome of which varies considerably over time. Some schizophrenics, for example, have reasonably good outcomes; others lapse into chronicity and become progressively more disabled. We must also confront the evidence that serious mental disorders are often exacerbated by other social problems of a nonmedical nature—poverty, racism, and substance abuse. Although psychiatric therapies can alleviate symptoms and permit individuals to live in the community, there is no "magic bullet"

> *"Although psychiatric therapies can . . . permit individuals to live in the community, there is no 'magic bullet' that will cure all cases of serious mental illness."*

that will cure all cases of serious mental illnesses. Like cardiovascular, renal, and other chronic degenerative disorders, serious mental disorders require both therapy and management.

Serious mental illnesses can strike at any time and among all elements of the population. The ensuing impact on the individual, family, and society is immense, for it often leads to disability and dependency. Rhetorical claims to the contrary, little is known about the etiology of serious mental disorders. Treatment—whether biological or psychosocial—does not necessarily eliminate the disorder. The absence of curative therapies, however, ought not to be an occasion to disparage efforts to find ways to alleviate some of the adverse consequences of illness. Many therapies assist seriously ill persons in coping with and managing their condition. "In the last analysis," a group of investigators recently concluded, "systems of treatment are not as yet able to cure, but they should be able to remove the obstacles that stand in the way of natural self-healing processes."

For too long mental health policies have embodied an elusive dream of magical cures that would eliminate age-old maladies. Psychiatrists and other professionals have justified their raison d'être in terms of cure and overstated their ability to intervene effectively. The public and their elected representatives often accepted without question the illusory belief that good health is always attainable and purchasable. The result has been periods of prolonged disillusionment that have sometimes led to the abandonment of severely incapacitated persons. Public policy has thus been shaped by exaggerated claims and by unrealistic valuative standards. Largely overlooked or forgotten are ethical and moral considerations. All societies, after all, have an obligation toward individuals whose disability leads to partial or full dependency. Even if the means of complete cure are beyond our grasp, it does not follow that we ought to ignore those whose illness incapacitates them. To posit an absolute standard of cure leads to a paralyzing incapacity to act in spite of evidence that programs that integrate mental health services, entitlements, housing, and social supports often minimize the need for prolonged hospitalization and foster a better quality of life. It has often been noted that a society will be judged by the manner in which it treats its most vulnerable and dependent citizens. In this sense, the severely mentally ill have a moral claim upon our sympathy, upon our compassion, and above all, upon our assistance.

Managed Care Benefits the Mentally Ill

by Keith Dixon

About the author: *Keith Dixon is the chief executive officer of a San Diego–based managed mental health care provider.*

It is a dreary fact, documented repeatedly, but one that still alarms: Mental illness and abuse of alcohol or other drugs is represented in as much as 20 percent of our adult population. Add in our seniors, children and adolescents (and perhaps those who hide such things from researchers' questions), and the numbers become staggering.

For every person with a mental health problem—primarily depression, manic-depressive illness, severe anxiety, alcohol and drug abuse, and schizophrenia—an average of four additional people are affected by the person's condition, and these conditions can sometimes prove fatal.

To some degree, all of us have been personally impacted by mental illness in our families or neighborhoods—even our presidents: one recently lost a good friend to suicide, and another came close to losing his wife to alcohol and drug addiction.

Less than half of the mentally ill receive competent, professional treatment, despite the advances achieved in psychiatry in the past two decades. We impact a relatively small number of patients with our treatment resources, and we do so at a tremendous cost.

The Cost of Mental Illness

In San Diego County, for example, taxpayers spend about $11 million each year on just 315 chronic patients with severe mental illness. Paying for 315 of our residents to attend Harvard would be far less expensive for taxpayers.

Nationwide, treatment costs for mental illness and substance abuse exceed $90 billion annually and have generally kept pace with our country's disastrous medical cost inflation.

Treatment costs have become a huge taxpayer burden and also a burden on

Reprinted from Keith Dixon, "Mental Illness Needs Managed Care," *San Diego Union-Tribune*, editorial, March 5, 1995, by permission of the author.

private employers who fund health insurance coverage of employees—costs that are reflected in the prices of goods and services and in the suppression of wages.

Yet the indirect costs incurred by government and businesses from those without competent psychiatric help are incalculable: lost wages and productivity, violence, crime, chronic unemployment, homelessness, inappropriate and preventable use of our very expensive medical system (e.g. emergency room utilization, treating the physical ravages of alcohol/drug abuse) and so on.

> *"Nationwide, treatment costs for mental illness and substance abuse exceed $90 billion annually."*

As taxpayers—and as competitive businesses in a global economy—it seems we cannot afford anymore to treat all mental illness in our community or in our work force, and yet we cannot afford not to. What, then, will become of our public mental health policy, and how will we pay for an enlightened one without raising additional taxes and/or cutting other worthy educational, correctional and social services?

The Role of Managed Care

Private companies have been developing innovative strategies to face up squarely to their dilemma.

The best of California's and the nation's private companies have embraced "managed mental (or behavioral) health care." Our public officials need to look at Federal Express, Xerox, General Electric, Wells Fargo, First Interstate Bank, Chevron, Southern California Edison, the Automobile Club of Southern California; and locally, at companies like General Dynamics, Toppan, a new health care purchasing consortium of biotech companies and, remarkably (perhaps ironically), a fair number of school districts and other public employers, such as Grossmont Union High School District and the joint purchasing authority of our county schools.

The Reorganization of Mental Health Care

Tempted to reduce mental health treatment costs by simply denying benefits to mentally ill and chemically dependent workers—a strategy analogous to public officials simply cutting mental health budgets and shifting consequences for doing so to other areas (e.g. police)—private companies instead fundamentally altered the way mental health care services are organized. The objectives: to make mental health care: 1) more accessible, more preventive and more clinically effective for employees so they remain productive workers, and 2) financially accountable to a budget and continuously more cost-efficient over time.

What many private companies embraced is a market-based strategy and structural reforms that reward providers of mental health care who can accomplish these two objectives at the lowest possible cost. The result is an ongoing reorganization of what has been an inefficient, cottage industry of isolated private practitioners and duplicative, competing psychiatric hospitals and units.

In the past, there has been little incentive for providers to promote wellness through services that might keep patients from ever needing intensive psychiatric care in the first place or from returning for a second (third, fourth, fifth . . .) time to expensive, inpatient settings.

In California, there are a score or more of competing, specialized managed behavioral health care companies who have built mental health care systems that operate at affordable costs.

Expanding Benefits and Reducing Costs

Managed care companies have expanded mental health benefits for private employers; reduced the costs of treatment; rendered preventive services through employee assistance programs; and are made accountable by a competitive marketplace for treatment quality, access to care and clinical outcome. The track record is there. But private managed care strategies have left the public mental health sector, to date, relatively untouched, and often our public officials are unaware of this industry's existence, methods or accomplishments. This needs to change.

> *"In the past, there has been little incentive for providers to promote . . . services that might keep patients from ever needing intensive psychiatric care in the first place."*

Dr. Mary Jane England, president of the American Psychiatric Association, testified to Congress on managed mental health care's accomplishments (and shortcomings) during the 1994 health care reform debate. She wore a button that said, in a parody of President Bill Clinton's campaign: "It's the delivery system, stupid."

All of us need to understand her message more clearly before we engage in another round of simplistic mental health and substance abuse services budget-cutting at the state and county levels.

The Public Sector Needs Managed Care

Cutting health care budgets needs to be done, but not without basic reform of the delivery system, a heavy dose of privatization of public programs and the realignment of financial incentives for providers to encourage prevention.

Otherwise, budget cuts will merely have the effect of dumping mentally ill patients on our streets or in our jails. This will shift the costs somewhere else without relieving our already overtaxed citizenry—and we will be turning our backs on some of our most vulnerable citizens.

Managed Care Does Not Benefit the Mentally Ill

by Susan Brink

About the author: *Susan Brink writes for* U.S. News & World Report.

Kathy Rhinehart knew the routine. Voices in her head. Paranoia. She thought the television set was talking about her. The lyrics of a song—a Carly Simon tune, she thinks—took on personal and ominous meaning. A 15-year history of manic-depression had taught her what to do when those symptoms hit. "I know when I need to be in the hospital," the Cedar Falls, Iowa, woman says.

But her insurer, one of the new managed-care companies specializing in mental health, thought otherwise. Rhinehart spent several hours in a hospital waiting room talking to doctors, nurses, and clerks, who in turn talked to managed-care representatives from Medco (since bought by Merit Behavioral Care Corp.), which administered her mental health benefits. Company officials eventually sent word back that she must go home. "I think they said it was because I wasn't suicidal," she says. But the voices got louder and more urgent, and she grew increasingly terrified. She returned to the hospital the next day, only to be turned away again. What had always worked—checking into a psychiatric unit for care and medication adjustment—wasn't working under the new managed-care rules.

Within two days, she saw another way out. "I had all my pills. I got the glass of water. I was ready to take them," she says. But before she swallowed anything, her boyfriend came home and rushed her to the hospital, where she was admitted. Now, she's learned a new aspect of the routine: "Next time, I'll just say I'm suicidal, so I can get into the hospital." (Ronald Geraty, executive vice president of Merit, would not comment on Rhinehart's story but said his organization works closely with consumer groups in establishing treatment guidelines.)

Demanding a Say

Administrators of health maintenance organizations (HMOs) and other managed-care programs are entering the once private sanctum of mental health treatment and demanding a say in who gets what kind of care. "Instead of working just with the patient, now there's an 800-pound gorilla in the room," says Jeremy Lazarus, Denver psychiatrist and consultant to the managed-care committee of the American Psychiatric Association.

Of the 180 million Americans with health insurance today, 75 percent are enrolled in plans with some type of managed mental health care coverage. That's up from 5 percent as recently as 1984. Back then, the vast majority of Americans had insurance policies without mental health coverage or with coverage that was extremely costly to the patient. Before managed care, a typical mental health benefit allowed for 30 days of inpatient care and 20 days of psychotherapy—usually with stiff copayments. The hospitals acted accordingly. "Lo and behold, everybody got 30 days in the hospital [and] 20 days of psychotherapy," says Clarke Ross, executive director of the American Managed Behavioral Healthcare Association, a Washington, D.C.–based trade organization. Treatment was built around insurance caps, not research.

Managed care has turned payment incentives upside down, paying set fees that encourage therapists to make their profits by shortening treatments. But therapists say the pressure to cut costs is restricting what kind of treatment is offered, and how long it can continue. Psychotherapy is often approved for three to five visits. Thereafter, the patient or therapist must argue for each subsequent visit.

> *"Administrators of health maintenance organizations . . . are entering the once private sanctum of mental health treatment and demanding a say in who gets what kind of care."*

Companies that pay the bills, the nation's employers who provide insurance for their workers, are taking a closer look as well. James Wrich, a Chicago consultant whose firm audits managed mental health companies for employers, worked with a large employer that once spent $10 million a year on mental health care for its employees. A managed mental health care company promised to provide comparable care for $7 million. When Wrich examined the insurer's books, he found that the managed-care company was spending only $2.3 million on direct care—with the rest going to profit and administrative costs. "It was never the employer's intention to reduce the direct-care expenditures that low. After the audit, they got a new managed-care company," says Wrich.

Trust in the Marketplace

Changing plans is precisely what a dissatisfied employer should do, says Keith Dixon, president of United Behavioral Health, a San Francisco managed behavioral health company. "We're a believer in markets. If a company is doing bad things to patients, we're hopeful the marketplace will drive them out," he says.

So far, market-style reforms have made the process of getting treatment more challenging for many patients. In many of the big systems, patients call a toll-free phone number and begin pouring out their problems to a stranger, who decides if a referral for psychotherapy is necessary. Valerie Raskin, a Chicago psychiatrist and author of *When Words Are Not Enough*, has seen people after they've gotten bad information over the phone. One such patient with a severe anxiety disorder had been treated successfully with anti-anxiety medication. When she became pregnant, she called her managed-care doctor and talked to a nurse who advised her to immediately stop taking the drug—common advice during pregnancy.

But without medication, she relapsed. "She had volleys of panic attacks, a heart-racing sense of doom. She slept no more than two hours a night for weeks," says Raskin. Her obstetrician could offer no one within the referral network with expertise on pregnancy and mental disorders. Rather than tough it out, the woman found Raskin and paid out of pocket for care.

Negotiating for Care

If getting into proper care is hard, staying in treatment can be next to impossible. A woman in group therapy was negotiating with her managed-care company for more sessions. "They decided that if she was well enough to do that, she didn't need treatment, so they cut her off," says Judy Roberts, director of the Washington State Coalition for Mental Health. The shorter time allowed for talk therapy upsets psychotherapists. . . .

Patients are more likely to get a drug treatment for a mental problem than ever before, though some studies show therapy is sometimes a better choice. A family doctor can be financially penalized by an insurer for referring a depressed patient to a psychologist. Writing a prescription can be less costly. "The training that primary care providers get in mental health is largely in the use of medications. So when you have a hammer, everything looks like a nail," says William Danton, psychologist at the University of Nevada School of Medicine. And therapists themselves report that they are increasingly pressured by the managed-care industry into prescribing drugs even when patients don't want them. Paul Ling, a Quincy, Mass., psychologist and cofounder of the Advocates for Quality Care, says, "I have personally been told that if the patient does not get on an SSRI

> *"Market-style reforms have made the process of getting treatment more challenging for many patients."*

[selective serotonin reuptake inhibitor—the new class of antidepressants including Prozac], they will not authorize any psychotherapy."

The heavy dose of bureaucracy in managed-care systems increases the fears of some mentally ill who need help. The stigma attached to mental illness keeps a lot of people silent about their problems. Professionals are united in the belief that for therapy to work, people must believe that their secrets will never leave the therapy room. But managed care's requirement that therapists prove that continued treatment is medically necessary gives people reason to worry about the HMO staff violating the sanctity of the treatment relationship. Ironically, the harder the therapist lobbies for more treatment for a patient, the more likely it is that increasingly personal details will be released to insurers. "Confidentiality goes out the window," Denver psychiatrist Lazarus says.

> *"Therapists . . . report that they are increasingly pressured by the managed-care industry into prescribing drugs even when patients don't want them."*

As an entire professional field reinvents itself, powerful groups are watching and offering counsel. The Institute of Medicine issued a report in the spring of 1997 calling on the federal government to monitor the quality of managed behavioral health plans. The National Alliance for the Mentally Ill, a patient advocacy group, issued a report card in September 1997 surveying nine of the country's largest mental health managed-care companies—and flunking all of them. Among the findings were that some plans still prescribed Haldol, a decades-old drug with side effects including severe and irreversible tremors, for schizophrenia rather than newer, more expensive drugs like Clozipine and Rispordol, says Laura Lee Hall, lead author of the NAMI report. Industry officials say that some survey results were based on outdated information.

Unfortunately, until the marketplace sorts out the good from the bad, patients are likely to continue doing what they have long done in the field of mental illness: Those with the resources will dig into their pockets and discreetly pay for care themselves.

Mental Health Should Be Treated on a Par with Physical Health

by Rosalynn Carter

About the author: *Former first lady Rosalynn Carter is chairman of the Mental Health Task Force at the Carter Center in Atlanta, Georgia.*

The Health Insurance Portability and Accountability Act of 1996 contained certain provisions for parity between mental and physical illnesses. Although it passed in the end, unfortunately this portion of the bill was hotly contested. I have been an advocate for mental health reform for more than 20 years, and each time there is an opportunity for real progress, the same objections are voiced by the same interest groups.

The main objection to parity for mental illness in health coverage is the belief that insurance costs will escalate dramatically. The fact is that it is much more cost effective to diagnose and treat mental illnesses in the early stages than to allow these illnesses to develop into serious problems that may require long-term hospitalization. Mental illnesses, like physical ones, can be defined, diagnosed and treated. Research has made clear that some major mental illnesses are related to chemical or structural problems of the brain. What we have learned about the brain just in the last decade has led to new medications and treatments.

Moreover, there is increasing evidence from many of our larger corporations—McDonnell Douglas, Digital, Honeywell, and First National Bank of Chicago, to name a few—that a comprehensive, managed mental health benefit is effective in dealing with mental health problems and also reduces the total cost of health care.

Appropriate mental health care is not free, but lack of proper care has devastating consequences, financial and emotional. In the workplace, both employers and ill employees suffer, due to absenteeism, higher turnover of jobs and diminished quality of work. Major depression now accounts for more "bed days"—

Reprinted from Rosalynn Carter, "A Positive Link of Mind and Body," *Los Angeles Times*, editorial, May 7, 1996; revised slightly by the author. Reprinted with permission.

people out of work and in bed—than any disorder except cardiovascular disease. This is unnecessary, when we now know that with therapy and medication, people can be treated for depression and live more normal lives as contributing members to society. And research has shown that therapy does not have to be long-term to be effective.

When we don't pay for mental health services through the health care system, we pay for the lack of these services through higher costs of medical care for physical illnesses, through the welfare system, the criminal justice system, in support to our homeless, in addition to lost productivity in the workplace and losses due to premature death from suicide. The indirect costs to society due to lack of treatment are far greater than the direct costs from treatment.

In the home, family members, including children, are affected emotionally. We must never lose sight of the human costs of decreased opportunity for people with mental illness to participate in the major activities of daily life in their communities. The cost of pain and suffering is incalculable.

In 1994, when we were working on health care reform, a national survey showed that 78% of people thought that mental health should be covered the same as physical health. This same poll showed that supporting this kind of legislation was the politically popular thing to do. There was 23% more support for a health care reform bill that included a mental health benefit than for one that did not. This indicates to me that the public was far ahead of Congress in wanting to help those who suffer the injustices of our current health care system.

> *"The indirect costs to society due to lack of [mental health] treatment are far greater than the direct costs from treatment."*

Individuals with mental illness long have experienced stigma and discrimination as a result of prevailing myths and false stereotypes. They have been excluded from the mainstream of American life in housing, employment and health care. We can correct this if we choose.

Every day we hear more and more from all levels of the health care community about how intricately linked are the mind and body—a positive outlook can make a tremendous difference in how quickly and fully someone can recover from a physical ailment. Creating a health care system that reflects parity between physical and mental health acknowledges the need to see people as whole human beings, and it recognizes the worth of every person regardless of his or her disability.

Mental Health Should Not Be Treated on a Par with Physical Health

by Robert J. Samuelson

About the author: *Robert J. Samuelson is a* Newsweek *contributing editor and a columnist for the* Washington Post.

Never before have so many people been so successfully treated for mental illness. Depending on how you read the numbers, between 6 and 11 percent of Americans annually receive some form of medical therapy for psychological problems. In 1950, less than 1 percent did. New drugs provide relief for victims of schizophrenia and manic depression who were once untreatable. Prozac, the best-known antidepressant, was introduced only in 1986. In 1995, worldwide sales totaled $2 billion.

It's this huge progress that ultimately underlies the proposal to require insurance companies to provide a "parity" of benefits between physical and mental illness. Though this is a bad idea that would drive up health spending, it's understandable in the context of so much change. Over a few decades, the stigma against mental illness has declined sharply. People more readily admit problems and seek help. Research has produced breakthrough drugs. There's less tolerance for making mental illness medicine's stepchild.

That's what most insurance plans do. A typical policy, for example, might allow lifetime spending of $50,000 for mental illness, pay for 30 days of hospitalization and require patient co-payments of 50 percent for outpatient services. Coverage for physical illness might be $1 million in lifetime spending, 120 days or more of hospitalization and co-payments of only 20 percent. One reason for the differences, of course, is the difficulty of defining mental illness. Who's sick?

American culture is obsessed with mood, dysfunction and self-fulfillment. Every stress or setback becomes a source of concern. There are no obvious bounds to family and marriage counseling or personal therapy. By regarding many ordinary anxieties and disappointments as ailments, mental illness becomes infinitely elastic—and, if covered by insurance, almost as expensive. Unfortunately, the congressional proposal (already passed by the Senate) tends in this direction. [The congressional proposal was amended to exclude mental health care parity. However, in 1996, Congress passed the Mental Health Parity Act, which mandates parity with certain restrictions.]

> *"One reason for the differences [in coverage for physical and mental illness] is the difficulty of defining mental illness."*

It would prohibit insurance plans from imposing "treatment limitations or financial requirements" on mental health benefits that are not imposed on "coverage for services for other conditions." The Congressional Budget Office estimates that the requirement would raise private insurance premiums by about 4 percent in 1998, or nearly $12 billion. Employers would respond, the CBO says, by cutting wages and other fringe benefits by almost $11 billion and dropping insurance for about 400,000 workers.

In truth, no one knows how much "parity" would cost, because the vague language would invite court challenge. But the more open-ended insurance is—the fewer limits on costs and coverage—the more it squeezes wages or causes insurance loss. One way to check spending would be to limit "parity" to "severe" mental illnesses: schizophrenia, manic depression, panic disorders, obsessive-compulsive disorders and major depressions. Afflicting 3 percent of Americans, these disorders can be disabling. Victims suffer hallucinations or suicidal gloom.

These disorders also involve the worst discrimination by insurance plans. A few decades ago, mental breakdowns were seen as freaks of personality. Since then, advances in neuroscience—the study of the nervous system—have shown that many stem from chemical imbalances in the brain. In this sense, they don't differ much from many physical diseases. So why cover them differently? Says Dr. Frederick Goodwin, former head of the National Institute for Mental Health:

"These are brain diseases. . . . You move two inches one way in the brain, and you have [the source] of epilepsy. You move two inches the other way, you have manic depression. I treat half my manic-depressive patients with anticonvulsants [drugs]."

Covering Big Losses, Not Small Ones

Even with drugs, periodic hospitalization may be required to cope with relapses. "Insurance is supposed to cover big losses and let people worry about little losses," says Harvard economist Richard Frank. Instead, the present system often covers people's early needs and exposes them to catastrophe. "Some families take enormous hits when their 19-year-old develops schizophrenia," says Frank. Once insurance is exhausted, many patients become wards of the state, going onto Medicaid or disability.

The trouble is that, in practice, neat distinctions can collapse. Diagnosing major depressions is still a gray area. Goodwin is skeptical about the workability of congressional legislation. Frank favors action but thinks the high patient co-payments (up to, say, an annual limit of $5,000) are a useful way to curb costs for less serious cases. But the legislation doesn't allow special co-payments for mental illness.

Mandated Treatment

The basic problem is that Congress is unwisely trying to dictate insurance coverage. Such "unfunded mandates" were the fatal defect of Clinton's health plan. Political pressures are skewed. Congress can confer benefits without incurring the political costs (higher taxes). If started, the process could become unending. Lobbies of patients and providers would besiege Congress to mandate a given treatment or test. All pleas would be emotionally compelling, because medical care denied seems cruel. No single mandate might have high costs. But collectively they could bloat health spending at the expense of other needs.

> *"The more open-ended insurance is . . . the more it squeezes wages or causes insurance loss."*

The right way to handle mental health is more tentative. The Federal Employees Health Benefit Program (FEHBP) is the largest buyer of health insurance, with more than 9 million beneficiaries. Let Congress instruct FEHBP to devise policies that balance extra coverage and higher costs. Some states have already mandated "parity" for insurers. The difference between these approaches and a sweeping federal mandate is that they all involve practical disciplines. For example, if states are too expansive in their mandates, they'll lose jobs to neighbors.

None of this would satisfy those who crave instant solutions. But it would provide experimentation and flexibility in an area of hard social choice. What should be recalled is that the greatest strides against mental illness have come through research, new drugs and shifts in attitudes. Political rhetoric notwithstanding, it is in these realms—and not insurance practices—that future progress also will be concentrated.

Mental Illness Should Be Destigmatized

by Les Campbell

About the author: *Les Campbell is a volunteer with the Alliance for the Mentally Ill.*

"Somewhere, homeless on the streets, there is Martin. He is a dangerous psychotic. Martin is cunning, and he is smart, and he is very dangerous, and he is at large."

So began this 1985 *San Diego Union* news article. It may have been written to inform, but the result was to inflame. After the "hook," it described a day in the life of a psychiatric social worker who went onto the streets to find people with mental illnesses.

The news article used phrases such as, ". . . looked at her with the kind of hope a dog has," ". . . turned to face her like a casement gun swinging onto its target."

And, speaking of a recent rape, the suspect ". . . could have been a homeless psychotic . . . could have been Martin." Most likely, according to well-documented statistics, the rape could just as logically have been committed by a so-called sane man.

Still, the media do not deserve all the blame for stigmatizing people who have mental illnesses. Violent patients are often released too soon from the protection of mental hospitals when timely treatment would still help.

In Los Angeles, David proved the point with clear evidence of danger. He doused himself with gasoline in a suicide attempt. But a court-appointed referee found no cause to hold him. Later, David drove his car into a crowd of pedestrians, injuring several, killing one.

Who, then, shall we fear? The Davids? The Martins? The courts? The professional referees? Do fear and stigma, created by patients who should have been cared for, but were not, need to exist?

From an informed society comes one answer: In Geel, Belgium, the mentally

Reprinted from Les Campbell, "Outside the Cage, Looking In: A Disturbing Look at How Society Defines the Mentally Ill," *San Diego Union-Tribune*, August 8, 1996, p. B11, by permission of the author.

ill live with 900 foster families where they work and take part in the community. They have done so since the early 1600s. The senior secretary of the organization that runs the program, Franz Vaneynde, says: "The sole difference that distinguishes this community from others is that the culturally conditioned, deep-seated fear of the mentally ill does not exist here."

> *"The stigma of mental illness is taught by omission in our schools."*

Civic-minded people in our own country agree on the right to live in comfortable housing with pleasant surroundings. But when a home for the mentally ill is established in their neighborhood, some people may qualify that right.

Typical of the problem, one neighborhood was upset when six mentally ill people moved in. A woman raved loud and long concerning the "threat." But 10 years later, not one single incident has supported her claim. Indeed, most are pleased and have extended acceptance that gives meaning to the often-repeated phrase, "Be a good neighbor."

Perpetuating Stigma

The stigma of mental illness is taught by omission in our schools. Neither elementary nor high school curricula includes accurate information on mental illness. Out of our fear of the unknown, the mentally ill are reduced in our minds from potentially valuable citizens to tainted eccentrics at best and fearsome maniacs at worst. Years past, they were chained, straitjacketed and hidden away in hospitals. When one escapes, it is too often reported, "Somewhere, homeless on the streets . . . is a dangerous psychotic."

But now that anti-psychotic medications have made possible the release of tens of thousands from state mental hospitals, how can we rid patients of this stigma?

Education Leads to Tolerance

Education is one answer. Why not let high school students, in their health-education classes, learn that the onset of most brain diseases occurs between the ages of 15 and 25?

Why not let them learn that one in every 100 in each graduating class eventually will suffer from schizophrenia and that no one knows how to prevent it?

Why not let parents learn these same facts, so they will know that mental illness could strike their own loved ones?

Why not let both student and parent benefit by hearing from people who, like Ellen, have been mentally ill most of their adult lives?

As Ellen tells it, mental illness can only be truly experienced from the inside. "To outsiders," she explains, "I am out of touch with reality. But, in truth, realities overwhelm me. How can I be 'cool' in such a tumultuous volcano? And how can you cope with my problems?"

Then she suggests, "Perhaps we could start by being more tolerant, for I may someday become as you, and you as me."

The Effects of Prejudice

Esso Leete, a founder of the National Alliance for the Mentally Ill's Consumer Council, describes the weight of this prejudice and discrimination on a mental patient:

"I can talk, but I may not be heard. I can make suggestions, but they may not be taken seriously. I can voice my thoughts, but they may be seen as delusions. I can recite experiences, but they may be interpreted as fantasies. To be a patient or even an ex-client is to be discounted. . . .

"In many cases, our weakest attributes are those we learned in the very institutions supposedly there to help us: i.e., withdrawal, dependency, fear, irresponsibility, lowered self-confidence, lost self-esteem and shattered personal dignity."

Mental Illness Should Not Be Destigmatized

by Richard E. Vatz

About the author: *Richard E. Vatz is a professor of rhetoric and communication at Towson State University in Maryland and the associate psychology editor of* USA Today *magazine.*

There is no more common cry in the mental health world than the cry to destigmatize mental illness. Over and over, primary players in mental health argue that the stigmatization of mental illness sufferers is the cause of underdiagnosis of those so afflicted and unfair treatment of the mentally ill. . . .

Stigma is a term defined by the *American Heritage Dictionary* as "a mark or token of infamy, disgrace or reproach." As used by the mental health industry, though, it invariably means an unfair, inaccurate, and dysfunctional reputation tied to a notion of mental illness that lacks any voluntary component. This view, in turn, is tied to the medical model stating that all of mental illness is analogous to physical illness that happens *to* people, eliminating any element of choice, control, or discretion.

Those in mental health fields see the stigmatization of mental illness as the reason that many people do not seek professional help. They point disparagingly, for example, to polls such as one conducted in 1991 by the National Institute of Mental Health in which 43% of respondents regarded depression as a personal failing, rather than an illness. They also cite cases such as that of Vincent Foster, the Clinton Administration aide who reportedly avoided seeking psychiatric help for fear that the stigma would cripple his reputation.

The Push to Destigmatize Mental Illness

The American Psychiatric Association (APA) has been behind a push to destigmatize mental illness. In May, 1994, for instance, they featured celebrities such as actors Rod Steiger and Suzanne Somers and humorist Art Buchwald, who attended the Presidential Symposium at the APA annual meeting, titled "Stigma and the Celebrity." In the July 1, 1994, *Psychiatric News,* the APA newsletter, they unanimously decried the stigma associated with mental illness.

In the piece, Steiger claimed that the stigma of mental illness "is as big a prejudice as racial or religious prejudice." He urged psychiatrists to apprise patients of
the additional burden of stigma, and
Buchwald noted wryly that "stigma
may be terrible, but it sure brings out
a crowd."

It is nearly impossible to pick up a
copy of *Psychiatric News* or any
article written by someone in the
mental health field without finding

> *"Stigmatization as a negative
> reinforcer can have a salutary
> effect, minimizing needless
> visits to mental health
> professionals."*

some references to stigma. The July 21, 1995, *Psychiatric News*, for example,
reports that the APA, in urging the U.S. Supreme Court to overturn a Colorado
law forbidding extension of civil rights protections to gay men and women,
filed a brief maintaining that "government measures that foster such stigma, as
by pointedly foreclosing opportunities for political participation for gay people,
only exacerbate those psychological harms."

An Authentic "Illness"?

There also is the National Stigma Clearinghouse, an organization founded in
1992 that is "concerned with portrayals of people with mental illnesses," which
attempts to "track and, if necessary, protest terms and images in the media that
unintentionally hurt millions of Americans." That organization, too, believes
that the fear of stigma can exacerbate the symptoms of mental illness. Nowhere
in any of the anti-stigma literature is there any consideration of the view that
eliminating stigma could foster in some cases the very self-defeating behaviors
and feelings known as "mental illness" by making them more acceptable—that
is, by normalizing mental illness.

There are questions that must be asked about the relationship between mental
illness and stigma: is mental illness an authentic "illness" or is it a personal failing; and what would the consequences be if there were no stigma and would
that still be the result if, as those in mental health argue, mental illnesses were
seen as bona fide illnesses? . . .

There is a type of stigmatization in the mental health field that is indefensi-
ble—the invidious labeling of patients with disparaging name-calling. Paula
Caplan, in her book, *They Say You're Crazy*, speaks of this in her example of
psychiatrists who refer to mentally retarded children as FLKs (funny-looking
kids). This is contemptible and, obviously, insensitive, but is far different from
the "stigmatization" cited as due to the normal connotations of being labeled as
having "mental illness" or seeking professional help.

Is it reasonable to decry the stigmatization of those who seek professional
help for mental illness? Indeed, stigmatization as a negative reinforcer can have
a salutary effect, minimizing needless visits to mental health professionals. One

of the reasons is that seeing psychiatrists for much of what is labeled as "mental illness" is discretionary; that is, if one does not see a professional practitioner, the "suffering" of many who are identified as "mentally ill" may solve itself, or require other strategies. Contrarily, in the case of serious somatic, or physical, illness, the condition will worsen and perhaps even be life-threatening.

When getting professional help becomes a routine method of dealing with life's vicissitudes, one may become unnecessarily dependent on the practitioner. Many so-called mental illnesses are problems in living that lend themselves to solutions through dealing with the conditions themselves; others are transitory and will solve themselves without professional intervention; and, finally, some are made worse by reliance on mental health professionals.

On the other hand, for serious brain diseases still categorized as mental illnesses, such as certain forms of schizophrenia, it is critical for family and sufferer alike that there be no barrier to the seeking of professional help. In these cases, though, it is unlikely that stigmatization will deter most people from getting the help they need.

An Economic Motive

There is a strong economic motive, as well, behind the fight against stigma. In a 1993 *Congressional Quarterly* piece, Russ Newman, acting executive director for practice at the American Psychological Association, decried the "stigma and attitude" of "why should I pay when it won't affect me?" Opponents of stigmatization quoted in this article cite the 1986 Rand Corp. finding that the more generous the health benefits, the more use of psychotherapy, and, in fact, mental health benefits "now total $104,000,000,000 annually and represent 20–30% of employers' medical costs."

Former first lady Rosalynn Carter, in a 1993 piece in *The Washington Post*, recognized the economic link to the destigmatization of mental illness: "I always thought that if insurance covered mental illnesses the way it does physical illness, a lot of the stigma associated with mental problems would be eliminated. More people would seek professional care before an illness became severe."

There has been concern expressed that the stigma of mental illness has affected the quality and number of mental health professionals who are willing to go into mental health care.

> *"In [severe] cases [of mental illness], it is unlikely that stigmatization will deter most people from getting the help they need."*

In the Aug. 8, 1993, *Congressional Quarterly Researcher*, James Scully, director of education at the American Psychiatric Association, stated that "The stigma attached to doctors who work in the field has often rivaled the stigma suffered by the mentally ill themselves." Indeed, there has been a depletion for years in the number of physicians who are going into mental health–related fields.

According to the *Researcher*, five percent of medical school graduates are going into psychiatry, and even that number is declining. Still, there is no reason to believe that stigma is a major cause of the decline, or at least any more of a cause than it ever was. At the same time, the field of psychiatry is having an identity crisis, with more of its functions being assumed by those in psychoneurology.

Practicalities and Costs

The mental health lobby, in a sense, has reaped what it has sown—depicting the mentally ill as having real brain disease, instead of people primarily with problems in living. This has been a major contributing factor to the stigmatization of the mentally ill.

What would be the consequences of genuinely rejecting the stigmatization of mental illness, and is it possible? The answer to the latter portion of this question is simply "no." The extent that stigmatization is removed from mental illness is the extent to which mental illness loses its *raison d'être* as a brain disease. It is this affiliation with the brain that provides the stigmatization. Without this dramatic link, the stigmatization will be tempered, but so will the acceptance of giving the mentally ill insured medical care.

The claim that mental illness is a real illness, and a brain disease at that, ensures the very stigma the APA and others reject. Thus, the very medical identity that authenticates mental illness as real illness makes stigmatization certain. It can not be said that people's thinking is diseased to the point that they don't know what they are doing or are out of control without stigmatizing them.

> *"Getting rid of the stigma of all behaviors labeled 'mental illness' would be a surefire way to ensure their increase in perpetuation."*

Jonathan Alter, in a 1994 article in *Newsweek*, "The Name of the Game Is Shame," dealing with out-of-wedlock birth, points out the benefits of stigma and hurting the "self-esteem" of people acting irresponsibly. He maintains that "shame" can be a potent negative reinforcer in the realm of having out-of-wedlock children, and it could be pointed out that it is a potent reinforcer in some of the areas of mental illness as well, especially in cases such as adjustment disorder and others that simply are catchall psychiatric classifications that could describe almost anyone with problems in living.

Redefining Mental Illness

Some mental disorders may be true illnesses, and therefore ought to be categorized as brain diseases. It is wrong, if not avoidable, to have them stigmatized. What happens, however, is that these illnesses, such as some forms of schizophrenia, are used to give credibility to the far more questionable phenomena, like former APA president Lewis Judd's "subsyndromal symptomatic depression," a combination of insomnia, fatigue, and low levels of depression. This was one make-shift "mental illness," described by Judd as the cause for nebulous "significant social disability," that never made it into the *Diagnostic and Statistical Manual of the American Psychiatric Association*, the APA's diagnostic bible.

The majority of mental illnesses are not genuine illnesses, but are problems in living that are amenable to reward and punishment. As the reward increases or the punishment (or stigmatization) decreases, the incidence of mental illness will rise. This is why, as the July 19, 1994, *Wall Street Journal* reports in its article, "Mental Health Law Protects Many People but Vexes Employers," the Americans with Disabilities Act (ADA) has led to the claim that "it will protect people whose mental illness can be treated but who may be unfairly stigmatized." In fact, the law is prompting questionable claims, including the use of the ADA, as the report warns, as a "crutch." Wallace Gasiewicz, medical director of General Motors' Warren, Mich., powertrain plant, states that "Everything related to psychiatry is confusing and muddled," and maintains that "I've seen people decide that their jobs weren't palatable and they want to change their job requirements, so they say they have job-related depression."

The Consequences of Destigmatization

Positive and negative reinforcement do have an effect on volitional behavior. In his book, *Heavy Drinking: The Myth of Alcoholism-As-Disease*, Herbert Fingarette cites many studies showing that heavy drinking is affected by rational considerations. Getting rid of the stigma of all behaviors labeled "mental illness" would be a surefire way to ensure their increase in perpetuation.

Steven Sharfstein, secretary of the American Psychiatric Association and president and medical director of the Sheppard Pratt Health System, a private psychiatric facility in Baltimore, suggested in 1993 that the reason, historically, that "psychiatry hasn't competed well with the rest of medicine" is that it has "labored under discrimination and stigma," leading to choices of hardware, such as a CAT scan over psychiatrists.

Yet, stigma encourages people to conform their behavior to health norms, but must not be allowed to discourage those who truly need help from getting it. That is why the end of stigma, if it were possible, probably would result in a surge of claims of mental illness that are positively reinforcing to the doctors who care for the mentally ill and the nearly endless number of people who could be among the recipients for their "illnesses."

Destigmatization of the majority of diagnoses of mental illness guarantees continued increases in their incidence and a lessening of negative reinforcement for the behaviors themselves. Perhaps when there is a serious downsizing of what passes for mental illness, it may be possible to destigmatize behaviors that genuinely are caused by real illness.

Bibliography

Books

Richard Abrams	*Electroconvulsive Therapy.* New York: Oxford, 1997.
Harold H. Bloomfield	*Hypericum and Depression.* Los Angeles: Prelude, 1996.
R.J. Bonnie and J. Monahan, eds.	*Mental Disorder, Work Disability, and the Law.* Chicago: University of Chicago Press, 1997.
Philip J. Boyle and Daniel Callahan, eds.	*What Price Mental Health? The Ethics and Politics of Priority Setting.* Washington, DC: Georgetown University Press, 1996.
Peter Breggin	*Talking Back to Prozac: What Doctors Won't Tell You About Today's Most Controversial Drug.* New York: St. Martin's, 1994.
Peter Breggin	*Talking Back to Ritalin: What Doctors Aren't Telling You About Stimulants for Children.* Monroe, ME: Common Courage Press, 1998.
Lincoln Caplan	*The Insanity Defense and the Trial of John W. Hinckley, Jr.* Boston: D.R. Godine, 1984.
Paula J. Caplan	*They Say You're Crazy: How the World's Most Powerful Psychiatrists Decide Who's Normal.* Reading, MA: Addison-Wesley, 1995.
Debra Elfenbein, ed.	*Living with Prozac and Other Selective Serotonin Reuptake Inhibitors (SSRIs): Personal Accounts of Life on Antidepressants.* San Francisco: HarperSanFrancisco, 1995.
Seth Farber	*Madness, Heresy, and the Rumor of Angels: The Revolt Against the Mental Health System.* Chicago: Open Court, 1993.
Lynn Gamwell	*Madness in America: Cultural and Medical Perceptions of Mental Illness Before 1914.* Ithaca: Cornell University Press, 1995.
Jeanne A. Heaton	*Tuning in Trouble: Talk TV's Destructive Impact on Mental Health.* San Francisco: Jossey-Bass, 1995.
Kay R. Jamison	*An Unquiet Mind.* New York: A.A. Knopf, 1995.

Bibliography

Stephen Joseph — *Understanding Post-Traumatic Stress: A Psychosocial Perspective on PTSD and Treatment.* Chichester, NY: Wiley, 1997.

David Allen Karp — *Speaking of Sadness: Depression, Disconnection, and the Meanings of Illness.* New York: Oxford, 1996.

Ken Kesey — *One Flew over the Cuckoo's Nest, a Novel.* New York: Viking, 1962.

Peter D. Kramer — *Listening to Prozac.* New York: Viking, 1993.

Kent S. Miller — *Executing the Mentally Ill: The Criminal Justice System and the Case of Alvin Ford.* Newbury Park, CA: Sage, 1993.

Jay Neugeboren — *Imagining Robert: My Brother, Madness, and Survival: A Memoir.* New York: Morrow, 1997.

Richard Ofshe — *Making Monsters: False Memories, Psychotherapy, and Sexual Hysteria.* New York: Scribner, 1994.

Jane Phillips — *The Magic Daughter: A Memoir of Living with Multiple Personality Disorder.* New York: Viking, 1995.

Terrence Real — *I Don't Want to Talk About It: Overcoming the Secret Legacy of Male Depression.* New York: Scribner, 1997.

Francine Shapiro — *EMDR: The Breakthrough Therapy for Overcoming Anxiety, Stress, and Trauma.* New York: BasicBooks, 1997.

Edward Shorter — *A History of Psychiatry: From the Era of the Asylum to the Age of Prozac.* New York: Wiley, 1997.

Lauren Slater — *Welcome to My Country.* New York: Anchor Books, 1997.

Ralph Slovenko — *Psychiatry and Criminal Culpability.* New York: Wiley, 1995.

William Styron — *Darkness Visible: A Memoir of Madness.* New York: Random House, 1990.

Thomas Szasz — *Cruel Compassion: Psychiatric Control of Society's Unwanted.* New York: Wiley, 1994.

Thomas Szasz — *Psychiatric Slavery.* Syracuse: Syracuse University Press, 1998.

E. Fuller Torrey — *Out of the Shadows: Confronting America's Mental Illness Crisis.* New York: Wiley, 1997.

Irving B. Weiner — *Principles of Psychotherapy.* New York: Wiley, 1998.

Thomas A. Widiger, ed. — *DSM-IV Sourcebook.* Washington, DC: American Psychiatric Association, 1994.

Bruce J. Winick — *The Right to Refuse Mental Health Treatment.* Washington, DC: American Psychological Association, 1997.

Periodicals

Aimee Lee Ball — "Are You Obsessed," *Harper's Bazaar*, March 1996.

Beth Brophy — "Kindergartners in the Prozac Nation," *U.S. News & World Report,* November 13, 1995.

Mental Health

Dennis Cauchon	"Stunningly Quick Results Often Fade Just as Fast," *USA Today,* December 6, 1995.
Mary H. Cooper	"Prozac Controversy," *CQ Researcher,* August 19, 1994. Available from 1414 22nd St. NW, Washington, DC 20037.
Geoffrey Cowler	"The Culture of Prozac," *Newsweek,* February 7, 1994.
Theodore Dalrymple	"Ill Deeds Aren't a Sign of Ill Health," *Wall Street Journal,* April 23, 1998.
Randi Henderson	"Relying on Ritalin," *Common Boundary,* May/June 1996. Available from 5272 River Rd., Suite 650, Bethesda, MD 20816.
Melinda Henneberger	"Managed Care Changing Practice of Psychotherapy," *New York Times,* October 9, 1994.
Ralph Hyatt	"Can Managed Care Accommodate Mental Health?" *USA Today,* July 1996.
Carol Hymowitz	"Shrinking Coverage: Has Managed Care Hurt Mental-Health Care? It Depends on Whom You Ask," *Wall Street Journal,* October 24, 1996.
Rael Jean Isaac and D.J. Jaffe	"Mental Illness, Public Safety," *New York Times,* December 23, 1995.
Daniel L. Judiscak	"Why Are the Mentally Ill in Jail?" *American Jails,* November/December 1995. Available from 2053 Day Rd., Suite 100, Hagerstown, MD 21740-9795.
Stuart A. Kirk and Herb Kutchins	"Is Bad Writing a Mental Disorder?" *New York Times,* June 20, 1994.
Gene Koprowski	"Studies Warn Against Feds Going Mental," *Insight,* August 26, 1996. Available from 3600 New York Ave. NE, Washington, DC 20002.
Peter D. Kramer and S. Avery Brown	"In His Words: Prozac Not Only Treats Depression, It Can Change Personality—Which Gives Pause to a Leading Psychiatrist Miracle Worker," *People,* November 15, 1993.
David B. Larson	"Have Faith: Religion Can Heal Mental Ills," *Insight,* March 6, 1995.
Leslie Laurence	"Who's Reading Your Mind?" *Glamour,* May 1997.
John Leo	"A Rough Day? No, Just a New Mental Disorder," *Conservative Chronicle,* October 29, 1997. Available from Box 37077, Boone, IA 50037-0077.
David Mechanic	"Managed Mental Health Care," *Society,* November/December 1997.
Sue Miller	"A Natural Mood Booster," *Newsweek,* May 5, 1997.
Peggy Papp	"Listening to the System," *Family Therapy Networker,* January/February 1997. Available from 8528 Bradford Rd., Silver Spring, MD 20901.
Frank T. Vertosick, Jr.	"Lobotomy's Back," *Discover,* October 1997.

Organizations to Contact

The editors have compiled the following list of organizations concerned with the issues debated in this book. The descriptions are derived from materials provided by the organizations. All have publications or information available for interested readers. The list was compiled on the date of publication of the present volume; the information provided here may change. Be aware that many organizations take several weeks or longer to respond to inquiries, so allow as much time as possible.

American Association of Suicidology (AAS)
4201 Connecticut Ave. NW, Suite 310, Washington, DC 20008
(202) 237-2280 • fax: (202) 237-2282
e-mail: amyjomc@ix.netcom.com
web address: http://www.cyberpsych.org/aas/index.html

The association is one of the largest suicide prevention organizations in the nation. It believes that suicidal thoughts are almost always a symptom of depression and that suicide is almost never a rational decision. The association provides referrals to regional crisis centers in the United States and Canada and helps those grieving the death of a loved one to suicide. It publishes numerous pamphlets and reports.

American Psychiatric Association (APA)
1400 K St. NW, Washington, DC 20005
(202) 682-6000 • fax: (202) 682-6850
e-mail: apa@psych.org • web address: http://www.psych.org

An organization of psychiatrists dedicated to studying the nature, treatment, and prevention of mental disorders, the APA helps create mental health policies, distributes information about psychiatry, and promotes psychiatric research and education. It publishes the *American Journal of Psychiatry* and *Psychiatric Services* monthly.

American Psychological Association (APA)
750 First St. NE, Washington, DC 20002-4242
(202) 336-5500 • fax: (202) 336-5708
e-mail: public.affairs@apa.org • web address: http://www.apa.org

This society of psychologists aims to "advance psychology as a science, as a profession, and as a means of promoting human welfare." It produces numerous publications, including the monthly journal *American Psychologist,* the monthly newspaper *APA Monitor,* and the quarterly *Journal of Abnormal Psychology.*

Citizens Commission on Human Rights (CCHR)
6362 Hollywood Blvd., Los Angeles, CA 90028
(213) 467-4242 • (800) 869-2247 • fax: (213) 467-3720
e-mail: humanrights@cchr.org • web address: http://www.cchr.org

CCHR is a nonprofit organization whose goal is to expose and eradicate criminal acts and human rights abuses by psychiatry. The organization believes that psychiatric drugs actually cause insanity and violence. Its members see it as their duty to "expose and help abolish any and all physically damaging practices in the field of mental healing." CCHR publishes nine books, including *Psychiatry: Destroying Morals* and *Psychiatry: Education's Ruin.*

False Memory Syndrome Foundation
3401 Market St., Suite 130, Philadelphia, PA 19104-3315
(215) 387-1865 • (800) 568-8882 • fax: (215) 387-1917

The foundation was established to combat False Memory Syndrome (FMS), a condition in which patients are led by their therapists to "remember" traumatic incidents—usually childhood sexual abuses—that never actually occurred. The foundation seeks to assist the victims of FMS and people falsely accused of committing child sexual abuse through publicity, counseling, and research. It publishes the *FMS Foundation Newsletter* and distributes information and articles on FMS.

International Society for the Study of Dissociation (ISSD)
60 Ravere Dr., Suite 500, Northbrook, IL 60062
(847) 480-0899 • fax: (847) 480-9282
e-mail: info@issd.org • web address: http://www.issd.org

The society's membership comprises mental health professionals and students interested in dissociation. It conducts research and promotes improved understanding of this condition. It publishes the quarterly journal *Dissociation* and a quarterly newsletter.

National Association of Psychiatric Health Systems (NAPHS)
web address: http://www.naphs.org

The association represents the interests of private psychiatric hospitals, residential treatment centers, and programs partially consisting of hospital care. It provides a forum for ideas concerning the administration, care, and treatment of the mentally ill. It publishes various fact sheets and policy recommendations, including *How You Can Help Reform Mental Health: A Grassroots Guide to Political Action.*

National Depressive and Manic Depressive Association (NDMDA)
730 N. Franklin St., Suite 501, Chicago, IL 60610-3526
(312) 642-0049 • fax: (312) 642-7243
e-mail: MYRTIS@aol.com

The association provides support and advocacy for patients with depression and manic-depressive illness. It seeks to persuade the public that these disorders are biochemical in nature and to end the stigmatization of people who suffer from them. It publishes the quarterly *NDMDA Newsletter* and various books and pamphlets.

National Foundation for Depressive Illness (NAFDI)
PO Box 2257, New York, NY 10116
recorded message: (800) 248-4344
web address: http://www.depression.org

NAFDI seeks to inform the public, health care providers, and corporations about depression and manic-depressive illness. It promotes the view that these disorders are physical illnesses treatable with medication, and it believes that such medication should be made readily available to those who need it. The foundation maintains several toll-free telephone lines and distributes brochures, bibliographies, and literature on the symptoms of and treatments for depression and manic-depressive illness. It also publishes the quarterly newsletter *NAFDI News.*

National Institute of Mental Health (NIMH)
NIMH Public Inquiries
5600 Fishers Ln., Room 7C-02, MSC 8030, Bethesda, MD 20892-8030
e-mail: nimhinfo@nih.gov • web address: http://www.nimh.nih.gov

NIMH is the federal agency concerned with mental health research. It plans and conducts a comprehensive program of research relating to the causes, prevention, diagnosis, and treatment of mental illnesses. It produces various informational publications on mental disorders and their treatment.

National Mental Health Association (NMHA)
1021 Prince St., Alexandria, VA 22314-2971
(703) 684-7722 • fax: (703) 684-5968
e-mail: nmhainfo@aol.com • web address: http://www.nmha.org

The association is a consumer advocacy organization concerned with combating mental illness and improving mental health. It promotes research into the treatment and prevention of mental illness, monitors the quality of care provided to the mentally ill, and provides educational materials on mental illness and mental health. It publishes the monthly newsletter *The Bell,* as well as various leaflets, pamphlets, and reports.

National Resource Center on Homelessness and Mental Illness (NRCHMI)
Policy Research Associates, Inc.
262 Delaware Ave., Delmar, NY 12054
(800) 444-7415 • fax: (518) 439-7612
e-mail: nrc@prainc.com • web address: http://www.prainc.com/nrc

The center provides information and technical assistance to various agencies concerned with the housing and other needs of the homeless mentally ill. It publishes *Access,* a quarterly newsletter that provides information on research, programs, and initiatives affecting the homeless mentally ill. It also provides free information packets on request.

Obsessive Compulsive Foundation (OCF)
PO Box 70, Milford, CT 06460-0070
(203) 878-5669 • fax: (203) 874-2826
e-mail: info@ocfoundation.org • web address: http://www.ocfoundation.org

The foundation consists of individuals with obsessive-compulsive disorders (OCDs), their friends and families, and the professionals who treat them. It seeks to increase public awareness of and discover a cure for obsessive-compulsive disorders. It publishes the bimonthly *OCD Newsletter* and brochures and educational materials on OCDs.

SA/VE (Suicide Awareness Voices of Education)
PO Box 24507, Minneapolis, MN 55424-0507
(612) 946-7998
e-mail: save@winternet.com • web address: http://www.save.org

The mission of SA/VE is "to educate about the brain diseases that, if untreated medically and psychologically, can result in suicide death; to make statements by members' presence through events like the Annual Awareness Day, protest, letter writing or other activities; to honor the memory of people who died by suicide; and to eliminate the stigma on suicide."

World Federation for Mental Health (WFMH)
1021 Prince St., Alexandria, VA 22314-2971
fax: (703) 519-7648
e-mail: wfmh@erols.com • web address: http://www.wfmh.com

The federation consists of individuals and associations dedicated to improving public mental health worldwide. It strives to coordinate mental health organizations in an effort to enhance mental health care in developing countries. It publishes a newsletter four times a year.

Index

Index

Index

CHD   - HI   CHD

CHD 25   195

- CHD 110   195   D   W

                                    T   107   96

risk = $\frac{25}{125} - \frac{10}{195}$ ⊖   1.93   4

                                        300   200

28+10   300

25                      $\frac{25}{25+10} - \frac{125}{175+195}$
25+10

                                                107
                                                 96
$\frac{25}{200} - \frac{10}{200} =$ $\frac{25 \times 20}{10 \times 80}$ 11

        D   W

Ex   25   10

no   65   70